WANTED: DEAD OR ALIVE

"What's the woman done?"

"She's carrying a paper to Double Bend. First, you've got to stop that woman. Next, you've got to get that paper. You'll get a hundred dollars for you and twenty bucks for every man with you."

"That sounds fair to me. How bad d'you want her?"

"The way I always want a thing done."

"If she rides too fast?"

"Shoot the horse."

"If she carries a gun...."

"She does carry a gun, and she'll use it. That's her kind."

"Well?"

"Treat her like a man."

"Is that straight? It don't go none too easy with a man that tackles a woman...not in these parts."

"I told you to stop her. I don't care how you do it."

Other *Leisure* books by Max Brand ®:

Max Brand®

Crossroads

LEISURE BOOKS NEW YORK CITY

A LEISURE BOOK®

May 2008

Published by special arrangement with Golden West Literary Agency.

Dorchester Publishing Co., Inc.
200 Madison Avenue
New York, NY 10016

ISBN 10: 0-8439-5876-6
ISBN 13: 978-0-8439-5876-8

Visit us on the web at www.dorchesterpub.com.

EDITOR'S NOTE

The text of the story you are about to read was derived from Frederick Faust's holographic manuscript. It was written as a sequel to his earlier novel, *Luck*, and appeared serially in *Argosy All-Story* in six parts (1/31/20–3/6/20) under the byline John Frederick, as was also the case for the earlier serial. For no reason that can be readily determined at this late date, following magazine publication it never appeared in book form. *Luck*, as the author intended it, was the first installment in the life of one of his finest and most memorable tragic heroines—Jacqueline Boone. *Crossroads* is the conclusion.

Destination—The World 1

How much hell *can* this fellow raise?" inquired a stranger in Guadalupe, after being regaled at some length by a tale of the manifold exploits of Dix Van Dyck.

And the answer was: "Partner, how much hell *is* there?"

Yet many held that there was nothing malicious about Dix Van Dyck. It was simply the spirit of what had been mischief in his boyhood. Now that he had passed the period of fisticuffs and entered that of six-guns, his pranks had serious consequences quite frequently, but his heart had not changed a whit.

Formerly, a fist fight satisfied all the yearnings of his hungry soul, but now that he stood something over six feet and weighed in the neighborhood of two hundred pounds of hard, fighting, lean-drawn muscle, an encounter with the brown fists of Dix Van Dyck was hardly preferable to a gun fight.

In another environment Dix unquestionably might have led a harmless and, in time, useful existence, but unfortunately he was born in the land of little rain and lived in a state where some eighty percent of the population is Mexican, where the laws of the legislature were printed in Spanish first and afterward in English, and where a Mexican considered himself of a strata a few degrees above that of any Anglo-American. It goes without argument that in such an environment Dix Van Dyck found a plenteous field for mischief, and he harvested his crop of deviltry with the most painful husbandry. Yet he escaped unpunished for many years. The reason was that there was in Dix Van Dyck an appealing element suggestive of the big boy run wild, and men found it hard to judge him sternly. Also it was known to all men that Dix was not the sort to hunt his six-gun by preference. He was perfectly contented to rely upon those bone-hard fists of his until the other fellow—probably from a strategic position behind a chair or from a corner of the floor—drew his gun. Then it was all over except the coroner's verdict. That verdict was usually "suicide."

Afterward there followed a period of anguish for Dix Van Dyck. For he did not like killings, and he swore off on gun play as religiously as a confirmed drunkard. But always the excitement of a prospective fight was too much for him, and the undertaker received another order. This would make it appear that Dix was a public nuisance. Yet men liked him. A man who fights squarely is judged most leniently in the Southwest. Moreover, the boyishly eager, almost wistful smile of Dix would have disarmed a heart of steel.

If he had confined his attentions to men of ill repute, all would have been well, but in an evil moment Dix crossed the path of a certain politician, one *Señor* Don Porfirio Maria Oñate. In the newspapers he was known as Mr. Oñate, but in private life everyone used the title he preferred. The worthy *Señor* Oñate was running for the office of sheriff of Chaparna County and approached Dix Van Dyck in a public place with a request for his vote. This was a rash step and would never have been undertaken by the noble don if he had not been too warmly inspired by tequila, that is apt to make the courage greater than the judgment.

The reply of Dix Van Dyck was of Homeric temper and

volume. He stated his opinion of *Señor* Don Porfirio Maria Oñate in full and completed his survey of the don's public career with some terse remarks about his ancestors. Any other man in the Southwest might have been tempted to fight, but even tequila was not as potent in the soul of Mr. Oñate as the fear of Dix Van Dyck. He stroked his mustache and smiled and hated Dix Van Dyck with his little, bright eyes, but he said nothing.

Afterward he sent his brother, accompanied by two accomplished cut-throats, to settle the long account with Dix Van Dyck. They came upon him from the rear when he was unarmed, and there followed a battle that still lives in the memory of the inhabitants of Chaparna County. Dix Van Dyck tore a shelf from the wall and with it brained two of his assailants. Then he strangled the third with his bare hands. Afterward he called upon *Señor* Oñate, but that gentleman was not at home, another proof of wisdom.

Three days later *Señor* Oñate was elected sheriff of Chaparna County, and Dix Van Dyck kissed his mother good bye, hugged his little brother, and departed for regions unknown to the north.

This might seem strange to some, for the last crime of Dix had been most manifest self-defense, but the dwellers in Chaparna County understood. It would have been impossible to get a jury that was not under the thumb of the new sheriff. It would have been a mockery, not a trial. So Dix Van Dyck mounted on a great horse, strong enough to bear even his weight on a day's ride, and disappeared into the hills.

He was not ill pleased by the thought of leaving Chaparna County, even under compulsion. Like the young Alexander, he was anxious for new worlds to conquer, and, once started along the outward path, he wondered why he had not made the move before. His mind was at peace; self-content warmed his blood. In the long holster his Winchester jostled softly. At either hip was the comfortable weight of a six-gun. The sweat of the tall horse was like incense in his nostrils, and the creaking of the saddle leather was sweeter than music to his ears. Behind his saddle a blanket was rolled in the slicker, and in the saddlebags he carried enough provisions for many a day.

The Arab seizes a handful of dates and another of barley and is ready for the desert. The Southwesterner travels almost as light. For guide Dix Van Dyck carried an instinct sure as that of a hunting coyote or a migratory bird. His destination was—the world.

Double Bend   2

He did not leave Guadalupe an hour too soon, for the new sheriff was hardly in office before a warrant for Dix Van Dyck appeared. A posse strove to serve it and rode hard to the north, only to find that their bird had flown into distant regions. They returned with the ill news, and Sheriff Oñate sat down to bide his time, for he had in fact what the elephant is endowed with in fancy— a memory that never dies.

As for Dix Van Dyck, he cared not a whit what was happening behind him. He had no sooner turned his shoulder upon yesterday than it was lost and abandoned with the shades of distant years. His heart went galloping into the future. So it was in the early evening that he swung into sight of Double Bend, a group of adobe huts and frame shacks huddling away into the purples that swung down from the shadowy mountains beyond.

Double Bend took its name from the windings of Coyote Creek, which flowed through its center. The main street followed the windings of that treacherous little stream, and men held that the inhabitants of Double Bend were as snake-like as the street they walked. All of this was unknown to Dix Van Dyck, for he had long since left far behind him the regions that he knew and where he was known. All that he saw in Double Bend as he passed down its sinuous main street looked very good to him. It gave the impression of a town that has been much lived in.

The window panes, for instance, were usually shattered. The wooden Indian that the proprietor of a general merchandise store had erected before his place of business was minus one arm and his legs had almost been shot away. From a saloon of capacious proportions strains of music and the roll of voices proclaimed that "a good time was being had by all."

So Dix Van Dyck hurriedly put up his horse in the stables, ate in the restaurant a great platter of ham and eggs with an enormous side dish of French-fried potatoes, and then bore toward the saloon and dance hall. The gasoline lamp flaring over its entrance was like the vortex of a whirlpool toward which all living things from many miles around gravitated with irresistible force. Buckboards littered one side of the street and horses the other, and under the glare of the lamp a continual stream of men passed toward the dance hall. None came out. It was like the yawning maw of some great monster drawing in an endless current of human food. At the door Dix Van Dyck paused and surveyed the interior.

His eyes kindled. He was a devotee of neither whiskey nor dancing, but here was life—life in plenty, action, confusion, clamor. In such places and in such moments the tang of the world came most sharply home to him. Moreover, there was a natural caution impelling the pause at the doorway. Inside might be a dozen foes, and a foe to Dix Van Dyck would not wait to give a warning. He would either flee or else start shooting from the hip.

Big Dix slipped into the shadow on one side and turned his leonine, ugly head from side to side in a slow survey. His trained eyes photographed a hundred faces—not one was known to him. The smile that had gone out while he made this preliminary survey now returned. He canted his head to one side and drank in the confusion of sounds that swept from dancing floor, bar, and gaming tables—all in one room.

"Rolls five for his point. . . . Come, Phoebe, talk to me, little black eyes! Rolls five. . . . Raise that ten. . . . Line up, gents, line up and name your poison. . . . Hey, Bill . . . I seen a gent over to Tuskogee. . . . My dance, Blondie. . . . Red seven! Show that card! By God, I say you will. . . . Say, boys, I'm some dry, where's the water hole, lead me to it, I can't see!"

Dix Van Dyck sauntered to the bar. On his lips the mischievous, boyish smile that all Guadalupe knew and feared was growing. In his quiet moments that eagle nose, straight, thin mouth, and forbidding eyes made him seem a man to be avoided and given ground, but his smile gave an expression of deluding gentleness to his features. Strangers, seeing him smile, were apt to invite him to a drink or ask him for a five-spot with equal readiness. But those who knew understood that smile meant a deep desire for action. It was like the grin of the pugilist who stands in his corner, rubbing his shoes in the rosin and waiting confidently for the bell.

First he examined the dancing floor, chiefly because the men were in movement there. But the monotonous whine of the violin and the regular movements of the dancers through the mist of smoke disgusted him. One of the dance-hall girls saw his smile and stopped before him expectantly. His face sobered long enough to return her glance, and she went on hastily, her query answered. Then he looked down the bar.

Whiskey itself had no charms for him, but he sometimes drank merely for excitement—a token, in Guadalupe, for men to vacate the barroom in which this grizzly happened to be quenching his thirst. The bar tonight, however, had no attraction for him. A drunken man staggered past him. He followed the uncertain

progress with contempt. Next he looked to the gaming tables. They were operating under full blast, the gamesters
stimulated by the dance music on one hand and the
high-power whiskey on the other. Crap tables, roulette,
chuck-a-luck, faro-poker—every table had a full house,
and Dix Van Dyck waited for an opening.

It was during this delay that he saw her enter and turned
full toward her to look again. Obviously she was not one of
the hired dancing girls. Neither had she come to buy
whiskey—a common occurrence. She loitered in the door
carelessly, as he had done the moment before, apparently
looking for a place in which she could amuse herself.

Booted, spurred, and with a regulation Forty-Five belted
around her waist, her appearance was not much out of
keeping with that of the average ranch girl. What distin-
guished her was, in the first place, an exquisitely slender,
olive-skinned, dark-eyed beauty and, in the second
place, an air of truly masculine detachment.

On account of her beauty Dix Van Dyck expected to
see a dozen men jump up and accost her. But instead
they merely turned their heads, stared at her, and then re-
sumed their occupations. He was thoroughly puzzled.
Apparently she was known. Apparently she was good.
But if so, what was she doing in this hellhole?

Now it must be understood that in the Southwest there
are only two classes of women. There are the bad and the
good. The bad are what bad women are everywhere—
very, very bad. On the other hand, the good are exceedingly good. They can travel alone anywhere, day or night,
and they are perfectly safe. In a country where the need
for men is great and where the place for women is small,
their value is proportionately high. In that country men
do not gossip about a woman, for slander meets the reply
of bullets. In that country a woman can take liberties
with a man that would damn her forever in the eyes of

Eastern society, but in the Southwest nothing is taken for granted about the weaker sex.

Chivalry wears no plumes, and knighthood bears no title, but there gallantry is a reality and not a name. To the Southwesterner a good woman is daughter or sister or mother. She can eat his food, ride his horse, draw his revolver, and even share his bunk. Yet she will not draw a whisper of suspicion until by her own act she confesses that she is not of the elect. Such an act is the entry of a place like this one of Jerry Conklin's in the Double Bend.

All this must be understood in order to read the confusion of mind with which Dix Van Dyck stared at the feminine intruder. He read in the glances of the men that deference that is accorded to only one type of woman in the Southwest. She was known, and she was respected. Then what was she doing here? He leaned back against the bar and scowled steadily at her. Something told him that he was on the trail of excitement.

As for the girl, she swept the great room with a calm eye, almost like the glance of an ennuied man looking for excitement. At last she approached a crap table. It was surrounded by a dense circle, two deep, every man intent on his game. But at her coming one of the men glanced up, recognized her, raised his hat, and stepped back to surrender his place.

The wonder of Dix Van Dyck made his face redden furiously. As for the other men at the gaming table, they turned toward the girl with broad grins, such as those who proclaim that the luck is running against the house. Dix Van Dyck caught the man on the stick—he who handles the dice for the house—in a keen scrutiny. The fellow was scowling blackly. The girl took the dice.

Her hand dipped in a pocket of her short riding skirt and came out with the glint of yellow. She made a few casts and lost. A low groan came from the gamesters.

Evidently they had wagered heavily on her luck. The girl stamped in vexation, which made Dix Van Dyck smile. At least, he thought, she was like other women in being a bad loser. She drew out another gold coin and tossed it on the table.

The Story of the Cross 3

After that, her luck apparently held consistently good. The others at the table were still wagering on her and with her, and the payer at that table did little besides constantly shovel out the coin of the house. However, the other men in the house paid little attention to the scene. In his part of the country Dix knew that such sensational winning would have drawn everyone about in a great circle to watch the big coin roll in. He gained a sudden and deep respect for a community where such prodigious luck passed with hardly a notice. It was like a crowd in a new mining town, where gold almost loses significance except when it comes raw from the earth.

At length, the girl left the table, and the payer wiped his sweaty forehead and turned a venomous glance after her retreating figure. She went straight to the roulette wheel, a small group following. Dix Van Dyck drew a little closer and saw that she had taken the most extreme chance that the game affords—she had placed a whole handful of gold on a single number.

The wheel whirled, the man behind it watching with anxious eyes. It slowed, purred, and clicked softly to a stop—and on her number. Stack after stack of coin was counted out and shoved to her—thirty-six for one. The payer watched her with a wistful eye. She placed her entire winnings again—and still on that most dubious of all gambling chances—a single number. Again the wheel whirled, purred to a stop, and again the girl won. The payer shook his head in gloomy doubt, and counted out the money slowly, stack by stack. Plainly it would not take much more to break the bank.

But, before he had half finished the count, the girl, as if impatient, picked up a handful of gold—less than her original wager—dropped it into her pocket, and said carelessly: "Keep the rest of it, Bill. I ride light. Keep the rest of it, and the next time a gent drops in here broke . . . and thirsty . . . buy him a drink and stake him."

The payer ceased in his count and stared after her with blinking, uncomprehending eyes while she strolled away to another table. Here, she lingered only a moment and then passed on to the dancing floor.

Dix Van Dyck waited for someone to follow her, someone to take the chair next to hers, but no one moved. She sat at a table alone. Men passed with smiles but without any close approach. If she had been a leper, she could not have been more sedulously avoided. Dix thought of many things: of some terrible, contagious disease, of insanity, or perhaps she was the sweetheart of some noted gunman.

Yes, that would explain it. Dix Van Dyck hitched his belt a little higher and laughed softly, unpleasantly, to himself. Most of his jests were of a nature that he alone could appreciate. He turned to a bearded, unshaven man next to him.

"Stranger," he said, "will you drink?"

"Don't mind," said the other.

"Red-eye?"

"Yep."

"Partner," continued Dix Van Dyck amiably, while the bartender was spinning the tall bottle toward them, "I been watching a little play that looks sort of queer to me. I'm a stranger in these parts, and maybe you could put me wise."

"Maybe."

"I been watching that girl over there to the table by the dancing floor."

"Jack?"

"Is that her name?"

"Yep."

"None of the boys don't seem much friendly with her. Can't she dance? Can't she talk? Or is she owned private by a gunman?"

The other grinned. "She can dance, she can talk, and there ain't any man in these parts fool enough to want to own her."

With this enigmatic reply he rested content, as if there were nothing more to be said. Dix Van Dyck blinked and drew in his breath. His very heart was eaten up with curiosity.

"Bad actor?" he asked.

"Ain't you really heard nothing about Jack?" asked the other with naïve wonder.

"Never."

"Follow me."

He led the way to the door of the saloon and squinted to right and left down the long line of tethered horses. One shape stood out through the half-broken gloom of the early night, a tall white horse, glimmering through the darkness. Even by that faint light the practiced eye of Dix Van Dyck made out an unusually beautiful piece of horseflesh.

"If you don't know the girl," said the stranger, "maybe you recognize the hoss? That white one down the line."

"Ain't nothing I can recognize him by," asserted Dix.

"Hmm," said the other, and scratched his head in the effort to find some clue that the other might be able to follow. "Ever hear of McGurk?"

"Sure," said Dix Van Dyck. "I've lived some way off from these parts, but I know McGurk is about the fastest gunman that ever fanned a hammer."

"McGurk *was*," answered the stranger.

"Dead?"

"Worse'n dead. Done for."

"Well?"

The other persisted in his irritating, roundabout way of telling what he knew, as if he wished to draw out the relish of a rare morsel. "Ever hear of Boone's gang?"

"Seems like I have," murmured Dix Van Dyck, "seems like I heard they was all cleaned up by McGurk."

"You heard wrong . . . a pile wrong," said the other. "That girl is Boone's daughter."

"The devil she is!"

"The devil she ain't. And mostly devil she is, at that. That white hoss there in the dark is McGurk's hoss."

"Is he here?"

"Nope, the girl rides the hoss."

The iron hand of Dix Van Dyck gripped the shoulder of his companion and his voice rolled, low and muttering, like approaching thunder. "Partner, I been asking you straight questions, one man to the other. Maybe I been asking too much, but in my part of the country nobody don't josh me when I feel serious. I'm a pile serious right now. Out with it. D'ye mean to tell me that girl in here finished McGurk . . . McGurk, who killed . . . ?"

"I know . . . McGurk who killed a hundred gunfighters. But all we know is that McGurk started on the trail of Boone's gang and that he finished 'em all except one young feller who beat it East and got married and this girl. We know McGurk started on that trail with a white horse. We know the girl come down from the mountains, riding that same white horse. Partner, them are the cards, and you can put 'em together any way you want."

Dix Van Dyck swallowed hard and then set his teeth. It was almost more than he could understand. He had a faint suspicion that the other was amusing himself with generous lies. If so, there would be an unhappy ending to the tale. He decided to draw out the man further. "Is that what scares 'em away from that girl in there?"

The other looked up with a scowl that changed almost at once into friendliness.

"Look here, pal," he explained, "you're all due for a cold trail. I'll tell you straight. When Jack Boone come down from the hills, there was another with her. He was one of the last of Boone's old gang . . . the best of the bad lot. All we know is what he told us. He said the girl had got a hold of a little cross . . . this sounds funny, I know . . . and that the cross give her good luck, but give bad luck to everyone near her . . . her friends, particular. He says that cross was what made her able to beat McGurk, and, as long as she had it on, there wasn't any man could handle her."

"That sounds all pretty damned fishy to me," grumbled Dix Van Dyck.

"Don't it?" agreed the other. "It sounded fishy to the lot of us. But the first thing we noticed was that this feller wanted nothing more than to get free of Jack Boone. He blew north and ain't been heard of since. Then Bud Ganton, a dirty half-breed with a record it took half an hour to read, made up his mind that he was going to get the loot that the girl was said to have. He started out from town for her cabin where she was living up in the hills. The next day the girl come riding in to tell the deputy marshal that there was a dead man out to her house. The marshal went out and found Ganton pumped full of lead and both his own guns out with a bullet fired out of each. Now there was only one thing Ganton was any good for, and that was a gun play. With his sixes he was a world-beater. I've seen him make a play, and he could make his gun talk French, I'm here to state. Nobody knows what happened exactly out there to the girl's cabin. But it was sure plain that Ganton had time to get out his guns and make a play before he dropped. The girl was too fast for him and drilled him clean. Now, if the girl didn't have something like that cross to help her out, how'd she ever have got away with Ganton?"

"If she was Boone's daughter, he sure taught her how to fan a six," answered Dix Van Dyck.

"Sure, but that ain't all the reason we got for thinking that little cross of hers makes her safe and raises hell for her friends. There was Luther Carey. He was knocked off'n his feet by Jack's pretty face . . . which she's some looker . . . and he said bad luck could go to the devil. He started on the trail for Jack. She warned him fair and square that it was a plumb cold trail and that he'd get bad luck if he stuck around. But Luther stayed. About a week later he was bucked off a little tame cayuse that a boy could've rid. He was bucked off and busted his neck when he hit the sand. I'm asking you, was that nacheral? No, I'll tell a man it wasn't.

"Then Hopkins, that Eastern dude that was a mining engineer. He come along and seen Jack and went crazy about her. We warned him fair and square, and she warned him, too, they say. But he kept going out to see her. One day he dropped down a shaft in the Buckhorn mine, and they had to go down with a broom and a shovel and sweep up what was left of him.

"There's two things we blame to the cross Jack wears. There's plenty of others. I could sit here all night and tell 'em to you. Take her luck with cards, for instance. You never see her lose more'n one out of every three passes. If she wanted to, she could break every game in the state. But money don't seem to mean nothing to her. Hang around her? Dance with her? Partner, I'd a pile rather jump off'n Eagle Bluff. It'd be an easier way of dying, but no surer."

The Imp of the Perverse   4

So saying, the stranger turned and walked back into the bar. Even the telling of the narrative seemed to make him need a drink.

Now, it was well known in Guadalupe that, if you wanted Dix Van Dyck to do a thing, the best way was to urge him toward the opposite. If there were two roads, one safe and one dangerous, it was thoroughly understood that one could always make Dix take the safe road by urging him to choose the dangerous. If the stranger at Double Bend had been inspired by an angel from heaven, he could not have spoken more effectively to make Dix Van Dyck seek out the girl, Jack. In fact, as he stepped back into the dance hall, his mind was already made up. He only waited for a convenient moment before approaching her. But, although his nature was strangely perverse, there was little that was wholly rash about Dix Van Dyck. In the first place, he believed with his entire soul every word that the stranger had told him about Jack and her mysterious cross. He had seen the effect of that cross in her gambling. Moreover, there is a deep element of superstition in those who live among Mexicans and prospectors. Luck becomes an almost personal god.

Because Dix Van Dyck believed thoroughly that this girl held good luck for herself and bad luck for all who came near her, he was afraid—deeply afraid. He felt a prickling chill run up his back as he looked at her. But it was the sort of fear that a man feels when he looks at a grim antagonist with whom he knows that he is about to fight. It was the sort of fear that mingles with one's desire to leap from a high place to destruction. It was the imp of perverse that lives in the soul of every man, but above all was present in Dix Van Dyck.

He was afraid. He would rather have faced a dozen guns in the hands of desperadoes than sit for a single second at the side of this girl. For this very reason he would not have missed the opportunity for all the gold in the world placed at his feet. He was shaken to his very soul with fear in advancing toward a danger against which there was no known method of fighting. And because of that nothing could stop him. He hesitated only long enough to survey the girl sharply, thoroughly, weigh her strength, estimate her character.

He could see only her profile, for she leaned forward with one elbow resting on the table, and her chin in the palm of her hand; the other arm lay across the back of the chair. An attitude of awkward repose in most people, but in this girl Dix Van Dyck felt a capacity for instant action. In the fraction of a second a sleeping dog can uncurl from the most clumsy position and leap a dozen feet away from danger. He felt the same possibility in this girl—a cat-like activity—a unconscious guard that remained alert even when mind and body slept. It even occurred to him that she might be perfectly aware of his scrutiny.

Once more his flesh prickled and grew cold. So he strode boldly up and took a chair near her. Her eyes swung around to him slowly, slowly as if a careful force regulated the movement. He found himself staring into pitchy black depths, wide, unconcerned, meaningless. He felt as if the eyes were looking through him and past him at some object in the infinite distance. For a man squints to see an object near at hand but stares with open eye at something far away. Judging by her eyes, he might have been a speck of white on the far horizon, an indefinite particle, whether cloud or sail. It whipped all the fighting instinct into his brain.

"My name," he said doggedly, "is Dix Van Dyck."

Her voice, in answer, was neither frivolous nor impertinent, but rather that of one who is wearied by the necessity of speech. "My name don't concern you, stranger. If you want to know it, ask one of the men. He'll tell you, along with a lot of reasons why you shouldn't be sitting here."

"Lady," answered Dix Van Dyck, "I've heard all those reasons. To put it straight, that's why I'm here."

The first spark of interest burned up in the dark eyes, and something like the ghost of a smile softened her mouth at the corners, as if in faint recognition of a kindred spirit.

"I've heard about good luck that follows you and bad luck that follows everyone around you."

"You don't believe it?" she asked, growing somewhat cold again.

"I believe it," said Dix Van Dyck calmly, "as if I read it in the Bible, but it ain't any real reason why you should sit here alone."

"Listen," said the girl, and she leaned gravely toward him, "I got an idea that I know what you are, and I like your kind. But you're on the wrong trail . . . a cold trail, partner. No matter what they told you, they didn't tell you enough, or you'd have been stopped. There's bad luck around me. That ain't all. There's hell!"

Her eyes widened, and she cast a glance over her shoulder—as if fate listened there, an impalpable presence, grinning invisibly at the warning she spoke to Dix Van Dyck. She had been beautiful even when she sat there impassively, but, now that a color was flushing the olive-tinted skin and life had come into her eyes, she was the most lovely woman Dix Van Dyck had ever seen. She thrilled him like a strain of music. She uplifted him like a passage of noble poetry. She lured him like the purple distances of the desert.

"Lady," he said, "speakin' in general, the only thing I want is action, and being near you promises a pile of it. If I bother you, I'll be on my way. If I don't, I'd sure like to hang around a while."

She considered this cavalier utterance with a frown and a thoughtful, sidewise glance that suddenly lifted to his face. "If I told you to go, would you?" she asked.

Dix Van Dyck flushed. "If you say the word, there ain't nothing I'd do quicker."

"Honest?"

The blood died away from his face and left it splotched with gray, tans, and purples. "Talkin' man to man," he said evenly, "it'd be some hard job to break away just now, but I'll go, if I have to."

"Then go," said the girl sharply.

The friendliness died from her eyes, and they became in an instant as black as they had been at the first. He pushed back his chair, setting his teeth in anger. But, even as he caught the edge of the table and put weight on it to rise, he knew that he could not go. It was like a desertion before the battle was fought. It was like cowardice under fire. He settled back in the chair, breathing hard, and glared at her.

"You're saying that to try me out?" he said.

"I never meant anything more in my life," said the girl.

"Yet," he persisted, "you was pretty friendly only a minute ago."

"Was I?" she queried with calm-eyed insolence. "Well, I'm tired of you now."

He felt a great desire to take that round, slender throat between thumbs and forefingers; he could almost tell how it would crunch under the pressure. Then he remembered with a cold rush of shame that she was a woman. A woman, and therefore a creature of infinite wiles. The thought held him. He studied her.

"Well?" she asked coldly. "Are you going?"

"D'you know," pondered Dix Van Dyck, his grim eyes boring into hers, "I got an idea that, if I get up and leave this table, you'll despise me. Am I right?"

The question had the effect of a sharp jerk on the reins. The girl straightened almost with a snap and her serious frown centered steadily on him.

Before she could answer he swept on: "Look at the way I'm fixed. All my life I've been hunting action. Most I could find was hounding a few yaller-hearted men. Now I get to you. Action just nacherally follers you around. I wouldn't have to hunt for it. I find you, and you start to give me the run. I ask you, man to man . . . is it fair? Is it square?"

There was a movement of her lips.

He raised his right hand suddenly and pointed. "Right now, you got a smile all ready to pop out, and you're fighting to keep it back. Am I right, lady?"

She could not help it. The smile came, and then a bubbling laugh. It ran on and on through musical variations like the sound of water trickling over rocks and plunging into tinkling shallows and chiming in deep pools. In all his life Dix Van Dyck had never heard a sound that so fascinated him. He could not tell whether she was laughing with him or at him. The laughter stopped. Sitting straight in her chair, she looked at him with marvelously bright eyes, the smile coming and going at the corners of her mouth.

A Fight against Luck   5

Do I get you right, Dix Van Dyck?" she asked. "Am I sort of a bait that pulls trouble your way? Is that why you want to hang around with me?"

"Jack . . . can I call you that?"

"Sure."

"Jack, you guessed right the first time. That's why I want to hang around. Here I am, six feet two, hard as nails, handy with two guns, and nothing to do. Can you beat that?"

"Nope," said the girl, and broke into her musical chuckle again. "Nope, you beat the world, partner."

"Thanks," grinned Dix Van Dyck. "I'll just oil up my guns and get in fighting shape, and we'll make a team of it."

She grew serious again, shaking her head. "It won't do. I can't let you do it. Look here, Dix Van Dyck, I like you more 'n any man I've run into in a long time. That's telling you straight. I'm not going to let you go to hell because of a fool idea. If you want action, just shoot out these lights, and I'll guarantee you all the action you want."

"But you see," explained Dix Van Dyck sadly, "the trouble a man makes ain't half so pleasin' as the kind he just runs into sort of accidental. Understand?"

"Yep."

"How long," said Dix Van Dyck wistfully, "before things most generally starts."

"Mostly different a lot," said Jacqueline.

"In the meantime," he said, "there's considerable room on the floor. Do we dance?"

She hesitated, as if she still wished to argue the question with him, as if she fought the temptation to let him stay, but then her head nodded with the rhythm of the music—she started up, and in an instant they were gliding across the floor.

There is a strange and dangerous potency in the dance. There is no need of polished, gleaming floor, of bright lights, of a numerous and accomplished orchestra, or of a brilliant assembly of women and men. There is no need of all this. Granted an age a little under thirty, a rhythm supplied by a rusty, stringed piano, the floor of a barn or the stones of a street, and the result is the same— an intoxication, a forgetfulness of the world, two bodies moving in harmony with a thought, and that thought one of beauty. Faces tilt up—a light comes upon them—in their blood is the fragrance of spring and the richness of autumn—the pulse of life runs quicker, quicker, races— and the two strike closer to the heart of things.

So it was with Dix Van Dyck and Jacqueline. She danced rather clumsily at first, as though she had almost forgotten the steps, but, before he became conscious of disappointment, she changed and grew more warmly alive in his arms. There was a cat-like lightness in her step so that the sway of her body followed him almost as if she were poised in air and drawn hither and thither mysteriously—at his will.

As for Jack, she glimpsed the glances of envy and admiration that followed her and knew that she was dancing divinely—knew it and was grateful to the man who held her. The incense of flattery had long been absent, and now it swept up gloriously until her nostrils trembled to inhale it deeply. She had been a creature of action, of masculine and terrible action, and, as such, accepted by the men and the women among whom she moved. Now she became, in an instant, femininely appealing, beautiful. A new and mighty strength filled her.

With all her heart she hated the bearded man who tapped Dix Van Dyck on his shoulder in the middle of the dance. They had paused at the edge of the dance floor and the man said: "Stranger, be on your way. You've started your own little hell by dancing with Jack, but someone else is liable to put on the finishing touch. There was a Mexican in here a minute ago . . . a bad one by the look . . . asking after a man like you. The deputy marshal . . . Glasgow . . . was with him. I sent 'em down the street, but they'll be back. Take my advice, and don't wait."

With that, he turned on his heel, and Dix Van Dyck, a towering figure in the crowd, stiffened and stared after him. Truly the arm of Sheriff Oñate was long.

"The bad luck," he nodded and stared down at the face of the girl.

"The bad luck," she agreed. "It didn't wait." She said it half ruefully, half carelessly, like one familiar with danger. "Take the back door," she advised. "It's the easiest way out."

"The easiest way," said the big man calmly, "is to get back to our table and wait for what comes. This ain't the finish. It's only the beginning of a long trail."

She followed him back to the table. It was only because she wanted a chance to argue the point.

"But you see," she explained, as they slipped again into their chairs, Van Dyck facing the door, "that everything is against you. The deputy marshal can call on everyone in the house, if he wants 'em. Besides, do you know the country in case you make a getaway?"

"Not a mile of it. I come from the south."

"What've you done that started the law after you?"

"Nothing. We've got a badman for sheriff down in Chaparna County. He's after my scalp."

"And you're going to sit here and see this through?"

"Sure. What would you do?"

She avoided the question. "It's a crazy idea. Take my word, the best thing is to cut and run. It's bad to have a sheriff after you. It's a lot worse to have a marshal, and Glasgow sticks to a trail like glue to a dog's tail."

Apparently he barely heard her words but sat stiff and straight in his chair, his keen eyes plunging into the future. By deep and sympathetic intuition she knew all that was passing in his mind.

His reason told him in no uncertain terms to take the advice of the girl and leave the saloon. But the same perverse instinct that had first made the man hunt her out, now held him in his chair, waiting for the surely approaching danger.

She knew at once that it was useless to argue longer with him. But the suspense began to make her uncomfortable and sick inside—the qualm that comes to the soldier before the battle. What made it doubly deadly was the noise that continued unabated throughout the rest of the great room. From the gaming tables, from the bar, from the orchestra, from the dance floor and the tables around it, the same unbroken stream of chatter, cries, curses, laughter poured out at them. It was like a grim parody of the whole of life. Into this gay throng death was about to come with silent steps, stretch out his arm, and beckon his victim. Then would fall an instant of silence, a few cries of horror, but almost at once the noise would be recommenced. Conscience would be drowned in the clamor of self-conscious gaiety.

"There's going to be a gun play," said Dix Van Dyck, "and I don't want you in the danger zone. Go to another table."

She shrugged her shoulders and smiled. He got the impression, somehow, that she valued her life less than anything in the world. He knew in fact that, when a woman turns daredevil, she passes beyond the limit of any man, but he was unprepared for this contemptuous indifference. He made no further effort to persuade her. His mind was too filled with conjecture. Was it indeed true that the girl was fatal to her friends? Or was the story half lie and half rumor? Against a common danger he was willing to take his chance, but to have his hands tied and the muzzle of his gun jolted by fate in the crisis of action was too much. It was superhuman—it was ghostly and paralyzing.

All of this Jack read in his face. She saw the keen eyes sink deeper under the bush of brow, saw his cheeks contract and the lower jaw thrust out, saw his forehead turn a sickly white, glimmering with perspiration. It was not cowardice. She had seen other men in her company face danger with the same aspect. But this man was different. Fear turned him cold, but it did not make him shake. It occurred to her, vaguely, that this might be the man who could break the power of the strange charm she carried. She could not stand the suspense of his silence any longer.

"How can you tell," she said, "when the man who's after you comes in?"

"I'll wait," answered the big, white-faced man, "until he makes a dive for his gun."

"Wait for that before you draw?"

"Yes."

"Then why not order your coffin now?"

"Because I take my chance on beating him to his gun."

"Beat two of them?" she repeated incredulously.

"Don't talk," he answered sharply. "I got to sit here and do a pile of thinking."

So she lapsed into silence. The face of Van Dyck, naturally homely, now grew horrible as the nervous strain of the wait told upon him. She began to have an odd feeling that she could hear the ticking of a clock somewhere through the din. It began very softly, click-click-clicking through the room and gradually rising to a crescendo, louder and louder and louder, till she wondered that everyone in the room did not hear it. It rose louder and more rapidly until she wanted to jump up from the table with an outcry of horror. Then she discovered that the mysterious beating was the drum of her own excited heart. She dared not rise.

It was a singular duel of courage between her and the man opposite. On him the danger rested. But upon her, she felt more and more strongly, would lie the blame for his death. For she did not dream of any other outcome to the encounter. She forced herself back to calmness and considered the figure of Van Dyck carefully, critically. It was that of the natural fighter, beyond a doubt, hard, lean, marvelously suggestive of activity in spite of its size. Her eyes centered on the hands. They had never worn gloves, it seemed, for they were as brown as his cheeks. They had never performed the labors of the range, for the fingers were long, sinewy, fleshless, and, when the fist closed, the row of knuckles stood out sharply. Nervous fingers. They hovered here and there. Sometimes, falling into a detached mood, it seemed to her that the hands on the opposite edge of the table were two spiders, deadly, long-leaping, and crouching, about to lunge at some prey. Perhaps at *her* throat.

Fear of the man grew slowly up in her. He was in an agony of apprehension. She knew he did not really expect to outlive the coming fight. She knew he believed in the potent power of the cross she wore and its damning bad luck. There remained his will-power and his pride. It made a terrible and silent fight—a man within a man.

Then that slender, long-fingered right hand grew tense on the edge of the table. He leaned back a little in his chair so that he would have free play to get at this revolvers.

The Camp Fire 6

You see him?" she whispered.

"Don't turn!" he warned her softly, fiercely. "I think I see the man. I think I see a Mexican I knew in Chaparna County."

"And the marshal?"

"There's no one with him . . . no one I can see."

"Thank God."

"Not yet. This Mex is a bad one . . . if he's the man I think. Pedro Alvarez . . . long record . . . snap shot."

"What's he doing?"

She yearned for a single glance back. But such a glance might have betrayed her companion to the hunter. Small things, she knew, frequently turned the odds in such battles.

"He's walkin' about . . . slow. He's looking hard."

"Dix Van Dyck, it ain't too late. Start for that back door before he sees you."

"You're right, Jack, I'm scared. Not of the Mex, but of that cross you wear. But I'm not too scared to fight. My hand don't shake none."

It was, in fact, as steady as a rock.

"Get your hand on your gun."

"Nope, I'll keep it here till he makes his move. I'm givin' your cross every chance to get in its work, see?"

"Maybe he won't sight you."

"Maybe."

"Then . . . ?"

But the words froze on her lips. The eyes of Dix Van Dyck had widened and narrowed suddenly, and into them came the gleam of recognition. She knew that somewhere behind her a man stood, staring at her companion. Death was there—its wings outspread—hesitating over which to strike.

Then the hand of Dix Van Dyck shot down, and a gun flashed with a crazy wobble over the edge of the table. The wobble came from the force of the explosion that kicked the muzzle of the gun high. No answering shot. She rose, whirling from her chair, and saw a tall, thin Mexican in an enormous sombrero, toppling backward. From his outstretched hand a revolver dropped. He struck a post, staggered, and then pitched forward on his face. With both his guns now in his hands Dix Van Dyck stood like one transfixed, staring at his work.

She caught at his arm. "Follow me. Glasgow will be here in a jiffy."

She fled before him toward the door, through it, and into the blessed dimness of the night. A form raced toward her.

"What was it?" shouted the voice of Glasgow in her ear.

"A Mex shot," she answered. "Your man's inside."

He leaped into the door of the saloon with his gun poised, and at the same time she saw the big form of Van Dyck lunge across the street, making for the stables. In a moment she sprang into her own saddle and waited.

In hardly more than half a minute there came a thunder of galloping hoofs over the wooden floor of the stable, and she spurred into place beside him. Behind them babel was issuing from the door of the dance hall and pouring out onto the street, but a winding of the way shut them from her view almost immediately.

He was well mounted, she saw at once, not on a horse

like the matchless stallion that carried her, but on a tall charger that covered the distance with mighty, swinging strides. He towered above her on this steed by a whole foot, and she felt suddenly reduced to impotence again, as she had felt when she sat opposite him in the dance hall, waiting. However, he reined in his horse when she reined in hers, keeping always half a length behind her. At length she reduced the pace to a gentle trot.

"No chase?" he called.

"Nope."

"What's wrong?"

"They know you're with me."

"Well?"

"They know I'm hard to catch."

He chuckled through the dark, and she added rather spitefully: "Besides, they'll wait for your bad luck."

"Bad luck be damned!" cried the ringing voice of Dix Van Dyck. "I've broken the bad luck tonight."

"Is it better," she queried almost angrily, resenting his confidence, "to be a free man in Double Bend or on the run in the desert with Marshal Glasgow behind you? I ask you that man to man? Is that good luck or bad?"

"Any way you want to put it," he replied carelessly. "It's the sort of luck I want. Besides, there's one more burr under the saddle of *Señor* Oñate, damn his eyes! Where'll we camp?"

"Up this cañon to the left a few miles. There's a good spring there and a circle of cottonwoods. We'll camp in the center of 'em."

"Risk a fire?"

"I tell you, they ain't going to hunt you tonight. They know you're with me. They know my hoss can carry double farther and faster than any of their ponies. Maybe they won't hunt at all but trust to your bad luck."

Over this he brooded in silence while they worked

their way up the rough bed of the ravine until they reached the circle of trees. They were ancient, mighty cottonwoods, nourished by the water from the spring.

In the center of the little grove they kindled a fire, for they found an abundance of dry wood and the whole, half-rotten trunk of a fallen giant. Then, propping themselves against their saddles, they sat on opposite sides of the fire. He rolled and lighted a cigarette, and she sat with her hands locked in front of her knees and her face turned up to the stars. Even the sailor has less love for the stars than the dweller of the desert. To the sailor they are guides and steering points, but to the desert dweller they are friends—the eyes of friends who look down through the long, breathless silence of the nights.

The two held their positions for minute after minute, unchanging. They were happy, for the quiet, the sense of space that was their proper environment. Now and then the flicker of the fire flashed clearly across their faces, but for the most part they were withdrawn and lost in the deep gloom of the night, and the glow of the fire with its thousand shadows actually helped to conceal them.

Tall, broad, black as the heart of the night, the cottonwoods fenced them in. There was but one way for them to look, and that was straight up, past the dizzy tops of the trees and on to the yellow lights of the stars. Up to these the girl stared, but the man, his head lowered to the palms of his hands and his face made ominous and ugly by the fire-shadows, stared steadily across at Jack. An age-old instinct, perhaps, directed them, for woman looks up—in acceptance—and man looks down—in doubt. By the flare and the leap of the fire he was studying her features, and every penetrating glimpse was like the reading of a new page in an endless story, each one strangely revealing.

Finally he got some fresh wood and piled it discreetly,

so that it made a thin little arm of flame, stabbing into the night, and by that light he could look steadily at the girl. She paid no attention. Her face was still raised, and her expression was one of deep, vague content. Looking at her in that manner he could well understand that no human thing in all the world was necessary to her. It gave her a singular charm—this independence of attitude. Also it was deeply challenging. It made him long to break through her reserve. Without knowing it, he adopted toward her little household gods the attitude of an iconoclast.

The Iconoclast　　　　　　　　7

Did y'ever hear about souls that get tangled up after death and come back to earth in the wrong shapes?" he said suddenly.

"I dunno," answered the girl. "Seems to me like I heard something about it. Why?"

"Well, I been thinking, wouldn't it be funny if the soul of some old sourdough come back and hopped into the body of a beautiful girl."

"Well?"

"It'd be kind of funny, that's all," he murmured contentedly.

"Hmm," said the girl. "Maybe you don't no ways mean me by that?"

He was much surprised. "You? Did I say you?"

"Which I'm sort of silent," she explained suspiciously.

"Well, it'd be a funny thing, eh?"

"That idea don't interest me none," she said coldly.

The silence fell heavily over them. Each knew each was thinking of the other. As for the girl, she did not understand very clearly the imputations behind the unusual question of Dix Van Dyck, but what she did feel most acutely was the challenge of his personality. It was, in a way, like a hand that had reached out and touched her on the shoulder, compelling her attention. She resented it keenly and strove to fasten her attention once more on the cold twinkle of the stars.

"D'you know," she said, thinking out loud, "that, when the stars are as bright as they are tonight, sometimes I feel just as if the old earth was pushing up closer to them . . . feel as if I was sailing right up through the air!"

"Hmm," grunted Dix Van Dyck. "That idea don't interest me none."

She admitted the counter thrust by nodding her head sharply and scowling across to him. His vast, boyish grin of delight met her eye, and she jerked her head back to stare once more at the stars. However, she was grateful that the night would obscure the burning heat of her face.

The stars, alas, had grown into a confused swirl of faint light. She found that she was making no effort to see them clearly. She was concentrating on the effort to find an answer to this insolent fellow. All the time there was that old sensation of surrounding strength—surrounding personality. The man was reaching out to her. For what?

"I feel," she said, "as if I was inside a house, and you was knockin' at the door. What d'ye want?"

"If you was inside a house and I was knocking at the door," responded the irrepressible Dix Van Dyck indirectly, "I got an idea that the door would stay locked."

"I got an idea," said the girl coldly, "that you're right."

This reply somewhat damped his spirits, but he rallied himself sternly to the trail. After all, she was only a girl. Yet, he began to guess more and more clearly at the soul of the sourdough.

"There ain't no use bein' strange," he assured her. "You might as well get to know me today as tomorrow."

"Tomorrow," she said calmly, "I ain't going to be with you."

"If you leave," he announced, "I'll follow."

"I'll go straight back to Double Bend," she said maliciously.

"I'll ride after you to Double Bend."

"To Marshal Glasgow?" she asked in real alarm.

"Why not? I'd take a chance with him."

"Some men was born fools, some educated fools, and some fools by choice, and I'm thinkin' you're all three rolled into one."

Nevertheless, she was much moved. Her voice told the tale.

"Now that this here partnership is begun . . . ," he started.

She cut in: "Who said partnership?"

"Why," he cried with a voice of much pain, "I thought all the time that was understood. Which was why I tried out the bad luck back there in the dance hall."

"Now," she answered scornfully, "you're lyin'. You done that for pure deviltry. I seen it in your eye."

"Anyway," he went on contentedly, "that was the way I understood it, so we'll leave it there."

"Will we?" she said with rising anger. "Am I going to have you trailin' me around the desert whether I want you or not? Say, Dix Van Dyck, ain't this a free country?"

"Are you pretty mad?" he asked cautiously.

"I am!"

"Well, that's good."

Her anger apparently choked back further words.

"Yes," he explained, "it shows we're on the way to being friends. That's what I've learned from women. Get 'em mad and they're two-thirds yours."

"I s'pose," she answered with dangerous calm, "that you know a pile about women. Kind of a heart-breaker, eh?"

"I know quite a bit about 'em," admitted the man easily. "You see, I ain't been doing much all my life outside of fighting men and making love to women. Takin' it all in all, I don't know which is the most exciting, but I'd kind of put a woman above a gun fight."

She thought at first that it might be pure banter, but he spoke so steadily and evenly that she was deceived. Then, remembering his manliness and courage earlier in the evening, she took pity on him.

"If you're playing me for the common run of girls," she said, "you're on another cold trail, Van Dyck. Men ain't a thing to me. Less'n nothing, in fact."

"That just goes to show," said Dix Van Dyck, "that you're built along my own lines inside. You see, girls have been less'n nothing to me, too."

"What you been doing then, lying to 'em?"

"Sort of. Mostly sort of angling around and waiting for the right one to come along."

"I s'pose," she said scornfully, "that I'm the right one."

"Nope. Not yet. You look all right, but I got to glance you over a bit more before I take you."

An inarticulate murmur of rage answered him.

"You *are* mad, ain't you?" he said with an open delight. "Let's see?"

Reaching over to the fire he raised a glowing brand, twirled it dexterously till it broke into a small flame, and raised it so that he could look fully into her face. She winced away a little and obviously wished with all her might that she could cover her face from his sight. She was scarlet with shame and pride and rage. That pride kept her from turning away. That rage made her drop a trembling hand on her gun.

"Van Dyck," she said furiously, and her voice shook like the voice of a fighting mad man, "I've pulled my gun for less things than this."

"But you can't make your draw on me?" he queried. "That sounds pretty good for me, doesn't it?"

She was silent.

"I s'pose," he went on, "that in the whole world there ain't nothing you hate half so much as you hate me."

"Stranger," she said, "you must be reading my mind."

"Sure," he said, "I have been for some time." His voice changed and grew deeply serious. "Tell me why it ain't possible for us to make a team, Jack? I been talkin' foolish, but I just wanted to get you worked up enough to begin really thinking about me. Look at the two of us. Here you are with every man, woman, and child in Double Bend afraid to sit down by you. Why can't we hit the trail together and run north? No, I don't mean double harness or anything like that. I mean travel like man with man. We'll hit new country where we're new. You'll get a chance to forget that fool cross, and I'll get a chance to live without fighting for a week or two. Shake on it?"

He stretched a broad palm beside the fire toward her, and he saw the instinctive jerk of her arm to meet his gesture. He held his hand patiently. At last he withdrew it with a sigh.

"Think it over," he said quietly, "I don't want you to make up your mind too quick."

Still no answer.

Then, suddenly, so that he stared where he sat and narrowed his eyes to peer at her, she said: "Van Dyck, are you talking as man to man or as man to woman?"

The solemnity of it took his breath. The light answer tumbled to his lips and fell heavily back again. She was sitting very straight, and he could make out the glow of her eyes as they reflected the firelight.

"If it's man to man, you'll go with me, Jack?"

"Right! Tell me straight, Van Dyck," she said.

The truth came up to his lips. It came and formed itself in words, surprising the speaker more than she who listened.

Plain Trails 8

I t's man to woman, Jack."

A pause came. Now that he had spoken, his mind swirled as he examined the appalling truth.

"I kind of thought so," said the girl. "I'm sorry."

He answered: "So'm I. Damned sorry, Jack."

"I was hoping," she said wearily, "that we *could* be pals."

"So was I," he said faintly.

She stood up. "I'm going to turn in."

"I'll sit here by the fire a while."

"Better not. You'll have a pile of riding to do tomorrow."

"But I got a pile of thinking to do right now."

"All right. Good night, Van Dyck."

Her hand went out to him. He shook it gravely with a reverent touch, and afterward with a vacant eye watched her preparations for the night. They were quickly made, and almost at once she lay wrapped in her blanket with her boots under her head. He bowed his forehead against his hands and pondered the situation gloomily. He was trying to retrace the course of the rough banter that had led him, at last, to this strange exposé of his own emotion. Then vague conjecture filled his mind of what she would do, and of how she would act toward him in the morning. He was in the position, in a way, of one who has striven to take the fort by storm, and, being repulsed, he must content himself with laboriously laying siege to the place and waiting for days and weeks and even months to tell. These thoughts in turn grew dim in his mind.

A pain in his back suddenly recalled him. He found that he had fallen asleep and must have sat in that cramped position for hours. Already the gray of the dawn was outlining the eastern hills. Every movement was a pain as he rose and stretched his limbs; the blood came tingling back, and he laughed at his own folly.

Then he turned to see if Jack was smiling silently at him. But she was gone. Perhaps she was foraging for wood with which to rekindle the fire. She was not there. He turned with a frown and swept the ravine up and down in search of her, but nowhere was there the glimmer of the white horse. Still scowling, he gathered an armful of dry wood and started the fire freshly. Perhaps she had gone for an early morning canter. Then, as the light flared, he glimpsed something white that stirred and fluttered under a rock.

It was a jagged corner of paper and, on it, scrawled almost illegibly as if it had been written by firelight, he read:

Keep straight up the valley; follow the river north on the other side of the mountains. I ain't leaving because I don't like you but because I like you too well.

Jack

He read it over once. He read it twice. He read it again before the full meaning trickled like light into his brain—light through a keyhole. Then he swore softly, steadily as running water. Once more his gaze swung around the horizon, but he could not even guess. She might have gone toward any point of the compass.

Dix Van Dyck felt the most tremendous loneliness of

his life. It welled up in him like water—it brimmed him to the throat. Over such rocky ground it would be very hard to trail her. He stared up at the mountains as if they could speak to him.

One by one and range by range, they were swinging up out of the purples of night and on their highest summit already there was a stain of rose and a stain of yellow—indiscriminate splotches of color startlingly vivid, as if a giant with an invisible paint brush were smearing them at random. But they were all unknown, all strange faces that looked down at him. He knew at once that he could never trace her in this rock wilderness. The very fact filled him with a limitless desire to find her—a strange mixture of emotions. Not love, exactly, but something like it. It was rather the sense of loss that comes to the prospector when he makes a rich strike, goes away for provisions, and returns to find that he has lost the location of his treasure—a lost mine in the desert. Men have been known to waste their lives following some such intangible clue, and Dix Van Dyck had this possibility of waste in him. The blood of the prospector who will follow the hope of a brave tomorrow across the desert year after year, rejoicing in the search rather than in the finding, was in his blood.

What Jack meant to him was merely a definite goal toward which he might strive. The energy that he had dissipated in a thousand careless and reckless ways now centered toward one purpose. She was his vanished mine, his lost treasure. She was priceless because she was unknown, guessed at. Her beauty, her strangeness, the singular superstition that surrounded and accompanied her, all had a part in making him turn toward her.

He set himself methodically to discover a way in which he might capture her again. It was, in the first place, obvious that he could never outstrip that glorious white stallion she rode. Even if he could, it was equally certain that he could never trace her through an unfamiliar country where the hand of the law might be lying in wait for him at any turn. One hold, it seemed, he possessed over her, however intangible it might be. She liked him. Perhaps she liked him for somewhat the same reasons that he liked her—because he was different, unknown to her either by type or example.

He had often stalked young antelope, lying prone in the grass within their sight and raising now and then a foot and leg to show over the top of the verdure. The antelope would stand, watching the strange appearance with bright, fascinated eyes, and then come a little closer to examine it. Always they kept on, with a curiosity greater than their caution, until at last they were within easy shooting distance.

He felt now, in the same way, that he had only to remain there quiet and at length the girl would circle back to the place. Yet this might mean a delay of days and days, and in the meantime the hounds of the law would be on his track. Moreover, the one thing in the world that he could least endure was inaction.

It was on this account that he chose the least promising way of reaching her. He skirted about among the rocks until he found the trail of her horse as she had ridden from the camp. Small, short steps they were at first, and the traces of the girl's boots went alongside. Apparently she had led the horse for a short distance from the place where Dix slept by the fire, and she had held back the stallion so that his steps would fall lightly on the rock. In a little way the double track ceased. The four prints of a standing horse were plain where she had mounted. Then the steps of the horse grew wider apart and more distinct. She had gone on from there at a trot.

The direction was straight across the ravine, at right

angles to the course she had told him to pursue up the valley, across the mountains and then following the river to the north. Dix Van Dyck growled to himself. Certainly she had intended to leave him in the lurch. He fastened his eyes on the rocky side of the ravine and trotted his horse up the steep slope. The signs were not hard to follow. The iron shoes of the stallion, striking the rock, chopped off little fragments that blazed away as plain to the practiced eye of Dix Van Dyck as if the course had been marked in ink across white paper.

He came now, however, upon a harder strata of rock where a glass would be necessary to follow the imprints even of iron shoes. But at this point the trail wound sharply to the right, as if the rider had swerved from the hard rocks by preference and chosen a course along the gravel at the side. This swerving trail puzzled Dix Van Dyck deeply. It was most unusual for a rider of the desert to change a course because of so slight an obstacle, particularly when riding a shod horse.

However, he did not waste time in wonder. He was too interested in the fresh trail. By the way the sand had drifted in upon the tracks, blurring them under the drive of the brisk wind, she could not have passed that way more than three hours before. His heart looked up with hope.

In this manner he came to the crest of the ridge along the left side of the cañon—a sharp crest, dipping down on the farther side almost as abruptly as it rose from the first valley. Just past the summit the trail veered sharply to the left and stopped in a maze of signs. It was a great slab of reddish stone, of copper coloring, but even that hard surface had taken numerous imprints. In a hundred places the stone was marked, and, as he read the sign, the horse had several times turned around and around here, as if chafing under a restraint that held him for an appreciable interval. Examining the ground at the edges of the rock, he caught the imprint of the girl's boot. She had dismounted here, then. The track was very fresh—not more than an hour old, as far as he could judge, though even the most experienced, he knew, often go astray in such matters.

Why she should stop here when she was barely started on her way he could not by any means imagine. A brief halt might be explained in a hundred ways, but here she must have kept the nervous, restive stallion for a full hour, or even more. Such marks could not have been made in a much shorter period. Finally he saw on a gravelly ledge a place where she had sat down.

Most certainly her actions were strange. He was so perturbed in the effort to unravel the meaning that he swung from his horse and sat down on the identical ledge where she must have been only a short time before. Then light broke upon him.

From that position, looking between two low ridges of rock at his left, he found himself staring down past the tops of the cottonwoods and onto the exact site of his late camp. There was still a faint column of smoke wavering up from the fire that he had hastily extinguished with sand—a slender mark against the atmosphere no more distinct than the tracery of a chalk pencil over a slate. She had stopped her horse in the shelter of the ridge and sat there to look back on the camp. She had seen him waken and stir about. She had waited there until she saw him take the trail after her. Did it mean that she actually expected him to follow her? Was that the meaning of the plain trail she had left?

He started up with an exclamation and swung into the saddle. Plain as writing down the slope her trail continued. He galloped along it with a reckless speed.

Oñate Talks Informally 9

I n the capital city of the state Sheriff Oñate was a personage to be sought out and flattered with ceremonious greeting. The vast majority of the electorate in that state admired him for a pomp of presence and a grace of manner that no one west of the Mississippi could rival. Represented by a man of such dignity, they felt confident he would get for them all they might wish. It is true that Sheriff Oñate did not achieve much in the way of arrests, but his own small office was an insignificant matter. What really counted was his position in the state.

It was known that, if he dropped a word in the ear of the governor, action was apt to result. What number of votes Oñate controlled even he himself could not estimate. At least it ran up into the thousands. Accordingly, in the capital, men listened when he spoke. He was more revered in a lobby of the legislature than he was in his office in Guadalupe.

The time of his coming was particularly well chosen. For the state election was within striking distance, and Governor Boardman, though he had lined his pockets comfortably during his term, was not yet in such a position that he could build a house with white verandahs that he had in mind. Accordingly, there was probably no one in the entire city so glad to see the great sheriff as the governor himself.

All of this the sheriff knew perfectly well. He knew also

that in his heart the governor hated the ground upon which he walked, and this merely increased the satisfaction of the benign Oñate. Straight to the offices of the governor he walked—walked, for he wished that many men might see him coming. That night many invitations to dine would wait for him at his hotel.

The man in the outer office had red hair and a pugnose. He was a newcomer also. For both reasons his reception of Oñate was far from cordial, for he saw in the smoky whites of Oñate's eyes that the man was of Indian blood, and the Irish remain the Irish the world around. He told the sheriff to sit down and wait his turn. Whereat the cheeks of the sheriff swelled with poisonous anger.

Luckily, the private secretary passed through the outer office at that moment. The effusiveness of his greeting made amends in some degree. With one eye Oñate enjoyed it; with the other he relished the red-faced discomfiture of the pug-nosed Irishman. He followed the secretary into the inner sanctum.

The governor had just signed an important letter and was screwing back the gold-chased cover of his pen while he pondered deeply whether or not he had made his terms a little too cheaply with a certain corporation. At sight of the sheriff he rolled to his feet—literally rolled, for he was a very plump little man and slid into and out of a chair with a singular undulatory motion. His pudgy hand met the soft palm of Oñate, and they smiled upon one another. If the color of their skins was different, the color of their hearts was the same.

"I have called . . . ," began Sheriff Oñate, tucking his hat under his arm and half bowing.

"Cut out the formality, Don Porfirio," said the governor breezily, "and try that chair . . . no, that one by the window. Here's a box of cigars . . . and here's a milder brand."

In slang the governor kept abreast of the times. If in other things he backslid a little, he did not lose votes thereby. So the account left a comfortable balance in his favor.

"Shoot!" repeated the governor and, so saying, he balanced his stubby feet on the edge of his desk and smiled again beneficiently upon his visitor.

"I have called," went on *Señor* Oñate, "to find out how the election promises and to learn what I may do."

He was never quite sure of his English, and the result was that he always spoke it with a painful grammatical correctness.

"Everything!" exploded the governor. "You can do everything, Oñate. I came into office by the flicker of an eyelash, and I'm liable to go out again by a lot bigger margin. Some of the boys don't like my policies. They claim that I'm too partial to the Mexicans." Here he winked broadly, the whole side of his face wrinkling with his mirth. "Of course, that's nonsense, Oñate!"

"Ah," murmured *Señor* Oñate, "naturally it is nonsense. You will smile, sir, to know that in my district the Mexicans think you hold a prejudice against them."

The governor still smiled but in a sickly fashion. "But you, Oñate, will round them out of such foolishness?"

"I?" said Oñate, and he waved his pudgy arms. "I do what I can, but, when ten thousand tongues start wagging, I cannot stop them all . . . not without great trouble."

The governor knew the symptoms. He waited for the request that he knew was coming and guessed at its size by the length of the prelude—an infallible token. The picture of the big house with the white verandah grew dim in his mind's eye.

"However," went on Oñate smoothly, "I do what I can. I talk here, I talk there. But at my heart, ah, *señor*, my heart is troubled with doubts."

"The hell it is!" exploded the governor, rolling half out of his chair. He gripped the arms of it and controlled himself with a mighty effort. "I'm sorry to hear it, Oñate. Let's have the reason."

As for *Señor* Oñate, he was rolling every second of the situation under his tongue like a seasoned gourmand. "I wrote not many days ago asking the governor for a thing . . . for so little a thing . . . it was merely to scratch with a pen on paper . . . so! But there came back a note of few words that said: "I will not do it." I was much grieved. I am still troubled."

"I refused you?" queried the governor in real astonishment. "What was it about? The matter's out of my mind."

"It was the matter of a man's life," said Oñate. His next words snapped out with a little harsh purr after each one. It was like the warning of the rattler before it strikes. "That of *Señor* Van Dyck . . . the swine . . . the pig . . . the dog who murdered my brother . . . my brother, Vincente!"

The violence of his emotions set him wheezing, and he fell back in his chair with heaving chest and closed eyes. In the moment during which he could see without being seen the face of the governor hardened into sardonic contempt. He smoothed it to a look of serious concern when one of Oñate's small eyes squinted open again.

"About that matter," he said, "I remember now. But your enemies advised you to send the letter to me. It would have been to your harm if I had done what you asked."

"To my harm? To mine?" cried Oñate, so surprised that he forgot both anger and grief.

"Exactly," explained the governor. "When I got your letter asking that Van Dyck be outlawed by proclamation, I looked into the thing. This is what I found. Van Dyck is a big, husky fellow who has run about getting into mischief all his life. But there's nothing venomous about him, and, though he's killed several men, he's always acted in self-defense. I can't have a man like that outlawed, Oñate."

"And my brother," said Oñate with ominous quiet, "is he not to be avenged?"

The heat that had been accumulating for some time in the governor broke out in a noisy surge. "Your brother," he said fiercely, "got two hired murderers and attacked Dix Van Dyck from behind. Van Dyck tore a shelf down from the wall of the saloon, brained two of the men, and strangled your brother, Vincente. It was a fine thing for a man with bare hands to do. And by God, he's not going to be touched for it! That's final!"

The sheriff, for a time, sat speechless. It was, perhaps, better for him that he could not utter a syllable, for during the interim the governor had a chance to quiet down, and very brightly there rose again in his mind the picture of the broad house, the white verandah, the stretch of green lawn, the pleasant vista down the hall and from room to room. For four years in his dreams he had wandered through the apartments of that mansion. And now he was destroying the thing he loved. He was throwing away perhaps ten thousand votes; he was signing his abdication. For whom? For a wild daredevil somewhere in the south country, a ne'er-do-well, a good-for-nothing mischief-maker. The sweat stood out upon the forehead of the governor.

"So!" breathed *Señor* Oñate at last, and heaved himself slowly from his chair. His basilisk eyes glittered against the face of the other. Between fat thumb and fat forefinger he reduced his cigar to a shapeless pulp; he dropped it on the floor; he ground it under his heel and into the fine, soft carpet. All the time his silent eyes were saying that such were the things he would relish doing to the chief executive. "So!" he said for the second time, tucked his hat under his arm (as he had seen a fine gentleman do once in a picture of olden days), and turned toward the door.

"Wait!" said the governor weakly.

But *Señor* Oñate proceeded toward the door, though with a shortened step.

"Wait!" called the governor, and enlivened by his alarm he sprang after the Mexican and seized him by the arm. "What the devil, Oñate, you're not leaving me like this?"

"I have stayed long enough," said Oñate, his voice still broken by panting, "to learn that what I have heard is true. You care for nothing . . . nothing but the *gringos*. Mexican gentlemen may be shot down in cold blood by white dogs who drink their blood. You do not lift your hand. You do not care. Pah! I have stayed long enough . . . too long!"

He turned once more toward the door, but this time the governor seized him by both shoulders and whirled him around.

"Come back here, Oñate! Listen to reason, man!"

Oñate waved both his short arms and, in so doing, brushed off the grip of the governor. "This," he moaned, "is my reward. I who have slaved for you. I who have brought you votes by the thousand and the ten thousand. I who have held you in my heart for a friend."

Grief, self-pity, raised real tears to his eyes. The governor was much moved. He pushed his visitor into a chair—so hard that he landed with a thump that cut short what promised to be a sob.

"Oñate," he said, "rather than break off our friendship, I will do what you wish. I will have the proclamation prepared."

Oñate seized both hands of the other. "My benefactor!" he cried and could only repeat with monotonous joy: "My benefactor!"

"After all," muttered the governor, "it is only one

man . . . only one life . . . and the fellow has been wild . . . too wild. I must put a stop to such things. This is no longer the wild West, and it's time people should know it."

He paced back and forth across the carpet, his hands clasped behind him. His voice rose. He might have been rehearsing a campaign speech. He repeated: "This is no longer the wild West!"

It was a good phrase. He smiled contentedly over it. It almost rubbed out the memory of the proclamation to be prepared and signed.

"And the price?" said Oñate, taking advantage of the smile.

"What price?" growled the governor.

Oñate bowed low. "The price on the head of the renegade?" His voice trembled with suppressed joy. "The price of blood that will draw out the pursuers . . . what price?"

"A price?" murmured the governor, and his rosy cheeks blanched a little. "A price on the head of this man?"

"In Double Bend," said Oñate rapidly, "he resisted arrest. He shot down a deputy marshal."

"Killed?"

"Nearly. In his heart he wished to kill him."

"White?"

"Mexican," said Oñate, and showed his teeth.

"Hmm!" grumbled the governor. He smashed his right fist into the palm of his left hand, rousing his own anger. "A common man-killer, by God!" he cried.

"It is true!" echoed Oñate.

"It's only just there should be a price on his head . . . it's . . . it's justice!" He had to swallow before he could finish the sentence.

"How much?" begged Oñate.

"Five hundred dollars," said the governor and repeated in a lower voice: "Five hundred dollars for a man's life."

"Five hundred?" echoed Oñate shrilly. "A good horse costs more. A thousand my friend, my dear friend, a thousand dollars. I shall talk for you in the campaign until my voice is hoarse . . . till it is gone!"

"A thousand dollars," said the governor. He turned his back and stared through the window. He felt as if he had taken upon his own shoulders the awful duties of Death, the Reaper.

Oñate took his cue. He backed through the door, calling: "In the morning, my friend, I shall come again. You shall command me in all things. *Adiós.*"

"After all," said the governor, "there has to be law and order." In front of him rose again the delightful mirage of the palm trees and behind them the broad, white verandah, a place of rest.

The Specialist in Pain   10

Let us consider for a time the case of the *Señor* Oñate now that a double blessing had descended upon him. In the first place, he was sheriff of Chaparna County, a rich office, for the county was near the border and a sheriff who would close one eye was heavily paid for that kindness. But there was one thing dearer to the heart of this gentleman than personal success, and that was the ruin of his enemy. He would sacrifice a thousand dollars if he could take five hundred from his foe. He would go hungry two days and nights if he could deprive his enemy of a single meal. Think, then, of the joy of the good Oñate when he saw, without personal sacrifice the destruction of Dix Van Dyck accomplished. It was not because of the death of Vincente alone that he hated Dix Van Dyck. It was rather because of that day when the big man damned Oñate thoroughly and conscientiously in the hearing of many people—damned him for a political blood-sucker, a species of cowardly vermin.

The memory of *Señor* Oñate was painfully clear. He could even recall the faces of those who had stood nearby—the *Americanos* with open grins of delight and the *Mejicanos* with a silent enjoyment that was no less profound. *Señor* Oñate hated them all—all who had witnessed that scene of humiliation. He remembered with a bitter coldness of heart how he had yearned with all his soul and striven mightily to draw his revolver and plant a Forty-Five caliber bullet in the midst of the teeth of Van Dyck.

All of this *Señor* Oñate remembered. He remembered also how the hand that twitched uneasily toward his hip had been frozen under the calm, all-seeing eye of Van Dyck. There was still room in Oñate's heart for gratitude to the Deity that he had *not* touched his gun in sight of the man-killer. After all, it was better this way. Even supposing that he succeeded with the gun play, Dix Van Dyck would have fallen forward on his face, dead before he touched the ground. A stupid act of revenge. Death robbed the victor of his triumph. Where was the pain in an instant oblivion? No, *Señor* Oñate saw far beyond such a petty revenge.

The blood of Indian ancestors flowed through his veins. In Mexico that is the blood of command. Juarez was pure Indian; Díaz was seven-eighths Indian. In Oñate there lived an instinct inspired by his Aztec ancestors who took prisoners in order to sacrifice them at the altar of their god or to torture them in a lingering, hideous death for their own pleasure. It was for this reason that he sought the outlawry of Dix Van Dyck. Men have lived long years as outlaws in the Southwest, but in the end they are sure to fall. They may leave their haunts and flee far away to escape the heavy hand of the law, but in the end an instinct as inevitable as the homing sense of the carrier pigeon makes them circle back, and they are caught. Moreover, from the date on which their outlawry begins, they are followed by the consciousness that their capture is preordained. They sever themselves from friends, for the best of friends may betray them for the price. Every stir of dead leaves may be the approaching footfalls of the captors. Every shadowy night may be the screen by which the trailers will stalk up to their prey. The mouth of every cave is like the yawning throat of a cannon; the head-hunters may lurk there. Every day is a lingering death.

All of this *Señor* Oñate knew perfectly. It was for this reason that he rubbed his fat hands together as he left the office of the governor. His heart was at peace with the world.

Still, he was not utterly content. No sooner did he know that a price would be laid on the head of Dix Van Dyck than he was beset with a mightly fear lest someone else might collect that thousand dollars. Not that he cared deeply for the money itself. He loved money for the power it gave him rather than for the coin. In this case, however, the money meant more than gold. It would be a symbol of his victory; a memory of the crushing of Dix Van Dyck. Moreover, and above all, Dix Van Dyck must know, when he fell, what hand brought him down. Half the sweetness of revenge would be lost if some other hand accomplished it. He himself would net the outlaw. He himself would take the thousand dollars. He would cash the reward in fifty twenty-dollar gold-pieces. Five neat piles that would make. Five handfuls.

In the evening, when he sat on his verandah drinking tequila and nibbling the slices of lemon, he would carry the gold in his pocket. He would count it with one hand, letting the heavy coins fall together in chiming showers. He would call out his son, Rodriguez, a tall and handsome youth, and tell him how a *gringo* had dared to insult an Oñate within the hearing of many men, and how that Oñate took revenge, carefully, without danger to himself, and how that made the revenge trebly sweet. At last he would take the gold from his pocket and pour it from one hand to the other for the admiration of his son. At the thought of these things the mouth of *Señor* Oñate moistened, and his eyes filled with tears of delight—for his was a simple soul that could be filled to overflowing by little things, the burning of an enemy's house or the death of an enemy.

It was, however, one thing to determine that Dix Van Dyck should fall by his direct power. It was quite another to accomplish this feat. He might, of course, hire a posse of noted gunmen to take the trail of the outlaw from Double Bend where he had been last seen. But the noted gunmen were mostly *gringos*, and they would have little enthusiasm for trailing one of their kind.

There was another alternative. It came to *Señor* Oñate that night while he sat on his verandah, sipping his tequila and letting the white-hot poison trickle, drop by drop, down his grateful throat. His house sat on the outskirts of Guadalupe, and, while the sheriff sat there on the verandah, he saw a tall figure of a man swing up the slope of the nearest hill, pause beside a great Spanish dagger, and then plunge into the gloom on the farther side. He knew by the gait of the runner, even at that distance, that it was El Tigre. At that the inspiration came to him. He stamped violently on the floor of the verandah. Instantly a house servant stood respectfully behind his chair.

"Bring one of the Indians to me," commanded Oñate, "and quickly."

The house servant disappeared as silently as he had come, and within a short time a second figure trotted up outside the verandah, jerked off his sombrero, and stood in an attitude something like that of a soldier at attention. A tall, somber figure, the sun in profile struck him and painted in black the cavernous hollows of the cheeks and the deep-sunken eyes. A hungry leanness in the eyes in the half light were like cavities of darkness touched with sparks of fire.

"Alvarado," said Oñate, his voice losing most of that terseness with which he had addressed the house servant and taking on a tone of mingled awe and fear, "find me El Tigre. I saw him run over the top of that hill."

The Indian, in place of answering, replaced the sombrero on his head, whirled, and swept up the slope of the hill with the long stride of the tireless runner. Oñate remained still and straight in his chair until Alvarado dipped out of sight over the crest of the hill. Then he slumped back in his chair.

Now the households of *ricos* are always numerous, but there needs some explanation for the fact that Oñate's establishment included Yaqui Indians. The Yaqui is to the Mexican what in the Middle Ages the Arab was to the Gentile. A Yaqui will walk many hungry miles to get one shot at a Mexican; and a Mexican will walk as many miles to avoid a Yaqui. The railroads in the Southwest had employed Yaquis and Mexican peons at the same time, but always the Yaqui had to be lodged and fed apart from the peon. In the eating hall a peon would rather storm the gates of hell than take a seat he knows is reserved for a Yaqui.

The conflict between Yaqui and Mexican was not new. It had been warmed and cherished by four centuries of hatred and murder. It goes back to the time when grim Cortez conquered most of the tribes but did not conquer them all. Neither did his successors. For four hundred years the war continued. Both sides used rope and fire and bullet and knife. Still the issue had not been decided. The mutual hatred had become an instinct; it is almost a religion. As the Algonquians, Mohicans, and Hurons once feared the Iroquois, so the Mexicans feared the Yaquis. Give a Yaqui a knife and he will trail two Mexicans armed with guns, and probably he will come back with his knife-blade reddened by something besides rust.

A Yaqui is made by nature to be the conqueror of the Southwest. He will put salt and tobacco in his pouch, sling a short-barreled rifle over his shoulder, and strike into the burning heart of the desert at a dog-trot that he maintains from morning to night, stopping only long enough to kill and eat raw meat. What that meat is he does not care. He will devour a prairie rat. He has been known to tear the flesh of a coyote, newly slain and warm. A fire is a luxury to him and cooked meat a delicacy, not a necessity. Running at his shambling trot, he will cover in ten days more miles than any other man in the world will cover on the finest of horses. In twenty-four hours he will cover a hundred and twenty miles the first day, and on the following days he will travel nearly as far. Moreover, he knows the desert, not because he has to know it, but because he loves it. He can follow a trail almost through the night, and some astonished travelers have sworn that he is gifted with an animal power of scenting.

He fights because he loves fighting, and, when a Mexican is in sight, he is filled with what amounts to a religious joy. With a rifle, to be sure; he is never perfectly at home. For that matter, few people in that world, outside of the whites, ever quite understood the use of powder and lead. Nevertheless, he achieves a tolerable accuracy with the gun, though he is nearly useless with a revolver. On the other hand, he is a genius with any sort of cold steel, and at a short distance he throws his camp hatchet or whips across his knife with as much accuracy and almost as deadly an effect as the six-gun of a border ruffian.

Taking all these things into consideration, it must be clear that a Mexican would rather take a rattlesnake into his household than have ought to do with a Yaqui. It is doubly strange, therefore, that *Señor* Don Porfirio Maria Oñate should keep six of these deadly fellows about him day and night. But his reason is perfectly clear.

El Tigre   11

T he only retrospective quality that the Indian possesses is a singularly acute memory for personal benefits and personal wrongs. One who harms him would better have trodden on the tail of a rattler. One who confers a favor upon him is installed at once in the innermost recesses of the Yaqui's heart. His vindictiveness lives as long as his life. Four hundred years ago the Spaniard named Cortez had committed certain horrible outrages in the name of exploring the New World. Because of that the Yaqui hated forever all Spaniards and all who are tainted with Spanish blood. But the Yaqui's memory of benefactions is almost as enduring. Give him a crust of bread when he is hungry and he will follow you to your home and lie across your threshold like a dog—a deadly guardian against all intruders. The life of your son and the honor of your daughter are safer in his hands than they would be in your own. In fact, so bitter has been the life of the Yaqui, so full of hatred and battling, that when he meets kindliness it takes a divine savor in his heart. His benefactor becomes his god.

It chanced that some years before *Señor* Oñate had crossed the border to claim a debt from a general, high in the service. It was not a large debt, and Oñate went more to irritate the general than with the hope of collecting it. As he knew beforehand, the general did not have a tithe of the sum. Even if he had had it, he would not have paid Oñate who lived among the *Americanos* so far to the forgetful north. But he showed Oñate, in lieu of payment, a most enjoyable time. Rather late in the evening, much heated with a wild mixture of Mexican drinks from mescal to beer, they visited the prison and paused particularly in front of the cell where six Yaquis were being held, awaiting the rope of the hangman. They were condemned for a murder. The evidence against them consisted in the fact that they had been found in the vicinity of a murdered Mexican. This was quite sufficient.

Señor Oñate regarded them with a mixture of terror and delight, as a child gazes on the harmless strength of the lion behind the bars at the zoo. A drunken desire seized him to possess these dangerous fighters, even as the child longs to have the lion's cub for a pet. Particularly he observed the lean face and meaningless eyes of El Tigre, a noted Indian. Memories of his exploits rang in the ears of Oñate. It was then that he remembered the debt of the general. He proposed on the spot that, if the Yaquis were given to him, he would discharge the debt. The general agreed. He had no direct authority over the prisoners, but indirect authority is all one needs south of the Rio Grande. A well-dressed man can order an arrest. A cavalier with a silver-mounted saddle can break up a mob.

The general saw the mayor, and the mayor saw someone else, and the next morning six Yaquis were escorted to a distant part of the border. Here they were informed that they owed their liberty to the ministrations of one *Señor* Oñate in the County of Chaparna, far to the north, and that he desired their presence at his house. This, as they very well understood, was all that was necessary. Thirty-six hours later a house servant, palsied with terror, ran to Oñate with the news that six Yaquis stood on his verandah. Something of the servant's terror was communicated to the master, but he understood something of what they must be. So he armed himself with a hollow dignity and went down to receive his wild guests. They were El Tigre and his five grim followers.

Now *Señor* Oñate, despite many faults, understood men. Instead of making a long speech to the Yaquis and enlarging upon what he done for them, or demanding an oath of faithfulness from them, he ordered that food he brought to them and pointed to an outhouse where they might sleep. From that moment they were his slaves. At first, they took it for granted that the Mexican wanted them for some special service, but, as soon as they understood that there was no particular mission for them to perform, they settled down calmly to the domestic life before them.

The five followers had no families, having lost wives and children by the bullets and bayonets of Mexican soldiery. But El Tigre had a daughter, secreted among the hills. He begged permission to be absent a week, and on the appointed day he returned, leading a tall girl, beautiful for her kind. She cooked for the six Indians, and they labored in the gardens of Oñate.

The scheme was perfect, except that now and then, toward the close of the day, a deep restlessness came over the Yaquis, and sometimes they would depart in a body, or one at a time, and spend the hours till morning prowling across the hills behind Guadalupe, like so many hungry wolves eager for a trail of blood. It was on such an errand, as Oñate well knew, that El Tigre himself had departed this evening, and he doubted whether or not Alvarado would ever overtake his leader.

However, El Tigre must have run at less than half his ordinary speed. In an hour he returned and stood, as Alvarado had stood earlier, hat in hand, stiff and straight, outside on the verandah and directly before Oñate. The

sheriff started when he glanced up and saw the appari-
tion. By this time it was completely dark, and he was
aware first of the steady, bright eyes of El Tigre, visible
almost as if they possessed the phosphorescence of his
namesake, and afterward he made out the gaunt outlines
of the Indian chief. El Tigre took the prolonged silence as
a command to speak.

"My father," he said, "has sent for El Tigre, his son."

"Your father," responded Oñate with an equal solemnity, "is sick at the heart with many troubles."

He waited, but it was not the habit of El Tigre to make
idle comments.

"There is a man," continued Oñate with sudden vehe-
mence, "whom I hate and who hates me."

He paused again, rather regretting his outburst. But the
purring voice of El Tigre, a harsh guttural, thick with a
hesitancy between words, like the one who seldom
speaks, answered: "The enemies of the father are the enemies of the son. El Tigre is lean with hunger. It is long
since he hunted. His ribs stick out through his skin because of his hunger. His tongue is dry because he wishes
to kill."

Oñate shivered a little and hastily swallowed the rest of
the contents of the glass before him. The warmth was
grateful to him. Suddenly he had an overly bright vision
of the six figures stealing through some far distant night
upon a trail visible to their eyes alone. He saw them slip
through the blackness toward the red eye of a camp fire.
He saw the bulk of Dix Van Dyck, Herculean among the
shadows thrown by the fire. He saw one of those stealthy
prowlers of the night creep behind, crouch, saw the
spring, the flash of the knife driven home, the leap and
outflung arms of the white man, his fall, face down,
among the red embers of the fire. Oñate shivered again,
but he grinned as he leaned toward El Tigre.

"The man is Dix Van Dyck, big man on a great horse. A great warrior. El Tigre will win much honor by that killing, and he will take a mighty load from the heart of his father. Moreover, there is a price on the head of the man, and El Tigre may hunt him as freely as he would hunt a coyote with traps or with guns. He was last seen at Double Bend."

"The heart of his father is the heart of El Tigre," responded the Indian, and without further speech he vanished.

Dolores   12

T he Anglo-American, when his heart is full, seeks action; the Mexican-American, when his heart is full, seeks words; the Indian, when his heart is full, seeks silence. So it happened that the next morning *Señor* Oñate, on his inevitable verandah, was ill at ease. He was happy, to be sure, and wore an automatic smile, but his thoughts were running to the north on the heels of El Tigre and his five companion bloodhounds.

These things being known, it is not difficult to imagine why *Señor* Oñate watched with interest the tall form of Dolores, daughter of El Tigre. She came from the squat door of the adobe hut, where the Yaquis dwelt, and moved onto a little hillock nearby. There she took her stand and screened her eyes against the glare of the sun while she looked north into the shadows of the hills. The wind fluttered the loose end of her crimson *rebozo*, and blew the dress about her, clinging at every curve. She was very tall, very slender, very erect. As she came down the hill again toward the hut, walking with the easy, swinging grace of youth, *Señor* Oñate felt a very great need of words. His heart, indeed, was filled to overflowing, for the *gringo* should know, before many days, what comes to those who cross the path of *Señor* Don Porfirio Maria Oñate.

He called: "Dolores!"

She swerved in the midst of a stride and stood stiff and

straight, looking toward him, as if she could not understand that he had called. He had never summoned her
before, but now she was the only creature in the world
who could entirely understand and sympathize with
him. Her father had taken the war path, and he had taken
it at the command of the sheriff.

Señor Oñate felt a sudden kinship with the girl. He forgot, for the instant, that she was a Yaqui. So he called
again: "Dolores, come hither!"

She came with the same buoyantly graceful stride, like
a young man, and her small feet paused beyond the verandah at a respectful distance. She stood much as her
father stood in the presence of the great sheriff. In place
of removing a hat that she did not wear, she took off the
rebozo that partially veiled her face. It was the ultimate
tribute of respect. It was like the act of a child who will
hide nothing from the eye of its father. The heart of *Señor*
Oñate was touched.

It was his habit to carry about with him pockets full of
trinkets. For a little gift here and there, given with a good
grace, is more to the childish heart than a rich bribe. He
fumbled now automatically in one of his loose coat
pockets and brought out a slender necklace of coral—a
flimsy trinket but very bright in the morning sun. He held
it high so that the light could catch at it and run flashing
from bead to bead. The face of Dolores, daughter of El Tigre, lighted a single instant with desire, and then the light
went out. Her eyes had grown luminous and darkened
again like the flashing of a red torch over a black pool—
a glimmer, and then a more profound darkness.

"They are yours, Dolores," said the sheriff, "to comfort
you for the loss of your father. He will come again in a little while. In the meantime you shall have these."

He flung them idly to her. Her hand darted out as
swiftly as the head of a striking snake. The beads were

caught by her and disappeared in the folds of her dress. Once again there was a flash of light in her eyes. It reminded *Señor* Oñate of the spark that flies from flint when iron strikes it. She straightened a little more, and her head went back. She was about to speak of her gratitude, and on such occasions an Indian never does less than Oñate.

"My father," said Dolores, and Oñate wondered at the timbre of her voice, deep as a man's and light as a girl's, "is filled with care for his children. I, Dolores, am not worthy. I am less than the desert rat creeping from mesquite to mesquite under the eye of the eagle that circles high in the air ... high ... a little speck on a white sky." She made a slow gesture, first raising her arm and then unfolding her slender hand. It suggested infinite height. "Yet, the care of the father is even for Dolores. He has made her rich. The heart of El Tigre shall beat hard when he sees the gift of the *Señor* Oñate. I am the child of my father. I am his slave. I am his shadow who does what he wills ... who comes when he comes ... who goes when he goes."

She drew the *rebozo* over her head again, turned, and made back toward the adobe hut. *Señor* Oñate watched her, swelling with the importance that comes from the knowledge of a good deed done. It made a little warmth in his body and lightness in his brain. But perhaps that came from following the easy, springing gait of Dolores. Like Diomedes, she rose a little with every step, as if her small feet scorned the ground. He matched her pride of gait against the humility of her speech and chuckled softly.

Afterward he followed stealthily toward the adobe hut until he gained an advantage post at the rear window. Through this he peered and saw Dolores squatted cross-legged on the floor of the hut. In the full current of the sunlight that slanted through the door, she dangled the string of bright beads, and, as the light made liquid brilliance of each bead, the face of the girl shone with an almost fierce exultation. With a soft little cry of delight she tossed the beads above her and caught them again with a dexterous hand as they fell. She poured them from hand to hand swiftly, so that it seemed at times as if she were handling liquid fire. She slipped them over her head and, catching up a polished steel mirror, surveyed herself from every angle.

Back to his comfortable chair on the verandah *Señor* Oñate carried the image of that smile. He forgot in time the head-hunt that El Tigre was carrying on in the northern hills. He forgot even the inevitable tequila that stood in a vase on the little table beside him.

Now, it is a dangerous thing to forget too much. It is also dangerous to think too much of one thing, particularly in a climate where the sun burns ideas home in the brain. There is nothing worse than brooding in the tropics or semi-tropics. When a man becomes too visionary, it is time for him to travel north and cool his body with snow and his thoughts with change. Of this *Señor* Oñate did not think. He gave himself up to visions like an opium smoker. The skin of Dolores, in fact, was hardly darker than his own. The complexion that he saw in his dreams, however, was almost an Italian olive. In those same dreams her smile grew softer. Her eyes grew gently conscious of him.

Now these dreams were endurable during the day, but, when the sun dropped from sight and when the night wind began to whisper drowsily through the leaves of the palms. . . . *Señor* Oñate awoke from his reverie and began to think of reality. This was no easy task. While he ate his supper, the vision crossed between him and his plate. It dazzled him. He sat, absent-minded, until the meat grew cold. Then he roused himself long enough to curse the waitress and the cook in a needless fury, although he remembered that a doctor of repute had once warned him against apoplexy. At this, trembling with alarm, he called for a wet, cold towel and reclined in a wicker chair with the towel wrapped about his feverish forehead. He began to curse cautiously, lest he should rouse himself again, the house, the servants, the country, the climate, the *Americanos*, the Yaquis, and Dolores. Here he paused and began to repeat the name over and over, like a musician lingering on a pleasing chord. He called for more tequila.

Meantime the name *Dolores* grew more and more fixed in his mind. He discovered that it was necessary for him to see her. At first he thought of sending for her. Then he decided that he could not speak to her in the hearing of his eavesdropping house servants. Moreover, he wanted the cooler, fresher air. He went out on the verandah again to think, but the moment he crossed the threshold, he was aware of a great yellow moon pushing up above an eastern hill. He watched it with a peculiar fascination. It rolled higher until it seemed to rest for a moment like an enormous, illumined blossom, in the crest of a Spanish dagger. It rose higher, hanging poised directly above the hut of Dolores, daughter of El Tigre. *Señor* Oñate walked toward the hut.

At the door he called her, his voice low and a little tremulous: "Dolores."

She stood a glimmering figure in the dusk. He could not see her face.

"Come out in the night, Dolores," he said. "It is cool. It is pleasant. Besides, you should see the yellow moon."

She stepped out and stood beside him. Still, he could not see her face, for the shadow of the hut struck across it.

The Trail   13

In Double Bend Marshal Phil Glasgow at length heard of a group of six Yaquis and their questions. He sought them out and led them in person up the ravine to the black embers of the camp fire beside which Dix Van Dyck and Jack Boone had sat. Then he turned his horse and rode back to the town. He asked no questions, and he offered no advice. Plainly they were on a blood trail, and in such affairs, as Phil Glasgow well knew, a Yaqui needs little help.

When he left them, they were sitting in a contented semicircle in the shade of the cottonwoods, but the moment he disappeared down the valley, El Tigre rose and moved in a wide circle about the remains of the old camp. The trails were days and days old, but there had been no heavy wind or rain to obscure them. A white man might have followed the trail. To the Yaquis it was an open book in which they read. They followed El Tigre up the ravine closely, and they talked as they went, grumbling over the significant marks.

"It is a trail of two, not one," said Alvarado.

"My brother is a fool!" said El Tigre, pausing to scan a mark on the ground with an eye that would distinguish between the tracks of a bobcat and a lynx at a dozen feet. "There are two, but one leads and the other follows. The first is a woman. She came here, leading her horse. A woman, for the marks are as deep at the toe as at the heel. Such is the gait of a woman. Here is the man . . . all heel and no toe. She came here first . . . led out her horse . . . mounted at this place . . . and went off softly . . . in the night. The man followed afterward and went by the trail of the woman. Here he spurred his horse . . . see where the dents of the rear hoofs are deep? . . . here he pulled his rein and came to a quick stop, for the four marks grind into the rock. Here he picked up the trail again."

"And here," cried another, taking up the tale at a point higher on the slope of the ravine, "he trotted a few hours after she had passed."

They followed at the dog-trot that eats up the miles ceaselessly, perhaps from morning to night—or even for twenty-four hours at a stretch—a tireless shamble that pays no heed to the ups and downs of the road.

"The woman is in fear," said Alvarado, "and rides from the man, Don Dix."

"She is not in fear," called El Tigre from the top of the cañon wall, "for here she waited until she saw that he was coming, and then she rose again hastily. The man followed to this place, saw her marks, and went galloping down the hill after her. Alvarado, we shall find them together at the end of this trail. She flees, but she leads him on, the way of woman with man. El Tigre knows. She hates him, but she would rather die than let him know. These two trails shall be one before we finish. One day . . . two days . . . they shall ride together."

After that they spoke little. The trail was clear as day before them. Now and then they were delayed, once where a drove of sheep had blotted out all signs for the distance of two miles, but on the other side of that tract Alvarado caught the sign again. They kept at their work all day and most of the night and found that the trail ran in a loose semicircle, heading finally into the open country to the west. They were putting eighty miles behind them every day, and yet they were only warming up to their work. Over a long march a walking man will beat the man who runs, but for a spurt of a few days there is hardly a human being who can keep pace with the Indian runner.

Then, at a cross-trail, El Tigre found a sign, bearing the picture of a man. It was written upon in both English and Spanish. The English was Greek to him, but the Spanish, being a Yaqui of much education, he managed to decipher plainly enough to put together the meaning. It announced that a reward of one thousand dollars would be paid for the capture of Dix Van Dyck, dead or alive. As if the sign had scared the girl, her trail diverged sharply to the right, and the tracks of the man followed as the course led straight toward the heart of the higher mountains.

"She fears," said El Tigre, "for the man from whom she flees. Now she will run fast to take him from the danger of men."

In this plan, indeed, she apparently persisted for some time, but at length her trail diverged sharply to the left and went straight to a town.

"She has gone," said Alvarado, "to betray him and take the price of his head. I also had a woman. She sent word of me to the *Rurales*. But I learned in time. I went in the hills and waited. After a while I came down by night and took her in the hut of another man. I cut her throat while she slept, and in the morning the man found her that way. It is so with this woman. She has gone to warn the town of the coming of Dix Van Dyck."

"I will bet the tallest sombrero in Juarez," answered El Tigre, "that she has not gone to betray him. She feared that two could be followed more quickly than one. She has gone to the town so that the man would leave her and go on alone. See, here his trail turns off from hers.

But he has the heart of a mountain lion. Look! How close he came to the town!"

His trail, indeed, ran back into the hills, and there they found the trace of his fire.

"See!" grunted El Tigre in his triumph. "He would not leave the woman. He has waited here for her to come."

They made a circle about the town, and to bear out his words they found her trail again on the further side. It was very fresh, not more than a day old. Also, before they had gone ten miles, the trail of Dix Van Dyck, heavy and plain, cut in on the lighter trail of the girl.

"Now she sees," explained El Tigre, "that he will not leave her track, and she rides hard to carry him quickly away from the danger of other men. It is well done! She is sharp-witted as a she-lynx with young. She rides very hard. She gallops. See, the strides are long and the forefeet strike hard, the way of a racing horse."

They had mounted, by degrees, a height of land. From this low summit they looked across a gully and up toward a loftier, more impassable range of mountains.

"She is going for rough ground," said El Tigre to his followers, "she will follow the bend of the valley . . . she will travel by the smoother ground. We will go straight across and climb where a horse could not go. We shall come before her in the valley, and then we shall take her, and afterward the man will come to us of his own will."

The mountains, in fact, were pierced by a deep gorge that wound into their depths, rising with a gradual curve. By cutting straight toward the crest of the range, climbing up the sides of almost perpendicular cliffs, a man on foot could reach the upper part of the valley by a rough journey of a few miles, whereas the horses, taking a gentler route, would travel many times that distance. Accordingly, the six Yaquis pulled their belts tighter and started across the gullies and up the ascent beyond. It took the better part of ten hours of bitter labor, but at the end of that time they had surmounted the crest of the big range. Below them, dropping down in declivities almost as sharp as those over which they had just climbed, the ground fell to the floor of a ravine, up which, according to El Tigre, the fugitives were sure to come.

It was the first light of dawn when they started their climb. It was late afternoon when they settled down to the vigil of watching. Even their iron endurance had been taxed by this trail, and now they stretched out in the shade of a bank and slept. El Tigre, gaunter but not less bright of eye than when he started on the journey, sat in a position nearby. From his place he could scan the heart of the ravine for miles.

It was a wild place without the wildness of the northern mountains where great trees and the noise of rivers are the soul of the wilderness and its voice. This was a region of perpetual silence. The river, that had once cloven its way down through the rocks, had long since been drunk to the last drop by the sun. It left behind a boulder-strewn channel above which walls of rock rose on each side, jagged, as if they had been hacked out by a monstrous saw in the hands of a giant—a giant, but a child who could not cut to a line. They were mottled in many colors, like the clouds over a lurid sunset, dull red and purple, and yellow with streaks of orange, and the polished brown taking on various tints from the slanting rays of the sun.

A valley of naked death. The rock-walls chiseled their way across the sky in bold, rough lines. Here the hand of creation had worked, but the mind of the worker had slept, it seemed. Here there was form, but here there had never been life. Never life during all the millions of years when the river cut its way, an inch to an age, through these hundreds of feet of massy rock. Never life since the futile river had been dried up, thousands of years before. A valley of death, indeed. Nothing lived here except the shadows which commenced to swing down the face of the cliffs, sweeping suddenly from crag to crag, and blotting out the raw coloring. Nothing except the shadows lived, the shadows and the patient eye of El Tigre.

The Trap   14

Down the long stretch of cañon that they commanded he saw at length a glimmer of white, lost
now and again among the boulders and reappear-
ing, each time more vividly. A rider on a white horse. El
Tigre awakened his companions and pointed out the approaching figure.

"The woman," he said. "We are the trap. She will be the
bait. We shall catch *Señor* Dix Van Dyck."

The others, following his motions, unslung their short-
barreled carbines and trotted in single file behind him
down the slope. The bottom of the ravine could not have
been better made to order for an ambush. Every rod of
its length there lay a dozen boulders behind which a score
of men could have lain in wait.

El Tigre chose a place where the path must of necessity
pass between two great masses of stone, each of them as
large as a small house. Here, a group behind each stone,
he ensconced his men, and they waited until stone rat-
tled not far away under the hoof of a trotting horse. The
sound came closer. It clanged in their ears. Then El Tigre
slipped from behind the rock with his carbine at his
shoulder. The others swarmed out, from behind and in
front, each with leveled gun.

As for the girl, she drew rein without a cry and sat her
saddle, looking calmly, contemptuously down at them.
Even under the steady muzzles of their guns she seemed

to debate whether or not she should draw her revolvers and attempt a fight for life. She had been too long on the fighting border, however, to attempt such folly, and her hands rose slowly, reluctantly above her head.

After that El Tigre worked rapidly. First he possessed himself of her weapons. Then he tied her hands behind her back with cord. Finally he removed the lariat that was curled beside her saddle. This done, he stood back, like a painter staring critically at an unfinished piece of his work. No one on either side had spoken during all this time.

At length the girl said: "If it's money you want, I haven't a cent on me. If you want my guns, take 'em. They're good ones. If you want my horse, I'll tell you before you start that there's not one of you could stay on his back for five minutes. If you want the saddle, take it, and I'll do with a blanket."

To this the others responded with blank stares except El Tigre, who shook his head. Then, reaching up to her shoulder, he tore a long, jagged-edged strip from the cloth, running clear to her wrist. Following his directions, Alvarado led the white horse back and forth and in a circle until the place was covered with a multitude of hoof marks. In the meantime El Tigre unsheathed his long hunting-knife and with the keen point pricked his forearm until there was a little flow of blood. With this he smeared the strip of cloth with a blotch at the top and with drops further down. From one of Jacqueline's revolvers he fired two shots and then tossed the weapon upon the ground in the middle of the pass.

"It is done," said El Tigre. "Lead the horse on again."

The mute procession continued up the ravine until they reached a pair of boulders situated in a manner almost identical with the pair they had just left. Here El Tigre gave the signal to halt, and in obedience to his gesture the girl dismounted. With her own bandanna he gagged her effectually. Then he fastened one end of the lariat around a projection at the base of one of the great rocks. The other end he held on the opposite side, noosing it loosely over a similar projection.

Now that his trap was laid, it was not in the Indian nature of El Tigre to continue the mystery. Under the questioning eyes of Alvarado he remained silent for a time, swelling with importance and exultation, then at length he said: "A white man and a bull, they are one. When the bull sees the red rag, he closes his eyes and charges. It is easy to dodge him then or to rope him. A white man, when he sees one of his women hurt, goes mad like a bull. He closes his eyes and charges. You shall see. This *Señor* Van Dyck, he shall come to the place where he finds the many tracks of the white horse. He shall find the gun on the ground and the barrel black with smoke. He shall find the cloth with the red stain. He shall say: 'She is taken by men and killed or hurt.' Then he will close his eyes like a bull and gallop up the valley hunting for death. So!"

El Tigre grunted and squinted his eyes. Only by great effort could he keep from laughing aloud in his triumph.

"The other white men, they hunt him with many guns. But El Tigre needs only a little rope. *Señor* Van Dyck comes like a mad bull with his eyes closed. He rides like thunder through the ravine. He comes here. Just before he comes, I pull the rope a little tighter. It rises from the ground. It strikes the legs of his horse. He falls, and the neck of *Señor* Van Dyck is broken. So!"

He grunted again and was answered by an admiring chorus from his companions. To kill was no novelty with them, but the manner of it was a constant delight. As for the girl, she had started and strained at her bonds for an instant when she understood from the swift Spanish of El

Tigre what he intended. But a moment later, recognizing her helplessness, she sank back against the rock, and her head fell on her breast to remain there motionless.

The Indians kept a sharp look-out, and in time there came through the gathering gloom of the evening the dull beating of heavy hoofs far away, rising to a clatter and ring as the horseman approached. Straight through the pass between the first pair of boulders he rode, his horse trotting hard.

He had scarcely passed through, however, when he drew rein with a force that jerked the big mount back on his haunches. In an instant he was on the ground and raised the fallen revolver of Jacqueline. With that in his hand he stood a moment as though stupefied. The sight of the torn cloth next caught his eye apparently, for he bent again and straightened with a bit of color in his hand. This time there was no delay. He vaulted with a single leap into the saddle, and, with his head lowered and his quirt flogging, he rode his horse at a full gallop up the cañon. A charge, as El Tigre had predicted, furious as that of a maddened and unrestrained bull—and as blind.

The rush of the pounding hoofs swept upon them. El Tigre tightened the rope, and the great horse, striking it with his flying forehoofs, lunged with a crash to the earth. No horsemanship in the world could have averted a fall under those conditions, and Dix Van Dyck, riding with his weight thrown forward in the saddle and far over the withers of the horse, was hurled like a ball from the sling out of the saddle and the length of a horse away. That fall should have broken his neck, but here and there on the floor of the cañon,—the last silt of a vanished river—there lay drifts of soft sand. It was on one of these that Dix Van Dyck fell, and the shock was broken.

While he lay there, Alvarado leaped forward and dove

on the prostrate body. He had better have plunged onto the prostrate body of a mountain lion. Van Dyck was breathless but not stunned. As the weight of the man struck him, he whirled to his back and grappled with the strength of a bear. One arm crushed the slenderer body of the Indian against him and locked his arms against his sides. The other hand caught Alvarado at the throat. One full grip and he would breathe no more. He strove to scream out, but only a hoarse, horrible whisper issued from his mouth.

El Tigre saw and understood. His carbine was leveled, but he dared not fire, for the shot might strike Alvarado who lay on top of the white man. Instead, he cried in a shrill voice in Spanish: "Give him life, *Señor* Van Dyck, and we will spare the life of the girl!"

It was not until then that Dix Van Dyck saw the figure of Jacqueline huddled against the rock, saw the leveled carbines of the Indians, and knew that he had come to the end of his trail. He rose, flinging the senseless body of Alvarado to the ground, and held out his hand to El Tigre. An Indian is true to his promises.

"It is a bargain," he said. "I give you your friend. Let the girl go free. There is no price on her head. Let the girl go free and I will go willingly with you. But"—and his revolvers being in the saddle holsters he could only draw his hunting-knife—"if you will not, you'll have to buy me for a price yet. Answer me, *señor!*"

The dignity of his ancestors, who had been chiefs of note, fell like a robe around El Tigre. "The heart of El Tigre is heavy," he said, "that he must take this white man against his will, but the girl shall go free."

His hand slipped with some caution into the grip of Dix Van Dyck.

"She is hurt," said the big white man. "Let me see to her wound."

"She is not harmed," answered El Tigre. "It was my blood that you saw on the cloth. It was I who fired the two shots from her gun and left it there." The gleam of his triumph came in his eyes.

"The cross!" muttered Van Dyck.

Partners

H e said aloud: "Nevertheless, I'm true to my promise. Let the girl go free and I'll follow you and make no attempt to escape."

"It is good," said El Tigre.

He cut the bonds of Jacqueline Boone and removed the gag from her mouth. She darted past him and ran to the side of Dix Van Dyck, resting her hands against his breast.

"I heard you," she said, speaking rapidly and in a low voice, "but take back your promise. There are only six of 'em, and we've got a fighting chance."

"Take back my promise," he repeated slowly, "and let the Indians take you along? I ain't that kind of a skunk, Jack."

"I know," she urged desperately, "but they can do me no harm."

"I know Indians," said Van Dyck. "Jack, take your hoss and ride out of my life. Forget me. From the time I was a kid, I was cut out for a wind-up like this. Now it's come, and I won't whine unless I get you mixed up in the tangle. Beat it, Jack, and forget me."

He turned sternly to the Indians, for one of them was approaching.

"Keep back, there, while I say good bye to the lady. El Tigre, call off your man."

El Tigre grunted acquiescence and summoned his

follower to fall back. He had no desire to press matters to a crisis. The honor of bringing in this desperado alive would make him the most dreaded Yaqui north of the Rio Grande. Already he basked in the sunshine of fame.

"Dix," said the girl faintly, "I'm sick inside. I thought I was leadin' you away from trouble, and instead I carried you right into a trap."

"It don't mean nothing," he assured her. "I've forgot it already. All I'm sorry about is we didn't get a chance to team it together. Seems to me, Jack, we was cut out for partners."

"Me, too," she answered, "but this is the end of it, Dix?"

"Yep. There ain't nothing more. Seems like it was a cold trail, eh?"

"A cold trail," she echoed miserably, "but I'll tell you this, Dix Van Dyck. All the time I was running away from you, I was wishing you'd catch me . . . sort of half wishing it. Understand?"

"Don't I!" grinned the big man, and his lean, ugly face softened almost to tenderness. "Honey, didn't I know that white hoss of yours could walk away from my plow hoss any time you give him his head? Didn't I know you was just sort of tantalizing me along? It was like a game of hide-and-seek, Jack, and I knew all the time that finally you'd let me find you."

"Did you know all that?" she asked, almost coldly. But she changed again, as swiftly. "There's ways out of the tightest holes in the world, Dix. I've come through some of 'em. You're going to get out of this. Partners can do a pile more'n any one man workin' alone."

"Partners?" said Dix Van Dyck.

"Partners," she asserted firmly. She was very grave. Her eyes were steady upon his.

Life had never been so dear to Dix Van Dyck as it was now when he must relinquish all hope of it. He held out his hand, saying: "No matter where this trail wound up, I'm glad I followed it."

And she, meeting his hand, answered: "Dix, I got an idea that this trail ain't ended yet."

"Good bye," he said.

"So long," answered Jack and turned toward the white horse. A moment later she was riding at a steady trot up the cañon.

The Indians, with Dix Van Dyck riding in their midst, took the opposite direction. Straight as a coyote running on a fresh scent, they cut across country for the town of Double Bend, a three-day journey. They had disarmed Van Dyck, but otherwise they treated him as if he were entirely free.

Even four centuries of pseudo-civilization had not entirely destroyed the Indian's faculty for reading character. He gained it during the thousands of years while he roamed the deserts and the forests of America, seldom meeting those of his kind, and on the occasions of those rare meetings he had to learn in seconds what the white man learns in years—or never at all. He had to discern whether the stranger was true friend or covert enemy. He had to know where he could trust blindly and where he must never close both eyes. As to El Tigre, he had centered one long glance on Dix Van Dyck when the tall man gave him the promise to attempt no escape. Thereafter, he gave his captive no further thought.

Driving straight through the mountains, they came at length to the banks of the stream known as the Blood River, not named because of any conflict near it but because the shallow waters seem to take on the color of the red earth over which they flow. Ordinarily a petty creek twisting a zigzag way through the mountains and fading away on the white desert below, the Blood River had been lately swelled by rains in the higher mountains and by melting snow. Now it belied its name and went, rushing and foaming along its course, a white streak among the burned, brown hills. A hundred yards below the point at which they struck the banks, it pitched over a cliff, and the roar of the cataract filled the air with mingling crash and booming.

It would have been the better part of caution either to camp on the bank of the stream until the waters fell—which they were sure to do within the space of thirty-six hours or less—or else detour to the left and follow the river for a half day's march when they were sure to come to waters so shallow that they could easily ford the stream. Alvarado advised this, but El Tigre carried in his mind the picture of the face of *Señor* Oñate, suffused with joy by the news of the capture. It was the payment of an ancient debt, and debts weigh heavily on the soul of a Yaqui. He could not delay. On his command they prepared to ford the river.

Dix Van Dyck, whose horse gave him a great advantage, entered the stream at the side of El Tigre. The others waited on the bank to watch the success or failure of the attempt. As for the rider, he was confident of his horse, for it was not the first time that they had forded a difficult water. He headed the charger almost straight upstream and drove home the spurs. Up to a point half way across Blood River the progress was swift and easy, but here the full current struck them suddenly and with vicious force. It spun horse and rider around and around, like a top, and, if chance had not aided them, they might have been swept in an arrow-like course toward the cataract below. But the feet of the horse struck a providential sand bank. From this point he straightened out and managed to reach the farther bank. He had scarcely gained the top when a cry of lament rose from the opposite shore.

He looked back and saw El Tigre, swimming for dear life in the very center of the current, borne rapidly along its course. Strong as the current was at the point where they attempted the fording, the banks of the stream narrowed just below and the water, compacting as if it entered the mouth of a chute, drove on foaming and raging with redoubled force. The cry from the Indians on the opposite shore announced the moment when El Tigre was borne down into the mouth of this deadly current. Fifty yards below him was a white ribbon of water—the edge of the cataract.

If it had been white men to whom he had given his promise to attempt no escape, perhaps temptation would not have entered the mind of Dix Van Dyck. As he sat his horse, he saw the foaming width of Blood River between him and all danger of pursuit. Before him stretched an easy, downward slope. In thirty seconds he could be beyond danger of rifle-fire. The urge for freedom came up in the throat of Van Dyck as the desire for flight comes in the heart of the young bird peering over the edge of the nest. Another moment and he would have been gone, bending low over his saddle horn to escape the following fire and driving his spurs home at every stride of the horse. But, even as he gathered the reins taut, he heard a sharp, keen cry over the roar of the falls. He knew well enough what that cry meant. It was the yell of a man who knows that his death is upon him. Turning in his saddle, he saw El Tigre throw up his arms and go whirling down the current. The edge of the falls was not thirty yards away.

It was the nearness of the danger and the horror of such a death that moved Dix Van Dyck to action. He spurred his horse, indeed—but it was toward the doomed man. As the horse plunged and floundered into the stream, Van Dyck threw himself headlong into the water. It caught at him with a thousand invisible hands and swung both him and the horse around in the current, until they faced shore again. The horse struck out furiously for land, only his head above water. The fear of death was on him, for he felt the grip and suction of the water. Not a dozen yards below was the edge of the cataract, and just above them, whirling around and around in his descent, came the body of El Tigre. Van Dyck worked himself back along the horse, caught the streaming tail, and flung himself as far as he could reach into the center of the current.

It was chance as much as skill, but his hand entangled in the long hair of the Indian. The weight of that double burden jerked back the horse himself. With only Van Dyck he might have regained the shore easily enough, but the burden of the two was like a dragnet behind. He fought hard, but where he gained a foot toward the shore, the water bore him a yard downstream.

Chance again rescued them. At the very crest of the waterfall the depth of the stream suddenly decreased at that side, where a number of boulders projected from the bed. The last swirl of the water had already caught Dix Van Dyck, and the tug of El Tigre's weight was almost more than he could bear. Sand had filled his eyes; his lungs were choked with water. Only an instinct made him persevere in the crisis. It was then that the feet of the horse struck against the rocks. He floundered, snorting and terror-stricken, to the shore. As he was dragged onto dry land, the head of Van Dyck struck a rock. Blackness swept across his brain.

When his senses returned, the Indians were grouped about him, working his arms to pump the water from his lungs. El Tigre had thrown them a rope, and they had crossed safely in that manner. Nearby stood the horse, his head hanging low from exhaustion.

Blood Money   16

The primary purpose of man, unquestionably, was to kill his enemies in order that he might live himself. Though this necessity has largely vanished, the instinct for killing remains. A man will dull the edge of his appetite watching a prize fight or the slaughter of a bull, but he is really never satisfied until he has brought down one of his own species—until he has attached a human scalp, in other words, to his belt. The Romans killed human beings in an arena; the Aztecs made it a religious ceremony. To *Señor* Oñate the killing of a man partook of both elements. It was a sport, and it was also a religious exercise. It filled his brain with a deep contentment. It exalted his soul with satisfaction and brought him, doubtless, nearest to his conception of his Maker.

On this day, therefore, he sat in his office swathed with manifold complacency. The day preceding a Negro, drunk, had resisted arrest, had broken from his captors, and had been shot through the back as he fled by *Señor* Oñate. So the sheriff was content. He sat in the sun with his heels cocked up on the ledge of the window. The yellow sunlight was hot and good. It made him thirsty. He saved his thirst. He let it accumulate like a spendthrift who saves his money for a year in order to throw it all away in one golden hour. In this way *Señor* Oñate allowed the flameless fire to eat deeper and deeper into his vitals, knowing that he could stop it at any moment, but preferring to let it prey on his vitals until, late in the afternoon, he should sit again on his verandah with green things in prospect, with house servants ever present, and with ice chiming melodiously against the side of his glass whenever he touched it.

In matters of the senses *Señor* Oñate was an artist. He demanded perfection—or nothing at all. He had been known to go hungry for thirty-six hours before a great banquet and then do justice to twenty courses. He had ridden for twelve hours over a burning desert in order to appreciate the cool, clear waters of a spring. In his earlier career he had no heart for the semi-comfort of the middle class. He lived in a rude adobe hut while his thousands accumulated. Then he stepped at a single stride into his mansion with its wide patio, its flowers, its pleasant rugs, its sense of much service and many silks that it carried like a woman of social position.

On this day, between his pleasant self-torture of thirst on the one hand and his memories of how the bullet had crunched its way through the back of the Negro exactly twenty-four hours before, the mental state of *Señor* Oñate may be described, without exaggeration, as closely approximating the ideal. It was hard for him to imagine any improvement, and yet such an improvement was at hand.

The Mexican door boy slipped noiselessly into his office and stood, as was his custom, with the door slightly ajar and one hand clutching the knob tightly. He had fallen into the habit of making his entrance in this manner, for it sometimes happened that *Señor* Oñate was displeased by the name that was announced, and on such occasions he was apt to seize the nearest book or paperweight and fling it at the face of the boy, round and as bright as polished copper. At times like these the boy could jerk himself back through the door with the speed of a snapping whiplash. He had one scar above his eye, but the other indentations were all on the door.

It was only habit, however, that made him retain a firm grip on the door today. He was sure of himself and his reception as he announced: "The Indian, El Tigre."

Joy illumined the face of the sheriff like a murky sunrise. He slipped from his chair, rubbing his fat palms together. "Quick!" said *Señor* Oñate.

The boy, with a grin, disappeared, and a moment later the door opened noiselessly. The tall form of El Tigre slipped through the opening. The interval, however, had been sufficient for *Señor* Oñate to wipe the last of his expectant smile from his face. He eyed the Yaqui as solemnly as an image of the great Buddha.

El Tigre, following the habits of his race, substituted action for words. He stepped to the desk and placed upon it a canvas bag. It jingled as he set it down. A small bag but it was plumply filled. It was almost as full as the overflowing heart of *Señor* Oñate. Then El Tigre stepped back toward the door.

"Wait," whispered Oñate, for he could not speak aloud at that moment. "Wait. You have him, El Tigre? But you have! This is the price! Ah-h-h!" The sigh came from the depths of his heart. "Wait," he repeated again, "you have done well. You have done very well, El Tigre . . . you and your men. Your father remembers you. So!"

He was anxious to be alone with the gold. Now he opened the bag and drew out a dozen pieces. They were newly minted; they seemed to speak of a new death. "Was it the knife or the gun, El Tigre?" He gripped the gold hard and waited, his breathing harsh and quick.

"He is alive," said El Tigre.

It was too much for the impassivity of *Señor* Oñate. He threw his short, fat arms above his head and shouted with joy. Now the revenge was perfect. It was the greatest day in his life. He could go to the prison at Double Bend. He could see his victim behind the bars. He could deride and taunt him. Torture is sweeter than death. "How?" he cried, and, remembering sundry tales of the prowess of Dix Van Dyck, he looked upon El Tigre with wide eyes of awe.

"It is much talk," said El Tigre, and fell silent.

Señor Oñate felt a pain in the palm of his right hand. He was gripping the gold too hard. Now he released his taut fingers. "I will not pay my son with money," said Oñate wisely, "but I will give a broad piece of gold to El Tigre and to each of his men in order that they may know I am their father. A piece of gold for each man"—he counted out five coins into the hand of El Tigre—"and two pieces for El Tigre. So!"

He held forth the last two pieces, but El Tigre glided a pace away.

"For my friends," he explained, "the money is clean. But it is wet with blood for El Tigre."

"What?" snarled Oñate. "Blood money? Who's talked this foolishness to you, El Tigre?"

"For the cost of one man's life it is not much," said El Tigre, "but for the cost of two men's lives it is very little."

"Two?" grinned Oñate. "Did you kill two, El Tigre?"

"I killed none," said El Tigre, "but I gave my life and my white brother returned it to me."

"Your white brother?" growled Oñate.

"*Señor* Van Dyck," explained the Yaqui.

"He? Your brother?" echoed Oñate, his voice shrill with anxiety.

"My life," said El Tigre, "it was in his hand like the shell of an egg. But he did not close his fingers. So El Tigre is here. But he cannot take the money. It is payment for the life of my white brother and payment for the life of El Tigre."

"Speak again, my son, slowly," demanded Oñate, "my head whirls."

"We put a promise on *Señor* Van Dyck and not a rope," said El Tigre.

"That," said Oñate, "was the way of fools. You trusted to his word?"

"I did," said El Tigre. "We came to a river. It was very swift. We should have waited till it went slower and smaller, but the heart of El Tigre was big to see the face of *Señor* Oñate and pay the gold into his hand. He tried to swim the river, and the river took him, as the wind takes a little piece of straw, and made him go around and around and carried him quickly . . . very quickly . . . to a great noise in the water and a great falling."

"Blood River Falls!" cried Oñate.

"It is the place," went on El Tigre. "I thought of my fathers. I was ready to die, though I am not old. Then my white brother was made sad in his heart to see a strong man die before the time. So he rode into the water and caught El Tigre by the hair of the head. And they came to the falls, and my white brother dragged El Tigre to the shore, and El Tigre lay there like a rag that is wet. When El Tigre was awake again out of a great sleep, he was sick inside and cold in the stomach. For he owed his life two times, once to my father, *Señor* Oñate, and once to my white brother. But he owed it first to *Señor* Oñate, so he paid that debt first, and he paid it with the life of his white brother."

The voice of El Tigre faltered and died away. At length he raised his head and concluded: "So El Tigre will go by himself into the hills where there is silence. He will go with his daughter. He will build a fire and speak with the spirit of his white brother and ask his forgiveness."

"Your daughter also?" asked Oñate anxiously. "Take Dolores with you? Why . . . ?" But he stopped, and the blood rose up and darkened his copper skin.

The Gifts of Oñate 17

S traight from the home of *Señor* Oñate to his own adobe hut went El Tigre with a swift, cat-like stride. Not the gait of the white man, who strikes heavily with his heels, but a movement that left him poised at every instant so that he could have leaped back or to the side without the loss of a fraction of a second. No white man can learn that gait. It is the heritage of some thousands of years of a hunting ancestry. In El Tigre it was peculiarly accentuated so that he seemed always stalking. This, as much as his fighting propensities, had earned him his name.

At the door of his hut he was aware of Dolores, standing at the window in the full glare of the sun. She was dressed in a Chinese kimono of dark green, flowered with gold. She held a small hand mirror before her and by that image brushed the black, silken length of her hair. The heart of El Tigre bounded with admiration first and then with wonder.

Coming behind her, noiseless as a shadow, he stretched out a hand and touched the silken fabric. He grunted with admiration, and that grunt was the first warning of his presence to Dolores. She started around with a sharp little cry, and at sight of her father hid the mirror and the brush behind her. Recovering, or seeming to recover, from her fright at once, she laughed softly at her own fear and slipped mirror and brush onto a shelf behind her.

"It is good," said El Tigre in their own familiar dialect, "to have soft cloth on a soft skin. Was the dress bought or stolen?"

"Stolen," murmured Dolores.

"Stolen?" said El Tigre, as if he had hardly caught the answer.

"It is a gift," said Dolores.

"A gift from what woman?" asked El Tigre.

"No woman. *Señor* Oñate."

"So!" grunted El Tigre. "Give!"

She slipped obediently out of the garment and handed it to him. He threw it carelessly on the beaten, ground floor. Next he stepped to the shelf. Both the mirror and the brush were backed with silver. These in turn he threw toward the kimono.

"Why?" asked El Tigre.

Her smile had come and gone even as her eyes flashed back at the rich presents in the dirt and then up at the grim face of El Tigre. "Our father was sad for Dolores who was alone. He gave these things to make her happy."

"Listen!" said the Indian, and raised a long, callused forefinger. Many a time it had pulled the trigger on a dead bead over the heart. He seemed now like a mother lessoning a child. "A man may have many fathers. *Señor* Oñate is my father, but a woman has only one father. Dolores, I am your father, no other."

"Dolores did not know," she answered.

"These things," he went on, "I shall carry back to *Señor* Oñate."

"No, no!" she cried.

"So?" grunted El Tigre.

"I will carry them myself," she answered, "and explain to *Señor* Oñate that I did not understand."

"That is good," said El Tigre, "for your tongue makes a music as swift as the raindrop running down the leaf of the dagger. But my tongue angers men. You shall carry them back yourself."

She folded a grass mat and pointed to the place for him to sit down, but he shook his head. "I have no time to sit down," he said. "I go on a long journey into the hills, and you must go with me. Make ready."

"A long journey?" she repeated in dismay.

"Quickly," said El Tigre.

Without answer but moving reluctantly, she set about the preparations. Now and again her dark eyes glanced with brilliant, bitter meaning toward the unconscious face of her father. He explained while she worked.

"Two prices have been paid for my life. One man I have repaid with the life of the other. There was no other way. His was the earlier debt. That was the price he asked. Now El Tigre is cold inside. He would go alone into the hills, build a fire, and talk with the spirits, but, because I have paid this price, I am not clean. I cannot speak. The spirits would come to me in bad dreams. They would lie to me. They would not tell me what I must do. Therefore you, Dolores, must come with me." The music of the name from his tongue was marvelous, and every time, just before uttering it, he made a little pause. It was as if he appreciated the sound himself—a little oasis in the harsh desert of his gutturals. "You, Dolores, shall go with me, and the spirits will come to you in dreams and tell you what I must do. For you are clean." His head went back. He half closed his eyes, and his grimly set lips softened to a smile. The girl stood stiffly as if she were seeing a sight of horror. Her eyes widened ceaselessly. "Come," he said and led her to the window.

He pointed far away. It was unusually clear, even for the crystal atmosphere of the Southwest, and far off beyond the deep blues and purples of the nearer ranges they could see the highest summits of the farthest ranges, topped with bluish-white of the snows that had fallen in the same storm that had swelled Blood River.

"It is for a time like this," said the Yaqui, "that I have kept you clean. I have saved you from men. Not a trace of the dust of their breath of desire has touched you. You are clean as the snows, Dolores. As clean as the snows and as cold in your purity. There is no stain on you. Even your thoughts are clean. The spirits will come to you quickly in your dreams. They will speak clearly to you. They will show you with words or with signs what I must do. For the weight of two debts was on me, Dolores, and one of them is still on my heart. Yet I am glad, for now you will help me.

"Dolores, my daughter, when the heart of a woman is pure as snow, it is richer than gold. Your mother, Dolores, was not clean. She was not like the snow. She was like muddy water, I saw this and made her speak the truth with her lips. Then I killed her, and since then no man has been my friend. I killed her and carried you away and made you grow straight in your mind like a pine tree that points at the stars. Now is the time. You shall pay me for all I have done."

As he spoke, his head lifted high, his face changed and exalted. She stole close behind him. Her hand went out stealthily, and inch by inch she drew out the shining length of his hunting knife. And the face of El Tigre himself was not more demoniac than the face of his daughter as she raised the knife. It hung poised above his back—her hand wavering like a leaf buoyed up by a gust of wind. Then the strength ran suddenly from her. The knife slipped from her hand and fell with a shiver of steel against the hard earth. She slipped in a shapeless heap against the floor.

El Tigre turned. He saw the naked knife. He listened to the deep sobbing of Dolores. His eyes traveled past her and lingered on the brush, the mirror, and the silken dress.

He understood. All the meaning of his name leaped into the Indian's face. He stooped as swiftly as a dropping hawk. One hand raised the knife. The other wound in the thick, black hair of Dolores, jerked her to her knees, and twisted back her head. There lay the soft expanse of throat and bosom, inviting the keen point of the knife. Its own weight almost would suffice to drive home the blade.

"You are about to die," said El Tigre. "Like your mother before you, you are about to die."

Her sobbing stopped. The great, grave, dark eyes stared up to him.

"Before you die," said El Tigre, "tell me the truth, as your mother told me. Who is the man?"

"*Señor* Oñate," said the girl.

"My father!" said the Indian, and drew in his breath.

"What could I do?" she pleaded, but not in a panic though the knife glittered beneath her chin. "You were far from me. In all things I was to please our father. He came to me in the night. He called me out to show me a yellow moon."

"Yet your eyes," said the Indian with a deep and child-like wonder, "are as clear now as they were when I left you. They are as clear as they were before you told me lies. You have not withered since the hand of Oñate touched you. But I have grown old. I have no strength to strike home. My eyes cannot see. I am as blind as an owl in midday."

His hand fell away from her tangled hair, and the knife went back into its sheath with a hiss like a striking snake.

"We cannot go into the hills," he concluded softly, sadly. "The spirits now would only lie to you."

Dolores turned her head and clenched her hands. It is not well that a Yaqui maiden should see tears in the eyes of her father.

T he course that the Indians took across the hills toward Double Bend with Dix Van Dyck in their midst had been straight as the flight of a crow from point to point. Yet it was no straighter than the course of Jacqueline Boone as she rode up the cañon. She rode straight, and she rode hard, pressing the white stallion to his uttermost speed, for she carried a purpose with her. It led her at a heart-breaking pace over the first slopes and then swooping down to the plains below.

The Indians were born with a thousand senses of direction that the whites can never acquire, but, as far as those things can be learned, Jack Boone possessed them. She had been born in the mountains. She had been raised with a gun in her hand. Men had been her companions, the law a stranger, comfort unknown. She had lived for adventure—as men live. So her course was straight—her sleeps short—and her days of riding long as she made for the capital of the state where Governor Boardman grew more corpulent from day to day.

A sense of guilt oppressed her, and a sense of coming loss. Guilt, because she felt that she had led Dix Van Dyck into the trap and that he would have fought his way out again if it had not been for her. Loss, because their savage partnership had been dissolved in the very moment of its beginning. Like El Tigre, she felt a debt. Like El Tigre, and with a soul as natural, as keen-purposed, and a will as tireless as the Indian's, she was resolved to discharge that debt.

There was nothing complex in the plan that she evolved. Naturally there was only one source from which relief for Dix Van Dyck could come. The source was the governor who could pardon the criminal. To Governor Boardman, accordingly, she was determined to go. She framed her plan accordingly. It was, as I have said, simple. Therein also lay its strength. It was so simple, so commonplace, so much to be expected in the Southwest that for these very reasons it was fairly sure of success. It is played with a money belt in one hand and a gun in the other.

With the money belt she went directly to Madame Sarah's shop. Madame Sarah had a French accent and Irish blue eyes. As a matter of fact she came from Brooklyn, but this made little difference in the Southwest. No one cared as long as her styles were a trifle more elegant and her prices double those of any other fashion shop in the little capital. Mothers were careful that their daughters should not go to Madame Sarah's, but they were somewhat prone to go there themselves. As for Jack Boone, she had not the slightest idea of the widespread reputation of Madame Sarah's place. But, when she picked up the paper, the first thing she saw was the broad advertisement of Madame Sarah's Parisian shop.

At the door the first doubt struck her. It was opened by a liveried gentleman of astounding height and a stomach line that made a perfect crescent. The model who trailed a flimsy creation of some sort of black net across the floor, stared at by two pudgy, overdressed women of the town, was Jack's second doubt. Her third doubt centered on the person of the little saleslady who came to meet her. She had acquired madame's French accent, which was not hard to do, for it consisted chiefly of a contraction of "the" to "ze," but she had not given up her habit of chewing gum. Meeting Jack, she took in the short, dusty riding skirt with a glance, shifted her gum, and inquired indifferently: "Madame wishes to make a purchase, or just to look over ze gowns?"

Jacqueline bestowed on the saleslady a glance of careful contempt that began at her slippers and ended on the well-trained lock that curled on the girl's cheek. "Send me the boss," she said.

The saleslady threw up her hands. "Ze which?" she inquired in a horrified whisper.

"The boss," said Jacqueline patiently. "Send me the foreman. If he isn't in, maybe I can get along with one of the straw bosses."

"Madame Sarah," answered the girl angrily, "ain't able to see you."

"You slipped on your lingo, friend," answered Jack, "but I got an idea that madame *is* in."

"I," said the girl reddening, "am ze saleslady."

"Go on," grinned Jack, "you got to let your skirts grow before you could sell me a hairpin. Who's the old girl with the glassware in her hair? Ain't that the boss?"

It was, in fact, Madame Sarah herself—the "glassware" was her diamond comb, the wonder of the capital. She was trailing a customer downstairs, her hands lifted in mute admiration of the latter's newly purchased gown. Jacqueline met her at the foot of the stairs.

"Ma'am," said Jacqueline, "I got more money than time. Can we get together?"

If the ear of madame was offended by this abruptness, her heart was not. She had seen women more strangely dressed than this spend fabulous sums on their clothes. Her sales, in fact, followed very largely the price of meat.

"We can!" she said with instant decision. "Pauline, will

you finish Missus Cary's business? Missus Cary, excuse? Ze gown, eet ees adorable!"

The accent in "adorable" came one syllable later than Mrs. Cary was accustomed to hearing it, and for the sake of that she would have forgiven anything. She felt as if the pavement of Paris were beneath her cramped, crowded feet. For the moment she forgot her corns. Madame Sarah turned the full battery of her smile upon Jacqueline.

"I want to get togged out," said Jack, "from head to foot, and I got forty minutes for the job. Am I in the right church?"

Madame Sarah bit her lip. She recovered in time to wave her rather plump and very bare arms in her most graceful gesture. "Ze Engleesh, it is ze str-range . . . what you call . . . ?"

"Ma'am," sighed Jack, "I'd like to stay and listen to you. It's a funny line of talk you carry, all right, and, if I had the time, I'd stay and enjoy it. But, if you can't talk plain English, I'm done. Split the pot and we'll call for a new deal."

Childhood memories surged through the brain of Madame Sarah. A glimpse of noisy, chattering streets flashed before her. *Split the pot . . . call for a new deal. . . .* "Honey," she said, and something like a cloak dropped from her, "I got you the first time. You *are* in the right church."

Jacqueline sighed and smiled. She extended her strong right hand. "Shake, partner. Say, that funny lingo acted on my brain like rust on a cylinder. I couldn't think. Now we'll make it snappy."

"Snappy's right," said Madame Sarah, squeezing the hand of Jack. "Maybe this ain't professional . . . but thank Gaw-wd I can be human once in a while. Now, deary, tell me what you want."

"Shoes," said Jack, "hat, and everything that goes in between clear down to the skin. I'll tell you what I want to do, and you tell me how to do it. I want a rig that'll catch the eye of a man and hold it. I want a rig that'll rope his attention and hold it while I brand him. Can you fix me up?"

A gleam came into the eye of Madame Sarah. Such a gleam had come in the eye of the Iroquois warrior when he heard the scalp yell. "Listen to me, deary," she said, "you don't need an outfit to rope the attention of any man in this one horse town they call a city. You could wear overalls and do the work with your eyes. But, if you want style, leave it to me. For the sake of talking English and canning that lingo, I'll cut my price in two. For a hundred and fifty iron men I'll make you a world-beater . . . everything from the skin out. Is it too steep, honey?"

"You could hit me again just as hard," said Jack, "and I wouldn't holler."

"Come upstairs," said Madame Sarah, a little downhearted at the thought of the hundred and fifty she had thrown away, "and we'll get a dressing room where I won't be overheard. I've got to watch my tongue around this shop the way a bulldog watches his chain. But *you* won't blow the news."

"I haven't heard a thing," said Jack. "Let's start the roundup."

It required, however, a good deal more than forty minutes. For there was a full-length mirror in the dressing room, and both of them called it into use many times. But in the end Jacqueline walked from the shop in a street dress only just startling enough to catch the eye of the capital. "For," as Madame Sarah had said, "it won't do to pile on the colors, deary. All you need is a background for that color in your cheeks and a shadow for your eyes. You'll *do*!"

This also was the opinion of Jacqueline. She hardly recognized herself when the "roundup" was finished. On the way out, she could not resist the temptation of lingering for a moment near the door and enjoying the fallen jaw of the saleslady with the forgetful accent. Then she went out to conquer.

Chivalry

19

As plain Jack she had entered madame's shop. As Miss Jacqueline Boone she stepped out upon the street afterward. She could not even think of herself by the abbreviated title. Only one metaphor, and an ancient one at that, fitted her case. She had burst from the cocoon, and now she fluttered into the sunlight, enjoying the beauty of her own wings. The new clothes, to be sure, were excessively strange and a burden in many ways. The rather tight skirts, for instance, cut short the free swing of her stride and reduced her gait to a sort of lame hobble. However, the soul of an actress is in every woman. She responds to make up as readily as she responds to the actualities of her situation—or even better. Give an Eastside washer woman fifty thousand a year, and inside of a month she will criticize the chef at the Claridge and speak movingly of the primitives of Italian art.

It is hard to believe that these instincts were not in Eve even before she tasted the apple. As for the hiss of the serpent, it may have been only the still, small whisper of a woman's heart. At least, Miss Jacqueline Boone heard something like that whisper as she walked slowly out of Madame Sarah's shop. She wore an afternoon street gown, and her hat was circled with artificial pansies and violets. The glow of that color was repeated like a dulled reflection in the flush that came tingling in the olive of her cheeks. The long gloves made her hands seem absurdly small. When she looked at them, she hardly recognized them as her own. They seemed more like something she had purchased in the shop. Most wonderful of all were the tiny black shining triangles that appeared in front of her skirt now and then: her feet—*her* feet—the things she was walking on!

Like a snake creeping out of an old skin, she slipped out of her former drab self. Before she had gone a block, she was pretty thoroughly at home in the brilliant markings of her new apparel. Her sense of power had always lain in an ability to ride any horse on the range except a few very bad outlaws, a sensitive trigger finger, a steady eye, and a heart that had known fear only twice. Once when McGurk was on the trail of her father's gang and once when she was with Pierre le Rouge. But McGurk was less than a woman now, and Pierre le Rouge, the last save one of the men of Boone's gang, was lost forever in the wide plains that sweep east until they reach the ocean of oblivion. She had been like a man, and more dangerous than nineteen out of twenty men at that. Now a new sense came over her—a sense of control, an electric thing that sparked and snapped in her vitals when men passed her on the street this day. Each of them, in passing, let his eyes widen the least trifle, and each one swerved a little toward her. A matter of mere inches but Jacqueline was conscious of the pull. Men dropped past her like trees past a galloping horse, and she felt them swirl into her wake as though she were traveling at a tremendous speed.

She pulled down the thickly woven veil from the brim of her hat. It did not conceal her, but it gave the impression that she wished concealment. The black lower line of the veil made her throat seem very round and soft and white. She had seen these things in the mirror in Madame

Sarah's dressing room, and they had thrilled her. Also she unfurled the light blue sun parasol and twirled it slowly over her shoulder.

As she sauntered along the street she was literally walking into a new part, a new life, a new self. Every man she passed gave her a keener self-confidence. The Lord had endowed her, she began to feel, with weapons more deadly than the six-gun that had been her father's last gift. To be sure, she was not yet familiar with the weapons. But at least she felt, as she had felt when her childish eyes first saw the oily blue barrel of a gun, that these things would kill from afar. She was not familiar with the new powers, and she knew that she was capable of only a walking part in this new self. If she had to speak, she determined to use the careful vocabulary that she had partially learned from Pierre le Rouge—a vocabulary of clean-cut words, many of them large, that one must pronounce slowly, giving the tongue plenty of time to strike the roof of the mouth or hit against the teeth, so that every syllable was distinct.

She came to the building with the wide steps in front of it. It was the widest set of steps she had ever seen. Also, there were columns above the steps, as tall and as straight as stone trees—the pride of the state. Somewhere beyond that granite forest was the great man she must see—she—Jack Boone, rough rider and gunfighter. She did not even know whether to call him "Governor," or "Governor Boardman," or "Mister Boardman," or plain "sir." She decided on the last term.

On the floor of the lower hall—in itself the most imposing apartment Jack had ever seen—one man was scattering sawdust and another was sweeping it up with a very long push broom. She stopped near the man with the push broom and smiled at him. He stood straight like a soldier and took off his hat. When she told him that she wanted to see the governor, he dropped his broom with a clatter to the floor and led her in person to the door. In the outer office she entered, there sat a dozen people and in one corner behind a desk was a red-haired man with a pug nose and blue eyes. He looked up at her with a weary scowl. She smiled and nodded. The scowl vanished. He rose. Her smile was repeated widely on his mouth. She stepped close.

"Do you think," said Jacqueline, combing her memory for the careful words and the careful pronunciation, "that it would be possible for me to see the governor?"

"Sure," said the red-headed youth, and she saw the eyes narrow as he peered through the veil. "Just give me your card to take in."

The heart of Jacqueline fell. It fell so far and so hard that she heard it bump. She was almost afraid that the man heard it also. "That's the trouble," she said. "I really can't give him my name."

"Oh!" said the red-haired man, and this time he looked *at* the veil, not through it. "Oh!" His smile went out. Then it came again slowly. It had a meaning that made Jacqueline uncomfortable, though she could not tell exactly why. "I dunno," said the man, growing a little careless in both manner and speech and leaning back to examine her more critically. "*Maybe* it can be done."

In the crisis she forgot to act a part. She leaned a little closer to him, and one hand went out in an impulsive gesture—a hand ridiculously small in that long glove. "I'm in trouble," she whispered, "great trouble. Won't you help me?"

The blue eyes of the man widened and held upon her as though fascinated. Then a color came up in his face. When he spoke, it was through set teeth, as though he were very angry—though obviously not at her. It was as if he wanted to strike someone standing behind her. "If that's the case," he said in a low, hard voice, "you can bet your last dollar that I'll go the limit for you." He turned away. "Wait here. I'll be back in half a minute."

As he passed through the inner door he seemed to be swearing to himself softly through set teeth. What he did was break into the office of the private secretary and bang the door with unnecessary loudness behind him. "Joe," he said to the secretary, "is the old man doing anything?"

"Nope," said the other, without looking up from his typewriter. "Old stunt of letting the people wait . . . make 'em think he's up to his eyes in work. That's all."

"Well, he'll be busy enough in a minute. There's a girl out there who won't give her name. She wants to see the old bluffer personally."

"Hmm," said the secretary, "can't be done. Better pass her on to me."

The red-headed man caught the secretary by the shoulder and gripped hard. "Joe," he said, "she's *got* to see him. Understand?"

"What's the dope?"

"I dunno. But she's a dinger, Joe. And she's wearing a veil so she won't be recognized. She's in trouble, see?"

"Oh!" said the secretary, exactly as the red-headed man had spoken a few minutes before. He added with a grin: "The old hound!"

"The damned cur!" said the red-headed man softly. "Wait till you see her, Joe, and you'll understand. I'd like to lean his head against the wall and punch it to a jelly."

"Oh!" said Joe. There seemed much meaning in this exclamation in the governor's office.

"She's a lady, Joe," said the red-headed man.

"A lady!" cried Joe, and he rose from his chair. "Bring her right in. Pete, politics are sure rotten, ain't they?"

"Ain't they?" agreed Pete fiercely. "I'll bring her in."

The Governor Meets a Lady

20

Governor Boardman looked up from the morning newspaper and glanced over his spectacles at his private secretary. "A lady?" he repeated. "What's she want?"

"Don't know," said Joe. "Won't give her name. Won't tell her business."

"Let her wait," said the governor. "Women don't come ahead of men in my office. Not yet!"

It was like a political dictum. He scowled back at his paper to dismiss the subject.

"She's wearing a thick veil," said Joe, apropos of nothing.

"Oh!" said the governor, reverting to the usual exclamation in turn. He laid down his newspaper.

"She says," continued Joe absently, turning toward his door, "that she's in trouble."

The governor started. He reddened and then frowned to cover his flush. "Wait a minute, Joe," he called.

The secretary turned, and the governor removed his spectacles and polished them vigorously—an unfailing sign of mental perturbation.

"What . . . er . . . does she look like?" he asked.

"A beaut," said Joe, irreverent of the chief executive's presence, "a knock-out, and a lady."

"A lady!" echoed the governor, sitting bolt upright in his chair.

"Right," said Joe. "Pete came in himself to tell me about her."

"Oh," said the governor.

He leaned back in his chair and patted his desk with a thoughtful palm. "D'you say she's wearing a veil?"

"Yep. A thick one. But it can't hide her."

The governor placed his spectacles in their case, closed the case with a decisive snap, slipped it into his upper vest pocket, and smoothed his hair. He scowled at Joe, but there was a certain wistfulness in his eye. "If she's in trouble," said the chief executive, "that alters the case. A woman in distress . . . er . . . should always receive consideration. Remember that, my lad . . . always!"

"Sure," said Joe, and turned on his heel.

The remark that had been made about the valets of great men should perhaps be extended to their private secretaries. As Joe, the secretary, went out by one door, Jack, the girl, came in by the other, and the red hair of Pete showed for an instant. "Good luck!" he whispered, and then the door closed with a click behind her, and she was left to the awful solemnity of the governor's presence.

Her eyes, at first, she could not raise to meet his glance and then slowly, inch by inch, her survey went up the creases of his trousers, numbered the buttons of his vest, paused with a start on his flowered necktie—ah, humanizing touch!—and passed with swift mental notation the fold of flabby flesh that overflowed his collar, and then more quickly went up and shocked against his eyes. She suddenly discovered that she was not afraid. She looked again, met a certain knowing half-smile on the lips of the great man, and knew that she was not even awed. He was leaning a little forward in his chair. She could feel her draw upon him as of a magnet upon iron. The knowledge that began with Eve dropped suddenly, as from a great height, upon Jacqueline. She knew that the governor was only a man!

She said: "Sir, may I talk with you alone?" Her voice was very low. In her uncertainty there was a hint of a tremolo in it.

The governor did not seem displeased. He rose from his chair. He tucked his pudgy hands into his trousers pockets. He beamed upon her. "Sit down, my girl," he said genially. "Certainly we can be alone."

"The doors?" she queried faintly.

The smile froze for an instant on the lips of the governor, went out, and came again. He locked each of the doors and placed the keys on the table near her. It was gracefully done. She thanked him with a smile and sat down gingerly on the edge of a chair.

"Make yourself comfortable," said Governor Boardman. "I'm told that you're in trouble. Well, just look on me as a father . . . or"—he corrected himself hastily—"as a brother, say. Or anyone you can talk freely and confidentially to."

"Thank you," said Jacqueline, and was silent. She had learned much, very much, in the last few hours, or she would never have thought of preserving that silence.

"Well, my dear," said the governor, "take your time. And perhaps you'll let me see your face?"

"Oh, no!" said Jacqueline, and shrank back in the chair, raising her hand hastily to her veil.

The governor smiled. In fact, it was almost a grin.

"I *am* in trouble," said Jacqueline. "Great trouble. A man. . . ."

"Brother, father, or . . . sweetheart?" asked the governor hastily.

"A . . . a . . . friend," said Jacqueline.

While the chuckle of the governor rolled in her ear, she hastily put the question to herself again. *Could Dix*

Van Dyck be any one of the three things? It alarmed her. For the first time she felt really uncomfortable. She became angry at the chuckle of the governor. It seemed to her that he was not only a mere man but in ways a very stupid man.

"His name is Dix Van Dyck," she said.

It was an effectual period to the governor's chuckle. He sat stiffer in his chair—as straight as his round body permitted. A little more and he would have rolled out of his seat. "Him!" said the governor ungrammatically.

"He," corrected Jacqueline, remembering Pierre le Rouge.

"An outlaw," said the governor with heat, "a man-killer. A price on his head for his outrages! Madame, if you have come on his behalf, there is nothing I can do for you except to express my sorrow that you have interested yourself in so worthless a man. Strange!"

It *was* strange, to his mind, that a woman dressed like this should be interested in a man who had been represented to him as a worthless, idling, drunken cowpuncher. Not even that. A loafer. He stared more keenly through the thick veil and made out only the deep shadows of the eyes of Jacqueline.

"People have told you lies," said Jacqueline coldly, and the desire to fight rose slowly in her and made her low voice as cold as the feeling of smooth steel. "People have told you lies. He's not a murderer. He's a man."

There was a singular accent on that last word. It made the eyes of the governor glance inward, and he winced. "The course of justice must not be interrupted," he said rather feebly. "When a man makes himself the enemy of society, he should be prepared to pay the penalty to society. Dix Van Dyck is . . . I beg your pardon . . . a ruffian and a born gunfighter. Society cannot tolerate such men. They destroy the very soul of order. And I, madame, represent the spirit of order in the state. You cannot expect me to intervene on behalf of Dix Van Dyck."

Something very like despair swept over Jacqueline. The tremble came again in her voice, and she spoke with both her hands held out toward Governor Boardman. "Then I won't ask for justice," she said. "I'll only beg you for mercy!" She saw his anger at least disappear. Half his weapons were torn away from him. She saw that she could not fight him with words, but she might win through entreaty. "He has always fought in self-defense. Give him one more chance. For my sake, I know he'll change. Sir, he has. . . ."

"This," he said, wiping his forehead, "ends a useless and painful interview. Madame, I regret that I can do nothing for your . . . friend."

She stood up straight by the table and caught up the keys with one hand. The other hand slipped into a fold of her dress. "You're all wrong, Governor," she said calmly.

"What?" he said, frowning as if he tried to clear his eyes.

"You heard me," she announced. "You're all wrong. You're going to take a piece of paper and sit at that desk and write a pardon for Dix Van Dyck. You can do it and you *will* do it."

"My dear girl," said the governor, "grief has made you hysterical. What can make me give him his pardon?"

"This," she said, and in an instant a long, blue-barreled gun shone in her hand and covered the governor. She held it at the hip. If she had poised it in the air and drawn a careful bead, he might have been foolish enough to attempt to overpower her, for he was not without courage. But he had seen experts handle guns, and he knew the meaning of that position at the hip—knew the meaning of that slightly crouched body. He saw a thousand things in that instant. He saw the red headline announcing his

death. He saw the face of Oñate if he should make out
the pardon. He reached for the edge of the desk as if to
grip it for support. By Providence his thumb was guided
to the button that rang for his private secretary. He recognized the button. He made the pressure long.

The girl had come a stealthy pace closer to him. Something about her had changed quickly. Her words came
sharply, smoothly, with a click, like the spinning of an oiled
cylinder. "The doors are locked. I got the keys. You haven't
got a chance, partner. You got a pair of deuces, and I carry
a royal flush. All I ask for is speed. Understand?"

The ashen lips of the governor said: "But. . . ."

A loud knocking came at the door. It was repeated, still
louder. She raised her veil with a hasty hand, and what
the Governor saw in the angry black eyes made him
shrink back as if she had covered him with another gun.

"You called for help, eh?" she murmured. "But that
won't work. Go to that door, open it, and tell the men outside you don't want 'em. If you make a wrong move, I'll
drill you, partner, quicker'n hell!" She drawled the last
word with a fierce relish. "I'll drill you and take a chance
on my getaway. Now, step fast. They're wearin' out their
hands on that door."

The governor obeyed. He was conscious, as he walked
toward the door, of the direction of the leveled revolver.
It was like something prodding him in the ribs. As he
passed to the side, his careful glance noted the small
forefinger curved around the trigger. A breath more pressure and his term of life would end. It gave him a feeling
of uncanny lightness. She tossed him the keys, and he
opened the door, though it was difficult for his trembling
hand to place the key in the lock. He waved a brusque
hand to the private secretary. "My mistake, Joe," he said
with white-faced cheerfulness, then closed the door, and
turned back into the room.

The Boss

is fear had lasted long enough for anger to take
part of its place. "I'm going to write out the pardon
for you," he said, "not because I'm afraid of your
gun, but because I always humor an hysterical woman."

"Partner," answered Jack calmly, "I don't care why you
do it, as long as it's done."

"Of course," he went on, "the moment you're gone, I'll
call in a marshal, explain how I was held up at the point
of a gun for the pardon, swear out a warrant for your arrest, and send a messenger to Double Bend to cancel the
pardon."

"That," said the girl with unabated cheerfulness,
"sounds smooth, but it wouldn't work. First, because they
don't make marshals in these parts that could stop me,
and because I'd come back and get you . . . and you
know it! Second, because you don't dare let 'em know
that a woman bluffed you out at the point of a gun.
They'd never stop laughin' in this state if they knew that,
Governor."

He had not thought of that. It made him wince and
turn yellow. Once more he saw the face of Oñate turning
yellow with vindictiveness when he heard of the governor's pardon. The image of the white verandah and the
cool, green palms died out in the governor's brain.

"Write," commanded the girl. "I'm a pile hurried."

He sat down at the desk and wrote, slowly—because

his brain was working in fits and starts, like a cold engine, but finally the words were set down and his name scrawled beneath the message. He shoved the paper slowly toward her. Even then his mind was working to discover a way to undo what he had just completed.

"Stick up your hands," said the girl as she received the paper in her left hand, "and keep 'em up while I throw an eye over this lingo. If you make a move to pull 'em down while I'm reading . . . trust me . . . I'll see you!"

He obeyed, sweating with mortification.

"It looks okay," she announced after she had finished reading. "The writing looks sort of wobbly . . . like you was drunk, old boy . . . but it's better to be drunk than be like you are sober. So long. Dix Van Dyck'll drink a long one to you when he gets this."

At the door she pulled the veil down over her face, slipped away the gun into a fold of her dress, and disappeared into the gloom of the hall.

For half a minute the governor stood staring at the door through which she had vanished as if he saw a specter. Then he leaped into action. He jammed his plump forefinger down on the button and kept it there until the private secretary fairly leaped through the door.

"Get Mitchell," groaned the governor like an expiring man.

It was, indeed, a political death that was taking place. Joe sped for the telephone. In half an hour Mitchell appeared. He was the power behind the throne in the state. For fifteen years he had controlled the legislature and usually the governor was his choice. He had dragged Boardman from the gutter to the gilded heights of the capital. And he was fond of his nominee for of all the men he had handled the present governor was the most pliable. He came now, in haste, but even in his haste his dignity would not have shamed the presence of a Roman senator, an old man of nearly seventy with a bush of snow-white hair and a slender beard of the same color. Long, lean, with high cheekbones and buried, small eyes, he looked like a fighter, and a fighter he was.

"I'm done," said the governor without rising to greet the great man.

"You usually are," said Mitchell, "once a month. What is it this time? The Mexicans or the copper men?"

"A woman," groaned the governor.

"Hell," said Mitchell, showing his first emotion, "that's worse than both together. What is it? Blackmail?"

"Looked like a lady," said the governor, "and came with a plea for Dix Van Dyck . . . the outlaw that was taken the other day. Oñate was interested in getting Dix Van Dyck. That's why I outlawed him."

"Put a rope around his neck for the sake of Oñate, eh?" murmured Mitchell. "I remember now."

"Of course, I turned her down. Said Van Dyck had to swing. She pulled a gun. What could I do? The little devil had hellfire in her eyes. I made out the pardon. She's ridden away with it straight for Double Bend, I suppose. I can't retract the pardon. If the state knows that a woman has made me back down, they'll never stop laughing at me."

"I could laugh myself," murmured Mitchell, "if it weren't for Oñate. He'll be furious when he finds out that Van Dyck is out again. How did the feud start between Oñate and Van Dyck? And who is Van Dyck? Was it land or booze or women or what?"

"Something Van Dyck said. Oñate sent his brother and two other men to kill Van Dyck. Instead, he got all three of 'em. That put Oñate on his trail. I had to railroad Van Dyck to keep Oñate. Oñate means twenty per cent of the state."

"Dirty business," said Mitchell, and then, being a graceful man, he waved his lean old hands through the air, "but little men have to die in order that big men may live. We can't ruin ourselves for the sake of any Dix Van Dyck. I'll tell you what you've got to do, Sam. You have to stop that girl before she reaches Double Bend. Before that pardon reaches the prison, you'll have to have Van Dyck strung up by a mob . . . anything will do. The great thing is to conciliate Oñate. Am I right?"

"Stop the girl? You might as well talk of stopping the wind. I've seen her. It can't be done, Mitchell."

"There's a gambling chance . . . better than an even chance. Stop the girl with peaceful means if you can, and get that pardon away from her. Stop her with bullets if you have to. In the meantime send off a messenger on the gallop for Double Bend. Oñate will be there enjoying the sight of Van Dyck behind the bars."

"But stopping the girl?" objected the governor, regaining his interest in life to some extent.

"Leave that to me. I'll telephone ahead down the path to Double Bend. I'll have a dozen men combing the trail for her. If she comes in reach of the trap, you can rest assured that she'll fall into it."

"And Oñate?"

"Give him a hint that the thing for him to do is to raise a mob and attack the jail at Double Bend."

"But," said the governor, "there's one thing in the way of that. Marshal Phil Glasgow is in Double Bend, and he's hell on mobs."

"Damnation!" roared the irate Mitchell, springing to his feet. "Are you going to let one man block your scheme? To hell with Phil Glasgow. Have him shot . . . tie him hand and foot . . . but don't let that pardon get to Double Bend. We've reached the turning of our tide. Without the Mexican vote, we've got nothing . . . and we lose the Mexican vote if we lose Oñate. He wants Van Dyck. Let him have the fellow. It's our contribution to hell . . . our cake thrown to Cerberus . . . yes, very good . . . our contribution to Cerberus. Ha, ha, ha!" Mitchell chuckled over his metaphor for he was a man of some classical education. He awoke with a growl. "But don't sit there like a blockhead staring at me. Get busy, Sam. This makes you or breaks you. Don't try to get that message to Oñate over the wire. You'll have to trust a messenger. Leave it to me to stop the girl."

"If you can do that!" sighed the governor.

"Is a slip of a girl," sneered the great man, "going to be the monkey wrench that wrecks my machine? Boardman, sometimes you talk like a fool."

The Shadow of the Bars

22

The greatness of a leader, it is said, can be accurately judged by the ability of his lieutenants. The leader himself may be capable, but unless he can choose the right men for the right place his hands are tied. Washington needed Hamilton, and Napoleon needed Soult, Lannes, Souchet, and the rest. As for Mitchell, while his scope was not so great, he had an equal need for men who would accept his word as the final law and act upon it unhesitatingly—wisely. He required smooth-tongued speakers for lobbying, silent powers to touch financial interests, stump-speakers to stir the brain, and preachers to rouse the emotions. He needed men with subtle brains and men with hard fists. He needed some who roared like lions and others who went as silently as the snake. Such were his requirements as boss of the state. He had the men. He had them pigeon-holed in the orderly recesses of his brain.

When he retired from the presence of Governor Boardman, therefore, he had merely to sit a moment by himself and comb over his resources. On this occasion he had hardly the leeway that he generally enjoyed. He had to find the right man, not in the state but in the little town of Godfrey that lay halfway between Double Bend and the capital city. Every town was mapped in the brain of Mitchell. He could name most of the streets. He knew the leading citizens. His system of espionage touched every channel of life in the state—financial, political, and social. Now he concentrated on the town of Godfrey, and out of that mental effort a picture rose in his mind—the picture of Bill Lawton.

What Mitchell wanted was not an officer of the law, but a man who would take his word in the place of any legal authority. He wanted, moreover, a man who would attack a woman as soon as he would a man. These were the two requirements that came into Mitchell's careful mind. There was another qualification that he did not think of until later. But in answer to the first two demands he saw the clear picture of Bill Lawton, hook-legged from a life spent in the saddle, a gait as clumsy as that of a salt-water tar when on foot, blunt, ugly hands ready for all work, a shock of iron-gray, dirty hair tumbling over a low forehead, little pig-eyes set close together, a negligible nose, and the loose mouth of a satyr.

He rang up the saloon of Bull Murphy at Godfrey. When the connection was made, he asked for Bill Lawton. He was perfectly sure that if he was in town Bill Lawton would be in the saloon. It was as impossible to imagine him elsewhere as it would be to imagine the sand away from the desert. In a moment the voice of Bill Lawton rolled back along the wire.

"Lawton?"

"Right."

"This is Mitchell."

"What Mitchell?"

"Cripple Creek Mitchell."

"The hell-l-l-l!"

"Are you broke, Bill?"

"Always."

"Want work?"

"Always. If it ain't hard."

"Can you get a dozen men . . . or half a dozen?"

"Half a hundred, if you want 'em."

"Then get 'em. I'll pay the expense. Tell 'em that. I want you to stop a woman who's riding between this town and Double Bend. She ought to be along early tomorrow morning. She rides. . . ."

"D'you say this's got to do with a woman?"

"Right."

"Then I can't get no half hundred . . . not in this town."

"How many can you get?"

"I dunno. Maybe half a dozen."

"Then get them."

"What's the woman done?"

"She's carrying a paper to Double Bend. First, you've got to stop that woman. Next, you've got to get that paper."

"How bad do you want her?"

"A hundred dollars' worth for you and twenty bucks for every man with you."

"That sounds fair to me. How bad d'you want her, speakin' of guns?"

"The way I always want a thing done."

"If she rides too fast?"

"Shoot the horse."

"If she carries a gun. . . ."

"She does carry a gun, and she'll use it. That's her kind."

"Well?"

"Treat her like a man."

"Is that straight? It don't go none too easy with a man that tackles a woman . . . not in these parts."

"I told you to stop her. I don't care how you do it."

"You're behind me?"

"To the limit."

"But I reckon you'd better raise that hundred to two."

"It's done."

"How'll I know the girl?"

"Very good-looking. Dark. Black hair and eyes. She'll probably be riding hard. Ought to pass somewhere near Godfrey early tomorrow morning. Will you be on the trails?"

"Trust me, chief."

"Good luck."

"S'long."

But, when he had hung up the telephone, Bill Lawton turned and wiped from his forehead large and steadily growing beads of perspiration. He went immediately to the corner of the barroom where his compatriot, the half-breed, Noony, still sat. To him he explained the situation, and Noony, before responding, shifted his eyes swiftly to all sides to make sure that no one was within distance of a whispering voice.

"It ain't lucky," said Noony, who was half Indian and half white, "to fool with a girl."

"It ain't," agreed Lawton. "You never said nothin' truer, Noony. But we got the big boss behind us."

"But, if a gang gets wind of it," answered Noony, "the big boss is a pile too far away to help us any. How many men you going to take?"

"How many?" queried Lawton. "You an' me. That's all. Take two men an' they'll keep their faces shut about a little deal. Take three an' one of 'em's apt to go to the district attorney and stay put. I *know*." He said it with sinister lack of enthusiasm. "But you, Noony, you know me too well to try any funny stuff."

The half-breed shrugged his shoulders as though something cold were running down his back. "I know," he said laconically. "But you think two's enough?"

"Where there's a woman," said Lawton, "it's almost too much. A woman ain't no good, Noony. I know because I've tried 'em when I was flush. A woman can make more trouble amongst a lot of gents than a barrel of whiskey and a pile of loot. I *know*. That's why I never take no chance with 'em."

"How d'you mean?" asked the half-breed.

"This," said Bill Lawton, and leaning forward with a ghastly grin he drew his forefinger slowly, with relish, across his throat. "After that," he concluded, "there ain't many men will want to fight for 'em."

"Going to do that this time?" asked Noony.

"What do you think I been talkin' for?" asked Lawton. "Money? Sure I'm going to do that this time! Think I'll let the girl come down to Godfrey and tell the boys what's happened? There's some of 'em already that don't like me none too much ever since I bumped off old Milton down at the cabin. And she couldn't make no mistake describin' this map of mine. God sure tagged and labeled me when I come into the world. They'd know me in a cityful. Even if we done nothing to her but take that paper off'n her, the boys would be out for my scalp. All she'd have to do would be to spill a couple of tears, and all the boys would go crazy. The sight of a woman cryin', Noony, is worse'n gambling to drive gents off their feed and make 'em ready for guns. I *know*. We'll stop this girl and hold her till we get the paper. Then I'll pull my knife . . . and you jest look the other way so's you couldn't give no evidence ag'in' me. Right?"

"Right!"

"Then where'll we lay for her?"

"She'll take the east trail, like as not," said Noony. "The big boss is after her. Maybe she knows she's wanted. She won't come near no town. She'll keep in the hills."

"Noony, there's what I call brain work! If it wasn't that I owed the boss a lot, I'd never tackle this job. But he got me out of the can when I was lingerin' around behind the bars waitin' to be knocked in the head. My God, Noony, there ain't nothin' so bad as jail . . . an' the shadows of the bars. They leave marks on you . . . inside. I got 'em with me still!"

A Man of Destiny

fter he had dismounted before the jail at Double
Bend, *Señor* Oñate approached the building slowly,
enjoying every step of his progress. A sense of richness surpassing filled his heart. Life to him was a gleaming river of tequila against a pleasant background of
Dolores and with a future rich in nameless possibilities of
political power and personal wealth. He began to feel
himself a man of destiny. The bright sun of the afternoon
meant as much to him as Napoleon's sun at Austerlitz. All
things conspired to please him.

The jail, for instance, might have been designed by
him in person for the incarceration of Dix Van Dyck. It
had formerly been a store with wide adobe walls and a
capacious cellar. The cellar was now used as the
prison, while in the upper story were the guards and in
one corner a saloon. In the cool gloom of the saloon
he paused for a drink, then he went in search of the
jailer.

The jailer, being politically dependent on Oñate,
greeted his coming with chattering delight. Hearing that
he wished to see Dix Van Dyck, he took up a lantern from
the corner of the room and lighted it. He explained that he
had received Sheriff Oñate's request that the prisoner
be made as uncomfortable as possible, and that he had
lodged him in one of the two cells that had been dug out
in a sort of subbasement—a place where little air filtered

through and where no ray of daylight entered. Sheriff Oñate grinned and nodded.

He followed his guide across the patio, down the first flight of stairs, and then they stopped before an iron-barred door. It was made of thick wood—oak, perhaps—and it sweated in the prison damp. The jailer produced a rusty key of unusual dimensions and, after much labor, managed to turn the creaking lock. When the door opened, the darkness of the interior seemed to roll out upon them like a palpable wave and with it came a faint, disagreeable taint on the air, partly of the underground, partly of that indefinably disagreeable odor of confined humanity.

The jailer raised the lantern above his head and, before entering the passage, peered into it. He was crouched, and there was about his whole bearing the suggestion of one entering a place of danger. Before he actually stepped into the damp gloom within, he loosened the revolver at his side and hitched his belt around so that it would be more convenient for the draw.

"I take no chances," he explained to Oñate. "Suppose *Señor* Van Dyck breaks from his cell and lurks here behind the door, ready to spring on me as I enter. I shoot him down, and there is no more to do."

"Has he tried to break out?" queried Oñate, adopting the undertone of his companion automatically.

"No," answered the jailer, "but he sits thinking like a cheetah all day and all night, and, when the time comes, he will strike."

"At least," murmured Oñate, his chuckle marvelously reduced as though he feared that he might be overheard, "he has enough to think about."

"*Señor* Oñate," said the jailer with an answering chuckle, "will have seen to that."

All this while they had been descending a steep and

circular flight of stairs cut into the hard, sweating ground—slippery underfoot. Now they came to the level bottom and stopped before a door of steel bars. The jailer raised his lantern high, and by that light Oñate saw a little cell hardly more than six feet by six feet. At one side of it, occupying fully half of the total floor space, was a raised wooden platform serving as a bed and a single blanket by way of bedding. On this platform sat a heavy-shouldered man with his elbows on his knees and his face in his hands. As the light struck him, he raised his head—very slowly—and turned toward the visitors. *Señor* Oñate sprang back with a little cry that turned into a curse.

"The bars," he whispered anxiously to the jailer. "Will they hold when he springs at 'em?"

The jailer turned on the sheriff with an understanding smile.

He said at length: "I also used to feel that he would spring at the bars when he looked at me like this, but he has never sprung. No, he is hungry for a kill, but like the cheetah he sits there night and day, waiting till his hunger grows too great."

"And then?" queried Oñate breathlessly.

"Then he will try the bars."

"And . . . ?"

"They will hold . . . and *Señor* Van Dyck will go mad."

Oñate ran to the bars in a sudden wild exultation. He shook them as though he strove to tear them apart and get at the prisoner within.

"Hear?" he called, his voice sharpening almost to a scream. "Do you hear? *Americano* dog . . . coyote . . . swine . . . do you hear? When you try the bars, you will fail . . . and go mad . . . mad . . . mad! Ha, ha, ha! Ha, ha, ha!"

He fell back from the bars, rubbing his plump palms

together. Then he turned to the jailer. "You may go. I will be alone with my friend Van Dyck."

The jailer nodded, surrendered the lantern, and went rather hastily up the narrow flight of the stairs.

"And so," went on Oñate, turning back to his victim, "this is the end of *Señor* Van Dyck . . . the man-killer? This is the end?"

The silence of the prisoner continued.

"It was I," said Oñate, "who went to the governor, my friend the governor, and made him put the price on your head. *Made* him, *Señor* Van Dyck. Do you hear? *Made* him! It is I who put you here under the ground like a dog in the dark. It is I who have hired the witnesses to swear away your life when the trial comes. It is I who will be there in the death room when the trap is sprung, and Dix Van Dyck drops through. Do you hear? Do you think of that?"

The prisoner smiled. "I only think," he said calmly, "of the feel of the throat of Vincente under my hands."

"Ah!" groaned Oñate.

"Of the way my thumb sank in the hollow of his throat."

"Dog . . . fiend!" gasped Oñate, and tore at the collar to loosen it around his fat throat.

"I felt him go limp," said Van Dyck.

"I shall tell the jailer," said Oñate. "There are many little attentions he can pay you."

"His tongue popped out of his mouth like a jack-in-the-box," went on Dix Van Dyck carelessly and in a meditative tone.

"I will have you tied hand and foot," groaned Oñate, "and I will have them drop water on you . . . drop by drop . . . until you scream and beg me for mercy."

"His eyes," said Van Dyck, "pleaded with me. I laughed into his dying face."

"Damn you!" screamed Oñate.

"I laughed . . . laughed . . . laughed!" repeated Van Dyck with slow emphasis.

The gun leaped from the hip of Oñate and poised in the dim light, wavering crazily.

"I shook him," said Dix Van Dyck calmly, "as you've seen a dog shake a dead rat. Vincente . . . he looked very much like a dead rat."

"Another word," gasped Oñate, "and I blow your head off . . . and pump bullets into your body."

"I shook him," said Dix Van Dyck, "and then I threw the body into a corner of the bar room and laughed again."

"Damn you!" breathed Oñate, and poised the gun, squinting his eye down the sights.

"Then I laughed as I laugh now at you," said Dix Van Dyck, and he broke into deep, heavy laughter.

"What keeps me from shooting?" panted Oñate in a sort of dazed wonder.

"Your cowardly heart," said Dix Van Dyck, "and the same fear that made your little brother, Vincente, drop on his knee before me and shriek for his life."

The door creaked above them, and a man ran, stumbling, down the steps.

"*Señor* Oñate!" he called.

"Get out!" snarled the sheriff. "I'm busy."

"Word from the governor!" answered the other and stood at the side of the sheriff. He was a Mexican, dusty as if from long and furious riding.

"Damn the governor!" answered Oñate after he had glanced at the face of the messenger. "I'm busy."

"It is life and death," muttered the messenger.

"Give it here."

He snatched the letter, tore it open, and read. He had hardly scanned the first half-dozen words when the paper dropped, fluttering, to the floor, and Oñate reeled back against the wall. His face was the color of ashes mixed with mud. The messenger, seizing him about the waist, would have supported the sheriff, but the fury of a madman gave Oñate super-human strength.

"Rather than that, I'll finish you myself, Van Dyck . . . wolf . . . devil . . . swine!" he screamed. He leaped to the door of the cell and fired point blank at the prisoner.

Bill Lawton Is Hard Hit   24

It was not the riding alone that fatigued Jacqueline Boone, though she had been in the saddle fifteen hours with only a few short stops. It was the continued thirst that not only tormented her but so sapped the strength of the white stallion that he came haltingly up the last slope. She had determined either to turn to the right and go to Godfrey for water or else make a detour to the left, for somewhere among the hills she was sure that at this season of the year she would find a stream of snow water.

This trail was new to her. It was the old path, the straight line from Double Bend to the capital, but in recent years the town of Godfrey had grown up and now the main-traveled trail passed through that village. On that course she would have known exactly where to find water; on this new trail she was almost helpless. Fortune, however, served her at the very point when she was about to turn from the trail to the left and make her detour through the higher mountains, for she found a tiny pool, oozing from the side of the mountain at the very edge of the trail.

It was hardly a spring. Only a small quantity of water seeped through a little fissure on the mountain edge, draining a great gravel bed above, and even this small quantity of water would not have been available for drinking had it not providentially trickled into a depression hollowed, as if purposely, in the top of a slab of rock. She checked her horse and the stallion, his ears flat back and his nostrils distended in the anguish of his thirst, made straight for the pool, but she drew the reins hard and surveyed the place.

Even here in the heart of the mountains her caution did not desert her. In a way it was a region to inspire caution, for a thousand men might have lurked within five hundred yards of her position and taken her hopelessly at a disadvantage. For a mile in either direction the valley made a perfect V, the cliffs on either side rough and straight at the tops and sloping more gradually at the bottom of the ravine. Down these slopes great boulders, detached perhaps by earthquakes, had rolled to every conceivable position. Behind these and behind the shrubs there were innumerable natural hiding places.

The eye of Jack swept the valley quickly and surely. For all her haste there was not a shrub or a boulder within easy range that she did not examine critically. Then she dismounted, and leaned over the pool. In the fever of her thirst she plunged her face into the water like a horse, and drank deeply with closed eyes. Raising her head to breathe, she kept her wet eyes closed and allowed the delicious coldness of the water to trickle down her throat. It was as she knelt there that a hand fell on her shoulder and something hard pressed against the center of her back. The muzzle of a gun, she knew.

She set her teeth but said calmly: "Well?"

"Stand up!" ordered a man's voice.

She rose. Her revolvers were drawn from the holsters.

"Turn around."

She turned and faced the most ominous pair she had ever laid eyes on in all her wild life among the mountains: the face of one round, gross, bestial and that of the other the opposite type of viciousness, thin, dark, hollow-cheeked, as if a fire consumed the man within. The same fire shone in the eyes of both.

"Look in the saddlebags," ordered the fatter and older of the two who seemed to be the commander.

The slender man moved instantly to the horse and opened the nearest bag.

"You're wrong," said the girl, "the money's in my belt. You're welcome to it. It's a pretty stiff stake at that, but . . . come easy, go easy."

She knew the ways of the lawless, and they love nothing so well as a graceful loser. The heavy-faced man, however, was not to be won.

"Shut your face," he ordered. "Noony, look 'em through."

It occurred to her that they might be looking for something other than money, but she shrugged the suspicion away. She had ridden far too fast to be overtaken. There was not a horse in the mountains that could have followed the pace of the white stallion even half the distance from the capital city to this point. She breathed easier. These could not be agents of Oñate or the governor. Noony was fumbling through the first bag.

"Nothing here, Lawton," he called.

"Try the other, Noony," answered Lawton. "Steady, there, I got my finger hard down on the trigger, my beauty, and I'll blow you to hell as soon as you bat an eye!"

She had started but not because she was about to make a move of resistance. The freedom with which the men called each other by name was the thing that made her start. It worried her. Among the outlaws she had known, no one was called by name except when they were alone together. Even then, names were not popular. Nicknames were chiefly in use.

If they were so free to call each other by names before

her, it must mean that they had nothing to fear from her testimony against them. This absence of fear again argued only one thing. They meant to get rid of her. It drew the color down from her cheek, but she was calm enough to examine Noony carefully.

She saw it now in the peculiar, hungry steadiness of his eyes. They were fixed upon hers. They burned into her mind. She knew that it is hard for any human being to face the glance of another except when he is bent on destruction. That steady glance worried her to the heart. Only one thing sustained her courage and that, strangely enough, was the chill touch of the little cross that hung suspended from her throat beneath her dress. It was like the light pressure of a reassuring and omniscient hand.

"Here!" called Noony suddenly. "She's got it, all right. It's something from the governor. It's going to Double Bend."

The face of Lawton hardened swiftly, and he drew closer by inches to the girl until his revolver was almost touching her breast. In his eye the will to murder was now a flame.

"Read it out," he said hoarsely, "and read it quick. I want to make sure before. . . ."

Noony began to read. Before he was half through with the legal phraseology, the brow of Lawton began to contract, but this time it seemed more in wonder than in anger. When the article was finished, he asked: "What'd you get out of it, Noony?"

"What it says," answered Noony. "This here paper pardons a gent named Dix Van Dyck for murderin' a few Mexicans."

"Murder?" said Lawton and stepped back from the girl a whole pace. "Murder?" he repeated, strangely moved. "And Mexicans?"

"That's what it says," nodded Noony, consulting the pardon again.

"This here Van Dyck," said Lawton to the girl, and he scowled terribly at her, "where is he?"

"In the jail at Double Bend," she answered steadily.

She heard him only faintly, so deeply was she concentrating on the touch of the little metal cross against her breast. She was wondering, dimly, how that strange power could free her now.

"Jail?" echoed Lawton, his former emotion shaking his voice again. "Jail, d'you say?"

"Sure," broke in Noony. "How'd the old governor be sendin' him a pardon if he wasn't in jail?"

"Noony," said Lawton in the same shaken voice, "you come here and take the drop on this girl . . . plug her if she moves. My hand ain't no good jest now."

Noony obediently crossed to them and leveled his revolver against the girl while Lawton fell back a little and mopped his forehead. The heat seemed on the point of overcoming him.

"Tell me, honest to God," said Lawton, "what kind of a murderin', no-good coyote is this here Van Dyck?"

"He ain't murdered no one and he ain't no good," answered the girl hotly. "He's never fired a shot that wasn't in self defense."

"Damn 'em . . . damn 'em all!" answered Lawton with rising warmth. "So Van Dyck's in jail. In jail . . . all alone . . . with the shadows of the bars. . . . God!"

"Steady up!" said Noony sharply. "Ain't you goin' through with this little game, Bill?"

"Wait," said Lawton. "I'm tryin' to think. Jail! What's he look like, girl?"

"He looks," said Jack instantly, "like the kind of gent that could pull a gun and shoot his man. He looks like the kind men like to have for a friend and hate like hell to have for an enemy. He looks like the kind that don't never leave no trail he starts. That's the kind he is. Big, ugly, with a steady eye."

"Noony," said Lawton, "is that kind of a gent to rot in jail and then get his neck stretched?"

"I dunno," answered Noony uneasily. "Ain't you goin' to finish the game after you've played it this far?"

"Shut up!" commanded Lawton sharply. "I got a pile of thinkin' to do. Girl," he said, turning to Jack, "what you got ag'in me?"

"Nothin'," she said calmly, "except that you were hard up and needed a stake. I've done some odd things myself, and I've seen a pile of odder ones done."

"Who might you be?" asked Lawton, coming closer to her again.

"Have you heard of old Boone and his gang?" Jack asked.

"By God!" said Lawton reverently. "You ain't Boone's girl? You ain't the girl they call Jack in these parts?"

"Right."

"The one that packs the cross . . . that brings bad luck on everybody but yourself?"

"It's that bad luck," she said sadly, "that brought Dix Van Dyck to jail. Lawton, don't you see, I'm tryin' to break the luck of the cross."

"Are we goin' to stop her?" asked Lawton moodily. "Are we going to play yaller dog, Noony?"

"I'm broke," said Noony sadly.

"My money belt's full," broke in Jack, "and you're welcome to it. Consider it a gift . . . a stake, if you want. You're welcome to it and no bones broke."

Bill Lawton considered her with his keen scowl. "For a woman," he said at last, "you look white, you talk white, and . . . by God, I think you *are* white. But I don't trust you none. Trust nothin' that wears a skirt. I *know.*"

"Besides," broke in Noony, "what about the big boss?"

Lawton started. "Him!" he said sharply. "Damn me, if I didn't forget plumb all about the boss. Noony, what we goin' to do?"

The girl listened and waited with her heart at her lips, but she was too wise in their ways to interrupt.

"I dunno," said Noony. "You say and I'll follow."

"Jail," muttered Lawton. "God!" He paused and then growled: "Bars in front of him. And him bein' a big man and a strong man. I know what he's feelin'. About this time of the day the long shadows of the bars is beginnin' to crawl across the floor. All hell's poppin' loose in him. Noony, what'm I goin' to do?"

"Hold her here. I'll slide down into Godfrey and telephone the boss. Maybe he'll find a way out."

"Do that!" said Lawton with great relief. "I'll take her down the valley to old Duffy's shanty. Ride hard, Noony. And see if there ain't some way out with the big boss. Noony, this hits me hard as hell."

The Dove   25

The bullet from the wobbling gun of Oñate flew wide past the head of Dix Van Dyck. He sat with his head back, still laughing, and his mockery maddened the sheriff. He raised the gun to poise it for a careful shot, but the messenger struck down his hand.

"There is another way," he whispered. "I know the mind of the governor. Read the rest of the letter. There is another way . . . a safer way. The governor. . . ."

"Damn him!" groaned Oñate. "I shall break him in little pieces . . . I shall make him laughed at by the state. . . . I shall . . . !"

"Too much talk," warned the messenger. "The big boss is behind this."

"He is!" cried Oñate and was silent, staring with wild eyes at the messenger.

"Yes," nodded the other.

"Mitchell?" repeated Oñate incredulously.

"Mitchell," said the messenger. "Best read the rest of the letter. Come. Upstairs after me!"

The sheriff followed him obediently with bowed head, like a man whose spirit is nearly broken. His breath was coming heavily, almost like so many soft sobs. In the light of the basement above, unable to wait longer, he shook out the letter again and read:

This in haste: I have pardoned Dix Van Dyck. The pardon is now on the way to Double Bend. You may be sure that the most extreme compulsion was used before I would sign the paper. A scoundrel entered my office under a lying pretext and shoved a revolver under my nose. He was desperate and meant business. I had to write the pardon. The man escaped. I have reason to think that a woman is carrying the pardon on horseback to Double Bend.

But do not give up hope. I have arranged to have her stopped on the way at any cost. She will, perhaps, be shot. At any rate, the pardon will be taken from her and destroyed. If this letter is in your hands before she has reached Double Bend with the pardon, you will know that she has fallen into our hands somewhere on the way, near Godfrey.

But in any case, lose no time. There seem to be many friends of this Van Dyck. Do not wait for the case to be brought to trial. It may be that men with money will back him. To show you that my sympathy and interest are behind you, I have labored hard to work out a plan by which you may have your revenge even more thoroughly than the law could give it to you, and a great deal quicker.

As soon as you have finished this letter, go out among your Mexican friends. Rouse them against Dix Van Dyck. It should be easily done. Paint him as the murderer of your countrymen. Make his fame black. Your friends will surely follow you. Attack the jail. Let your mob capture Dix Van Dyck and carry him away into the hills. Or, if you wish merely to kill him, you can finish him as soon as you reach him in the jail. That should be plain to you. I'm surprised that you have not thought of this before. Certainly it will not be hard to overpower the officers of the jail.

As soon as you have read this, burn it at once and do not let a scrap of it remain.

Oñate folded the paper carefully.

"Give it to me," said the messenger. "I was instructed to see that it was destroyed."

Oñate smiled slowly and broadly upon his country-man. "You fool!" said he. "You *have* seen it destroyed."

"I am his trusted man," said the messenger darkly. "Give me the letter, *señor.*"

"Bah," answered Ornate scornfully, and he drew out several pieces of gold from his pocket—as an incontestable proof of his affluence he always carried his money in this way—and dropped them, jingling, into the hand of the messenger. "Have you not seen the letter destroyed?"

The messenger smiled in return. The smile made him so like Oñate in expression that for the instant he might have passed as the man's brother. "I myself," he said, "burned the letter to a crisp and crushed the crisp into ashes. ¡*Adiós, señor!*"

In place of answering *Señor* Oñate watched the fellow pass out of the room, and he followed him with the unchanging smile. Peace was coming slowly back over his soul. As he paced with careful step out of the jail, he paused for a moment in the yellow, hot sunlight to let the full sense of the new idea flood through his brain. His smile persisted, and it went out only long enough for him to curse himself for not having thought of the idea before. It was simple; it was perfect. Its perfection lay in its simplicity. His smile persisted all the way to his house. The letter of the governor crinkled comfortably in his pocket. He would not have exchanged the possession of that letter for a fortune paid to him in cash.

Hitherto the governor had served him—for a price. Hereafter the governor would be his abject dog—for nothing. In the fullness of his soul he burst into song as he trotted his horse softly down the path to his house. The title of his song was "The Dove."

Señor Oñate had a house in both Guadalupe and Double Bend. To be sure, the house at Double Bend could not compare with the broad grounds and the roomy mansion at Guadalupe. Nevertheless, it was probably the finest building in the town and worthy of the affluence of Oñate. The garden was small but perfect of its kind, and in the patio bloomed the choice blossoms that he prized the most. He maintained two servants in this place, and at every meal, three times a day, the servants prepared a repast worthy of Oñate's tastes and set a place for him at the table. One servant stood stiffly behind the chair during all the dinner hour. It pleased Oñate to think of that servility even when he was absent. Moreover, this extravagance was more talked of among his countrymen and more admired than any other of his attributes. It showed more than wealth; it showed almost omnipotence.

To this dwelling in Double Bend, only the day before, he had sent El Tigre and the girl, Dolores. Usually he dropped in on his servants without warning to make sure that they were following the adamantine rules he had laid down for them. But this time, since he expected to stay some days in Double Bend, he had sent El Tigre and his daughter to prepare every detail of the house for his reception. Dolores would attend to his comfort. El Tigre would guard his safety like a watchdog. What is there more for the soul to desire when one may purchase both safety and comfort? If *Señor* Oñate was at peace with the world, surely there was a reason for it.

For some time after the return of El Tigre from the manhunt, he had been worried about the attitude the Yaqui would adopt toward him since his affair with Dolores had begun. His worries, however, were not long lived. He knew, to be sure, just what the attitude of the average Indian would be toward such an affair, but in El Tigre, apparently, love for his benefactor overruled all pride. Naturally the Yaqui often saw his master and Dolores together, but on such occasions he assumed a blindness absolute and satisfying to the soul of Oñate, no matter how suspicious the soul of the Mexican might be. When her father was near, the girl would fall suddenly into silence and formality, but the moment they were alone again, her little caressing manners returned. She was not the first girl to enter his life, but none had grown upon him so completely and so swiftly as Dolores.

From that first evening when he repeated her name and found it beautiful, the very thought of her had been sufficient to paralyze his reason and his judgment in a delicious sense of pleasure and possession. He did not stop to ask if she loved him. It was quite enough for him that he owned her.

Sometimes, indeed, when he turned suddenly and unexpectedly upon her, he would find her eyes dwelling upon his with a cold and dangerous solemnity. He only prized her the more for this. Who would content himself with a common house cat if it were possible to reduce to subjection, utter servility to eye and voice, a beautiful, wild panther, or the spotted, terrible cheetah? Not Oñate, to be sure! He loved the caress and whisper of her voice because the hiss of the snake was not far hidden behind the sound. He loved the soft touch of her hand because the same soft fingers were so apt to curl suddenly around the hilt of a knife. A little more subservience and she would have become as dull to him as any bought thing. As it was, no matter how he showered her with gifts of jewels and silks and robes and beautiful toys, the danger from her was only postponed, not destroyed.

He had never won her completely and that was the stimulus that made him woo her continually. Possession is nine points of the law. It is also nine points of boredom. *Señor* Oñate was never bored. He needed her as he needed tequila. She returned to him like thirst, many times a day.

The Whip

26

*S**eñor* Oñate did three things when he reached his house. He called for a table to be set in the patio. He called for tequila. And he called for Dolores. The three things were done. The table was set instantly. The house servants trotted in their haste. The tequila was brought also on the run in a silver bucket of ice. Two glasses were placed on the table. The house servants stood anxiously, awaiting acceptance or dismissal.

"Tell Dolores that I am hurried," he commanded, having surveyed the preparations and found them good. "Tell her to come at once. Go!"

They disappeared on hasty, padding feet. The thought of the continued presence of their great master seemed to weigh upon them like the dread of fire and famine and drought. They did all things together, as if one brain were not enough to comprehend the orders of Oñate.

Oñate let the smile grow out again upon his lips when they were gone. He waited. He had come to lose all taste for food and drink unless it were served to him by the slender hands of Dolores. He waited. His thirst grew into a hollow fire. It became illimitable and went, hot and tingling, through his veins. Still Dolores did not come. He smote the bell till it jangled again. The servants leaped into view, breathless.

"Dolores!" commanded the master, scowling.

"She says," they stammered in one voice, "that she is

sleepy . . . that she will not arise until the sun is setting. We begged her on our knees to come in haste. We told her that *Señor* Oñate was hurried. But the spirit of a devil. . . ."

"Fools . . . dogs!" bellowed Oñate, smashing his fat hand against the top of the table. "Go again . . . run . . . drag the girl-demon to me by the hair of the head. Go!"

They fled, wild-eyed.

The pause began again. Oñate, with one eye upon the iced tequila and the other upon the absent vision of Dolores, leaned back in his chair with eyes closed, and waited. Any one knows that when one closes his eyes without sleeping, every second is prolonged. But Oñate did not think of this. Presently he began to pant. He struck the bell again and this time so furiously that it rolled from the table and fell with musical clatter on the brick pavement of the patio.

Once more the servants came. They stood at a distance from his hand and abased their eyes before his red stare.

"What can we do?" said one of them, almost sobbing in terror and rage, and he showed a long rent in his loose jacket. "I gave the girl your message. I would have laid hands upon her. But she drew a knife with the speed of light and struck at me. By an inch only, *señor*, I escaped with my life. The ass, Pedro, who stands here beside me . . . coward and pig! . . . he would not move to help me. Then from outside the door we spoke soft words to her. She laughed, and we heard her lying down again just as the bell rang."

Oñate stooped to snatch up his whip that he had carried idly with him, also because he had found through long habit that the lash was of use in many ways. Swift though his stroke the servants were even swifter. They vanished again through the door. In a little time he heard their raised, pleading voices at the door of Dolores.

A small, cruel smile came on the lips of *Señor* Oñate. He began to draw the lash of the whip slowly through his hands. It was stained in places. It was these stains that made him smile.

His anger all the while grew apace. It was no longer hot. It had grown cold. He wanted to kill. He had almost forgotten the tequila. And then, different from the padding haste of the servants, he heard a step. His hand closed hard on the handle of the whip, locking tighter and tighter. He would strike her across the throat; he would leave her marked as his slave. It was time . . . good time . . . that she had learned the hand of Oñate and his mark.

The servants scurried before him.

"She is coming," they stammered. "Dolores will be here at once, *señor!*"

He stared at them. They were beyond the reach of his whip, so his eyes wandered past them. The blood was beginning to pound in his forehead, and he wanted to take a deep breath of cold air for he felt as if his rage would stifle him.

The slow, regular, soft step came closer. Then he knew that she was standing beside him, for he caught the faint, faint rustle of silk stirred by the wind against silk. A delicate perfume reached him, something to be guessed at rather than known. He could almost hear her breath. It was marvelous how acute his senses had become where the girl was concerned. In another instant he would turn his head and whirl the lash. Then he heard a faint, light click of ice against crystal-thin glass. It arrested his thought. It charmed him, in a way, as the eye of a snake is said to fascinate the bird.

"¿Señor?"

He opened his eyes slowly, his smile beginning. There she stood, as he had known she would stand, with two fingers of the dark-skinned, perfect hand holding the slender glass. Her dark eyes, as was her way, looked just past him. They never seemed to focus directly on his face. Sometimes he felt as though she were speaking to someone behind him. He had even turned, once or twice, when he knew that there was no one near them. He took the glass.

"Dolores," he said, making his voice hard, "there is a devil in you."

"Yes, *señor.*"

He let his eyes rest on her, irritated by her calm. She was dressed, *rebozo* and all, in dark red, the color of blood just after it has stained the skin and congealed. It glowed only where the slant sun of the afternoon struck it, and then it seemed like hot blood itself. Low on her forehead, hanging just below the edge of the *rebozo*, was a large emerald pendant from a slender golden chain. It was his latest gift.

"I must drive out the devil in you, Dolores," he said.

"Yes," she repeated with monotonous regularity. "Yes, *señor.*"

"With the whip," he said, and the word brought a terrible fury on him. The lash of the whip would bite through that thin silk and leave welts on the flesh. Every time he touched those welts she would flinch and remember that he was absolute lord. "With the whip," he repeated hoarsely.

Her eyes focused on him at that, slowly. She smiled and that maddened him.

"I would not whip you, but the devil in you," he said.

"The devil," she said, "should be whipped."

"But?" He waited, for he saw a glint in her eyes as cold as the light of the emerald.

"But it would be dangerous. Devils are dangerous, *señor.*"

"Ah?" he queried, and a strange pleasure came to mingle with, rather than abate, his rage. "What would the devil do?" he asked.

"Dolores cannot tell," she answered. "She has not asked the devil what he would do, but she knows that he has teeth." She touched the wide scarf that was knotted at her waist, and beneath the knot he made out the gleaming handle of a knife.

"It is well," said Oñate quietly. "Some day I shall kill you, Dolores."

"Yes, *señor.*"

"But now, fill your glass."

"I am not thirsty."

"Fill your glass."

She obeyed. The servant, Pedro, who stood nearby with widely staring eyes, chuckled harshly.

"I drink to the devil in your eyes, Dolores."

"To the devil in *your* eyes," she echoed. But she only touched the glass against her lips and set it down untasted.

"Dolores!"

"¿*Señor?*"

"You did not drink?"

"I am not thirsty, *señor.*"

"Dolores, empty your glass!"

She turned and flung the contents in the face of Pedro. He fled, cursing, stamping, crying out to Manuel, his companion. The tequila was like burning fire against his eyes. But Dolores turned back to Oñate. As she trailed her fingers across his forehead slowly, cool fingers, soft as silk, she said: "I have waited for you, *señor.* You have been long away."

"Dolores, you are lying to me."

"Indeed, *señor*, I am not."

"Dolores, you do not care for my coming or my going. Is it not true?"

"Surely it is not true."

He turned, half incredulous, half eager. "If you lie to me now, Dolores, I will take your own knife and cut your tongue in two. I will split it and give you two tongues. You need them both, you little demon!"

"I do not lie," she persisted calmly.

"Will you swear it?"

To his astonishment she raised the cross at her throat.

"Dolores!" he cried, astonished and delighted.

"*¿Señor?*"

"Swear to me."

"What shall I swear?"

"That . . . let me see . . . that you have truly missed me while I was gone."

"I swear it, *señor.*"

"Ah, Dolores! Swear still more. Swear that you have yearned for me to come again?"

"I swear that I have yearned for you to come again."

"My love!" whispered the sheriff, and held out his pudgy arms to her. She merely flicked the tips of his fingers with a careless hand. He dropped his arm scowling. "Why did you yearn for my coming?" he asked sharply.

"Because, *señor,* I have seen a *mantilla* of lace . . . fine lace that is yellow with age. I wish one."

"Devil . . . cold-hearted devil!" said Oñate between his teeth.

She chose that moment of rage to slip into his arms. They closed around her, fiercely and then tenderly.

"Dearest!" whispered the sheriff.

"The *mantilla?*" murmured Dolores.

Fear

27

Two days before he would have flung her from him in a sullen rage. Now he merely snarled and drew in his breath—his rage lasted no longer than that. "You shall have the *mantilla*," he promised, "oh, little, heartless one!"

He passed his hand slowly over her hair. It made him think of patting the terrible black head of a panther. She left his arms, having received his promise, with a movement so subtle and graceful that he could not follow it. All he knew was that one moment she was close to him and the next moment far away on the other side of the table, pouring him another glass of tequila.

"Will I ever know if you truly love me, child?" he asked, watching her with lazy content.

She considered the question with those hazy eyes that focused just behind his chair and always filled him with the same uneasiness. Then she used his own word. "Dolores is a *child*. How can she know?"

"Why?" asked the sheriff.

"You are fat," said the girl, "and old."

"Still," he argued, keeping back his anger from his voice, "you do not leave me, and you are free to go."

"I am not ready," she said, "but, when I am rich with your money and have many fine clothes, I will go."

"So?" said Oñate.

"I have spoken," she answered, and yawned so that he saw the flash of her white teeth.

"What will you do when you leave me, Dolores? Will you ever again find a master as gentle as I am?"

Her eyes misted with content as she considered a pleasant prospect. "I will go in my fine clothes to the dance hall," she said, "and look at the men. When I find the one I want, I will smile at him, and he will come to me . . . a white man."

"So?" snarled Oñate.

"It is true. He will come to me . . . a big man with a straight, thin mouth . . . a lean man with very hard muscles. He will tell me to follow him, and I will go to his house."

"So?"

"It is true. I will follow him and give him my jewels that you have bought me. I will give them all to the *Americano.*"

"He will get drunk," commented Oñate, "and, when he comes home, he will beat you for pleasure."

"It is true," said the girl, and yawned again so that her small, gleaming teeth showed. "I will know that the man who beats me is my master. I will be his woman."

"She-devil!" he broke out. "What keeps me from lashing you?"

"Fear," said Dolores instantly.

"Fear?" he echoed, with a rising passion. "Fear? If I put a knife between your ribs, beautiful fiend, beautiful Dolores, what man would question me for it. Fear?"

"Fear," she repeated. "You are fat and old and as slow as a snake after it has swallowed a rabbit. I could kill you in many places before you struck me once."

"So?" said Oñate, and having gathered up the whip stealthily, he leaned suddenly forward and struck at her viciously.

She swerved from her chair as the falling leaf is jerked aside from its straight descent by a gust of wind. The whirling lash brushed the flying end of her *rebozo*. The next instant her knife point was at the throat of Oñate.

"Grunt, pig!" said Dolores.

His eyes were green with fear, but he managed to pant. "It was only play, dearest."

She touched his throat with the point of her knife—so lightly that it only tickled the skin. "It is pleasant," said Dolores, "to play. But *Señor* Oñate is too fat to make a game." She put back the knife under her scarf and stepped backward to her chair.

"How long will it be," said Oñate, "before I take you as you sleep and wring your neck?"

"It is hard to tell," said Dolores and yawned again, stretching her supple limbs with infinitely slow pleasure. "Now I am tired. Will the master let me go to sleep?"

"No," he said surly.

She had risen as she spoke. Now she slipped back into the chair. It was always that way. She obeyed him implicitly at the very moment when he thought her revolt was hopeless. The sense of mastery made his blood warm.

"No," he repeated again, "you will sit there till I am tired of looking at you. So you will leave me, Dolores?"

"I have spoken, *señor.*"

"Leave me forever," he mused.

It made him prize that instant of possession the more. She knew it, and he knew she knew.

"Not for always," said Dolores. "In two years . . . three years . . . I will be no longer beautiful. I am not like white women. They are lovely forever. Two years . . . then I will begin to get fat . . . like you . . . my skin will wrinkle like paper that has been many times folded and cannot be smoothed out. Then the *Americano* will beat me again and throw me from his door."

"So?" grinned Oñate. "You know that, little devil of mine?"

"I have spoken. Then I shall come back to you."

"Good!" grunted Oñate. "I will beat you with this same whip and put you in the kitchen to work. I will marry you to Pedro and teach him to beat you twice a day."

"No," said the girl calmly, "when I come back, you will take me in your arms and speak many small, foolish words to me."

"I?" repeated Oñate furiously. "I take you back when you are fat and wrinkled and . . . a hag?"

"It is true," she smiled imperturbably, "for I will always be beautiful to you."

"Bah! You are crazy as a horse that has not had water for two days in the desert."

"No. I will always be beautiful to you because you need me."

He stared at her, his little eyes widening to a strange degree. He had always feared her supple strength, but this was the first time that he had come to fear her mind. He peered at her as though he were seeing her for the first time.

"Because I love you?" he queried huskily.

"Yes."

"Child, I am not a fool. I use you, but I do not love you."

"You are a fool," she answered, "and, when I am gone, you will love me. A horse loves his master even in spite of the spurs."

"And you," echoed Oñate, "are my master?"

"Is it not true?" she asked indifferently. "Have you not felt my spurs?"

He spluttered a tremendous curse and stared at her with what amounted almost to superstitious fear.

She took his glass of tequila and raised it to his lips. "Drink, *señor*."

"She-devil . . . she-devil!" he stammered.

"Drink, my master."

"Dolores, when you smile at me, I know that you have been telling me cruel lies."

"Yes. I cannot help the lies, *señor.*"

"I believe you, Dolores mine."

She held the glass and tilted it when he drank. Afterward he leaned back in his chair, breathing heavily. He was trembling like a man who had been talking for his life, pleading with a cruel and inexorable judge. She touched her cool hand against his forehead and trailed the soft fingers across his eyes.

"My master," she murmured, "is weary. He must sleep."

"Not till I'm drunk, Dolores. What you have said has started a fire in me."

"Then Dolores will put it out again."

"You cannot put out the fire of suspicion, Dolores."

"No? We will see!"

"Can you open my eyes and then close them?"

"Perhaps?"

He whispered something.

"What was that?" she asked rather sharply, and bent her ear to his lips.

"Nothing," said the sheriff.

"I thought it was a prayer," she said.

He opened his eyes again and grinned suddenly up at her. "Sometimes I think that, if I make the sign of the cross, you will vanish into thin air."

"Dolores did not understand."

"Perhaps not," muttered Oñate, "but then the devil does not understand his own deviltry. Another drink, Dolores."

But she stiffened suddenly and stepped away. Her face had grown as blank as though a mask had dropped over it. The sheriff knew that El Tigre was behind him.

García—Friend

H e turned swiftly in his chair, and in the shadow of the arched doorway to the left he caught an impression of movement. Not the actual figure of a man stepping out of sight, but a feeling that something had at that moment disappeared from the passage.

"Tell me," he demanded, turning back to the Yaqui girl, "was that El Tigre?"

"El Tigre?" she queried in surprise.

"What did you see?" he asked suspiciously.

"The shadow of the house on the bricks. The yellow flowers against the wall."

"Only that?"

"If there was anything else, Dolores has forgotten."

He knew she was lying. As he lay brooding, for the first time he wondered if the Indian held a grudge against him and concealed it. He decided that it would be well to get rid of El Tigre and all his company. But, before the decision was clearly formed in his brain, Manuel shuffled to his side.

The servant brought word that the telephone had rung, and someone was asking for the master of the house. When he had the receiver to his ear, a moment later, a voice came faintly from the distance over the hum of the wires: "This is Mitchell."

"This is Oñate," he answered.

"The pardon was stopped on the way," called Mitchell.

"Ah," said Oñate.

"But not destroyed," went on the big boss. "It is only delayed until sunset tomorrow. At that time the messenger will start again with the pardon. If you want to act, act quickly. I can't get the pardon destroyed. I have tried. Does this give you enough time?"

"Plenty," answered Oñate. "I'll have things ready by dark tomorrow. Good bye."

He hung up the receiver and called Manuel, giving him instructions to bring García at once to the house. Then he went back to the patio and sat silently, oblivious of Dolores. He was thinking hard, and the half hour that elapsed before the coming of García flew on wings for the sheriff.

The jingle of silver spurs made him glance up out of his reverie at last, and he saw García, a tall, thin man with shoulders stooped, as if from too much labor over a desk. His black hair bushed out behind. His forehead was heavily wrinkled. If his eyes had not been so close together, he would have given the impression of a close and continual student of weighty affairs. As it was, he looked a good deal like a professional musician. One would not have been surprised to find him wearing Windsor ties and loosely cut clothes. He bowed silently to Oñate, accepted in silence the chair to which the sheriff waved, and sitting down, fixed his melancholy eyes on the great man.

"García," said Oñate without waste of formality, "I am in trouble. I need you, and you, I know, need money."

"Yes," nodded García.

"How much?" asked the sheriff.

The eyes of García turned slowly to Dolores.

"It is nothing," said Oñate carelessly. "We can speak safely before her. She sees nothing, when I tell her to be blind. She hears nothing, when I tell her to be deaf. Dolores?"

"It is true, *señor*," she answered in her soft voice.

The glance of García dwelt on her for another blank moment and then swung back to Oñate. "I have lost at faro," he said, "but I have the system at last. With a hundred dollars I can break the bank tonight and pay you back tomorrow."

"Good!" said Oñate, and, covering a smile by bending his head, he thrust his hand into his trousers pocket and drew out five twenty-dollar gold pieces.

García pocketed the amount without comment or thanks, saying only: "Money grows on trees for *Señor* Oñate."

"There is a man," began Oñate sharply, "in prison here."

"Aye," said García, "the *gringo* who killed Vincente."

"You have seen him?"

"I know of him."

"I had him put in the jail. I had the price put on his head. García, tomorrow by midnight the pardon of *Señor* Van Dyck will arrive." He waited for a moment, but García would give him no suggestion—no help. "Before that time he must die."

"It would be well," said the gambler.

"It *must* be well, García."

"Ah?"

"You have the gift of speech."

"So?"

"Words come easily to you. You brought me a dozen votes every time you spoke before the last election."

"More, *señor.*"

"More, perhaps. García, our friends in Double Bend think much of you . . . all except the *Americanos.*"

"Yes, *señor.*"

"You see what I mean?"

"Alas, *señor*, I am a child in the dark."

"Van Dyck must die."

"That is very true."

"The law will not kill him before tomorrow at midnight, and by that time he will be free."

"Then he must be killed before?"

"Yes."

"Teach me how to reach him in the prison."

"Not you alone but many must reach him."

"Many?"

"You are blind today, my friend."

"I try to see, but the light is dim."

"Go to the house of a friend. Speak to him. Tell him of the deeds of *Señor* Van Dyck. Tell him how the *gringo* has killed our countrymen. Tell how he lies helpless in the jail. Teach our friends that now is the time we must cut the head of the snake."

"And then?"

"García, you are a fool. Do you not see? A mob must rise. You must talk many words among them. Teach them to think of Dix Van Dyck as a killer of men. Tell them that, unless they act by dark tomorrow, he will escape from them. Then he will rage among them like a mountain lion among sheep. He will kill them like dogs wherever they meet him. He will be worse than a devil among them. Then put words in the mouth of Dix Van Dyck. Tell our friends what he has said of them. Make him seem to threaten some of them by name. Trust me, García, you will not talk long before those men you name will be talking in turn. They will ask for blood. They will talk of attacking the jail."

"This may be done," mused García, "with very few words."

"True," exclaimed Oñate, "and, when they are ripe, explain how easy it will be to take the jail in one rush. The men who guard the jail are our friends also. A dollar here and a dollar spent there will be enough. They will fire their rifles in the air. They will allow themselves to be bound hand and foot . . . and the jailer will point out the key to Van Dyck's cell. Do you see now, my brother?"

"The light comes to me, *señor*," said García.

"While you are talking to our friends, do not let them be thirsty. A dry throat makes a weak hand. That is plain. Here is more money. I will give you Manuel and Pedro. As you talk, they will carry the liquor you buy through the crowd. Let them all drink. Not beer but strong mescal. It will turn their blood to fire. You will feel the flames rise and fan hot in your face while you talk to them. For see, they are like children, and they only need to be led. Is it clear, García?"

"It shall be done!"

"Heart of gold! García, you are a worthy friend. It is well to have such friends as you. But listen to me closely. It must not seem that I have anything to do with the work. I am sheriff!"

The solemn face of García loosened for an instant into a smile. It came and went quickly, as the sharp bark of a coyote that quavered that same second in the distant hills.

"True. You are sheriff, and a sheriff should put down a mob by force."

"You are right. I should save prisoners for the fangs of the law. Ha, ha, ha, ha!" The laughter of Oñate was inextinguishable. "But," he went on at last, wiping the tears of pleasure from his eyes, "I will not be here when the mob rises. I shall wait till the early afternoon to see how your work is proceeding. Then I shall take my horse and ride slowly away. You understand, *señor*?"

"Perfectly."

"One thing more. It is not necessary that *Señor* Van Dyck should die quickly."

"No?"

"Let him die slowly, García, for the sake of our long friendship. Let him die very slowly. Whisper it through the crowd. Carry him with you into a cañon near the town. Carry him where there is silence . . . and the dark of the night . . . and much mesquite. Mesquite will make a fire, and with a fire many things may be done, *señor*. Is it not true?"

Señor García regarded the sheriff with narrow eyes. "It is true again," he said slowly, "that many things may be done with fire."

"And when the crowd is drunken?"

"Yes, they will think of those things to do."

"But you, García, you will not drink, and therefore, when the time comes, if they forget things that might be done, you will be there to help them think. Here, for instance, is a pleasant thing."

He leaned close to the ear of García and whispered for a long moment. As he did so, the face of the slender man changed by degrees. It grew a sickly olive-drab. The wrinkles of his forehead grew deep as if they had been traced in the hollows with a thick pencil. At last, when Oñate leaned back again, García stood up and shook himself like a dog getting water out of his fur.

"I thank the dear God for one thing, Oñate."

"Yes?"

"That you are not my enemy."

With that, he left the patio.

Señor Oñate leaned back in his chair and rubbed his fat palms together. His eyes gleamed so brightly that, if it had been dark, they would have shone by their own light.

"Is it not well done, Dolores?" he asked. "Could even your cruel Indian heart think of better things? Eh?"

There was no answer. He turned around and found that she was gone and for how long he could not tell. He began to call aloud to her and mutter to himself.

"Dolores! The she-devil has stolen away from me . . . Dolores *mia*! I shall tie her tonight while she sleeps and teach her a lesson with a whip . . . Dolores! But if I did that, she would knife me tomorrow . . . Dolores!"

Stud Poker 29

I t was mid-morning of the next day when Noony trotted his horse to the door of the shanty where Bill Lawton sat with Jacqueline and swung from the saddle. He found the girl sitting on a box in a corner of the shanty with her hands folded calmly in her lap and staring placidly into the distance. Bill Lawton himself sat cross-legged on the hard packed floor and laid out some greasy cards on a plank in a game of Chinese solitaire. Neither of them showed the slightest excitement when he entered. He came carrying his saddle which he flung down in the corner.

"I telephoned to big boss," said Noony. "I told him we was done with the game and didn't want the coin. He was mad. He raised hell. He said the girl had bribed us. I told him she hadn't, and we'd do everything we could . . . except stop the pardon. He said: "Delay her until tomorrow at sunset, and I don't care if you send her on. Let her bring the pardon to Double Bend then." So I said we would. When the sun goes down tonight, ma'am, you're free to beat it. That is, if it's agreeable to Bill Lawton."

"It sure is," said Bill, "that's only fair to the big boss."

"If we keep her till then," went on Noony, "we get the coin just the same."

"The hell we do!"

"Sure."

"Then there ain't no doubt about us keepin' her."

"D'you know what it means?" asked the girl very quietly.

"What means?"

"Your big boss sayin' that it was all right if you kept me here till sunset?"

"What d'you see in it?"

"They'll kill Dix van Dyck at sunset. That's what it means."

"It ain't possible!" said Lawton.

"Ain't it?" she asked contemptuously. "I tell you, Lawton, I *know* they're going to bump him off. The big boss holds me here. Then he telephones to the cur Oñate at Double Bend and tells him how much time he's got."

Lawton stirred a little uneasily. "Don't be imaginin' too much," he grumbled. "It don't do no good."

"Easy thing, too," went on the girl. "All they have to do is walk down and shoot Van Dyck through the bars of his cell. They unlock his door. They stick a club in his dead hand. They tell the judge the next day that they done it in self-defense. Ain't that simple, Lawton?"

The big man stared at her in silent horror. "Simple?" he echoed. "It's hell!"

"Is it?" responded Jack. "But maybe that's what'll happen to you the next time they get you in the pen, Lawton. You ain't got many friends among them runnin' the jails in these parts. Am I right?"

"The next time they get me," said Lawton, "they'll carry me in feet first in a wooden box. That's me! Besides, if this Dix Van Dyck was half the man you call him, he'd never let himself be taken that way."

"D'you know how he was taken?" asked the girl, a slight tremor coming in her voice.

"Spill it," said Noony, "but don't you pull no sob stuff. My nerves don't like it none."

"El Tigre got me first . . . El Tigre and his gang."

"The Yaqui, eh?"

"Yep. He got me, and then he tackled Van Dyck. Dix let 'em take him without a fight, so's I could get away. That's the only way they could ever have landed him, partners. I ask you, ain't that the sort of a pal you'd like to have when you're in a hole?"

They were both silent, scowling at the floor.

"I ask you," she continued, "are you goin' to let 'em shoot Dix Van Dyck full of holes while he's lyin' helpless in the jail? Tell it to me straight, strangers!"

"By God . . . ," began Bill Lawton.

But the cold-blooded half breed cut in: "Come clean, Bill. Are we goin' to throw off the big boss and get him on our trail for the sake of a man we never seen? This here girl's in love with him. I can see that. Are we going to take all she says for gospel? If he's in jail, there's a reason for it. I say, let him rot there if he's going to start rotting at sunset today. That's me!"

"Noony," said Lawton, though a little reluctantly, "I guess you're talkin' reason. Here's your coin, Jack. You and me not bein' particular kindly just now, I ain't going to take a loan from a woman that's hating me in her heart. You got to stay here till sunset, and Dix Van Dyck's got to take his chance along with the rest of us."

She knew it was final. Her eyes blinked, as though a light of blinding intensity had been thrown across her face, and she swayed back against the wall. The two men stared at her in concern.

"It ain't easy," said Noony.

"It's hell," said Lawton. "Here, girl. Here's your coin."

He tossed the money belt she had given them to her feet. The jingle of the money seemed to rouse her. Her eyes opened, and she stared first at the money and then at Lawton with a growing comprehension.

"She's hard hit," whispered Noony to Lawton, "but she don't make no holler. She's a woman in a thousand, Bill."

"Nope," said Lawton, "there ain't another woman like her in the world. Look at her set her teeth and straighten her face. But there's all hell breakin' loose inside her."

The eyes of the girl were resting, with a growing light, on the pack of cards that Bill Lawton was shuffling over and over again—merely to employ his fingers while he thought.

She said with sudden gravity, and a hint of eagerness behind her eyes: "Partners, I've lost. I see that. Me and Dix was partners, but he's a cold trail now, and I ain't followed a cold trail twice in my life. He's dead. All right, I ain't going to waste time mourning for him. There's other things in the world. So, let's forget him. In the meantime we got to kill a pile of hours from here to sunset. Lawton, how about some stud poker?"

"Poker!" repeated Lawton, with his eyes on the money belt whose weight he had tested in his fingers only the moment before. "That's my middle name, partner. How about you, Noony?"

"I'm in," said Noony, and immediately took his position cross-legged beside the board where Lawton sat.

The girl followed his example. They cut for the deal, which fell to Lawton, and he tossed out the first cards with a careless flip of one hand—an act that looks easy but that takes long practice. It insured, however, honesty in the deal, for the bottom card showed at every turn of the dealer's hand, and it would have been almost impossible for him to bury cards on the bottom of the deck.

Fortune fluctuated very little at the beginning of the game. The girl lost steadily to both Noony and Lawton, but she paid no attention to her losses. If she had been a man and ten years older, they would have looked upon her as an experienced gambler and therefore confident in her ability to win in the long run. She lost stakes large and small without betraying the slightest gloom. They watched her with admiration. Next to speed and endurance in a horse, there is nothing so much admired in the Southwest as the ability to lose money gracefully.

That is because it is an art hard to acquire. When a man works for forty dollars a month and works hard and long hours every day for his money, he is not apt to lose it with a smile. The hearts of Lawton and Noony warmed, therefore, as she lost stake after stake to them, large and small.

They eyed her with wonder. She seemed, indeed, to be merely playing to kill time, as she had at first suggested. Now and then she cast a covert glance through the door and toward the mesquite bush from which the shadow was growing shorter and shorter as the hour approached noon. Otherwise she showed no uneasiness. She seemed to have accepted the fate of Dix Van Dyck with equanimity and to have cast the thought of him away from her. A cold trail, indeed.

However, her manner changed sharply after a time. Until half her money was gone, she played with careless indifference, and Noony and Lawton accumulated each a comfortable stake. At this point she began to play with more attention. She slipped her left hand, now and then, into the bosom of her shirt near the throat, and seemed to be fumbling something there.

In spite of her closer attention to the game she still lost, and now a sort of angry incredulity possessed her, like that of one who has bet his money on a sure thing at the races and refuses to believe his eyes when the "sure thing" trails farther behind at every post while the flying leaders enter the home stretch. Now she played with her left hand continually clenched inside her shirt—a singular position. Her wagers grew larger and larger. Still she lost. And now she followed the game with a frenzy of silent terror. The money still continued to slip from her.

Finally there remained half a dozen gold coins in front of her. She placed them on a single hand with the air of one who takes chance by the throat, and then sat with eyes closed and her hand over her cards. At last she jerked her hand away and exposed her buried card. Both Noony and Lawton had called her bet. Her three fives beat the two pair of Noony, and the pot was shuffled toward her.

The effect on the girl, however, was so strong that she became almost hysterical. It was relief—enormous relief. She laughed. She sang a fragment of a chorus. She hummed another tune. In the next hand, barely glancing at her cards, she wagered twenty dollars and forced the betting up, from card to card, until a hundred was staked before her. She lost again.

To the astonishment of the two men they discovered that she had wagered everything on a pair of queens. They had known that she was bluffing, but they had not dreamed that she could bluff so well. The loss did not daunt her. In the next hand she played the rest of her money, and on this occasion she won her second large wager. Thereafter, luck followed her closely. Out of every four hands she won two, and the two she won were sure to be the ones of the highest wagers. They tried bluffing her, but she would bet recklessly on a hand as low as a pair of eights. Finally Lawton halted the game and consulted Noony in a whisper outside the hut.

"She knows the cards," he said, "and she's reading the backs of 'em. She marked 'em all. Maybe with her fingernail."

"Change the game, then," suggested Noony.

"To what?"

"Draw for aces. Nobody can't beat that game."

"She won't change her game. See if she will?"

But when they returned and proposed a change, she accepted eagerly.

"Are you tired of stud poker?" drawled Noony.

"No," she said, "but drawing for aces is faster. I want action."

They exchanged glances of wonder and commenced the draw. She won again.

Dolores Finds a Man   30

Undoubtedly there was more of the child than the woman in the soul of Dolores. It was an impulse of childish curiosity that carried her away from the house of *Señor* Oñate while he sat talking with García. She went to her room first and wrapped herself in a dark blue cloak, and then walked straight to the jail of Double Bend. The jailer had seen her only once before, but he remembered her perfectly, for the favorite of *Señor* Oñate was not one to be lightly forgotten. He smiled at her amiably when she appeared at the door of the jail.

"I have come from *Señor* Oñate," she said coldly to the jailer, "and I bring a message from him to *Señor* Dix Van Dyck, the man whom El Tigre captured. Let me see him at once and alone."

If the heart of the jailer beat faster with anger at this haughty speech, he taught it to beat more calmly again at once by simply recalling the greatness of Oñate. "Alone?" he objected. "That is against the rules."

"However," said the girl in her faultless Spanish that she had learned from the grave vocabulary of El Tigre, "it is the will of the sheriff. Let me see *Señor* Van Dyck at once, sir."

"If it's an order," said the jailer, "let me see the writing."

"Order?" she repeated with a rising emphasis that made her voice shrill. "If you send back to *Señor* Oñate for a written order . . . !"

"Well?" said the jailer who could not be bullied too far.

She changed her tactics with the speed of light. Both her hands went out to him, palm up, in a graceful gesture of entreaty. She smiled upon the jailer. "If I go back and say that I have not given his message, I shall be beaten, *señor*." Then she drew the cloak tighter about her with a little shudder, as though in fancy she already felt the lash on her soft shoulders. The jailer was a man, and being a man, as the logic book tells us, he was mortal. He looked upon Dolores and her smile. He sighed.

"If it is that," he said at last, "I shall step past the rules with one eye closed. You shall see Dix Van Dyck."

So he went to his safe and took his big, rusty key. With this in his hand like a truncheon, a sign of dignity and power, he led the girl down the first flight of steps in the basement, and finally unlocked the door that led down the last passage. The musty stench and the gloom rolled out to meet them. The girl recoiled with a little exclamation, a harsh guttural in her native tongue, instinct with horror. One passion possessed her—the passion for liberty that ennobles her race.

"I have asked," she said with a gesture of dignity and repulsion, "to see a man, not the kennel of a dog."

The jailer handed her his lantern with a grin. "Down to the bottom of those steps, my girl," he said, "and you'll see the kennel of Dix Van Dyck."

"A man?" she said in the same tone of horror. "A man down . . . there?"

It might have been the horrors of hell that her slender forefinger indicated. The jailer was touched by the implication that he was at fault.

"It was an order, not my wish," he said, "and we have no strong place to keep fighting men. No strong place but this one."

"Is he dangerous?" she asked curiously.

"Is a wild mustang dangerous?" returned the jailer, perfectly willing to retain this beauty in conversation. "Is a mountain lion dangerous when she has hungry young ones in her cave?"

"So?" said the girl. "Yet El Tigre took him!"

"It is true," nodded the jailer, "but he took him by a trick. He paid the price. For the sake of the woman Dix Van Dyck went with El Tigre."

"Then he is a fool . . . an ass," said the girl scornfully, "to have paid so much for a woman. He could buy a dozen women for a tenth of that price."

"It is true," said the jailer. "He is a fool."

"And yet . . . ," said the girl, and paused. "He has killed men?"

"Count all your pretty fingers and all your little toes, my dear," said the jailer, "and he has killed more men than that."

"It is true?" she gasped, incredulous. "El Tigre is not so terrible as that."

"He would eat three like El Tigre," answered the jailer calmly, "and still think he had done a small day's work. So we took no chances and put him here. Also the sheriff ordered that it be done."

"So!" said Dolores. "I will go down to look at him."

She raised the lantern over her head and peered down the flight of sweating steps with a shudder of disgust.

"You are not afraid?" queried the jailer in admiration.

"Bah!" she said, though her voice was hushed. "He is soft flesh, and I carry sharp steel." She touched the hilt of her knife and began to descend the steps with sudden eagerness.

"You should have been a man," said the jailer, calling after her. "We could use men like you in the jail."

At the bottom of the steps, as the jailer had promised, she found the bars of steel and behind them the form of what seemed to Dolores the largest man she had ever seen. It was shadowy at first and so huge that she stopped short and bit her lip to keep back the cry of terror. Then she made herself approach the bars more closely, holding the lantern as high as she could reach. The light fell on a large, shaggy head that turned slowly toward her. She stopped short again, awed by the glimmer of the eyes. Then she saw a rough face, unshaven for many days. But the sharp, hard line of jaw and cheekbone could not be disguised by that stubble of unkempt beard. It did not cover the high-arched, cruel nose, or the shag of eyebrows over the light of the undaunted eyes, or the straight line of the thin lips.

She gazed, fascinated. She drank in every detail of the picture again and again. Still the man stared back, unblinking. This man had thrown himself away for the sake of a woman! She would have as soon suspected that there was a heart of love in a wild wolf—a timber wolf.

"I am Dolores," she said, "the daughter of El Tigre."

He made no answer.

"I have not come to look at you because my father brought you here."

Still he would not speak.

"I have come because I want to thank you for saving the life of my father, El Tigre. He is like a tiger. He speaks little, but the heart of El Tigre is very heavy because you must die."

The man stood up and looked down at her. Standing erect, he was too tall for the ceiling, so he had to stand with his head bent forward. It gave the impression that he was peering down at her from a great height.

"Go tell El Tigre, Dolores," he said, and there was a marvelous lack of harshness in his voice, "that Dix Van Dyck holds no grudge against him. El Tigre is a square-shooter. Tell him that Dix Van Dyck says so. If I ever get out of this hell hole, I'll never make a move to harm him. Is that clear?"

"Alas, *señor*, you will never leave this place alive."

"No? Dolores, I'm a hell of a long ways from being dead."

She shook her head.

"What d'you know?" he asked and strode forward with a single long stride to the bars.

Standing there in the keener light of the lantern, she did not think him so vast, but she found his face more terrible. She could have believed anything desperate and cruel about a man with a face such as that, but she could not dream that he would throw himself away for a woman. She felt an overmastering desire to see the face of that woman.

"What d'you know?" repeated the giant.

"I cannot tell."

His hands shot through the bars and caught her shoulder with a tremendous power. One pressure of that hand would have crushed her throat, and she knew it. All the blood rushed to her heart, but still she did not make a move to draw her knife.

"There's crooked work going on," said Van Dyck, "and you know what it is. Out with it!"

She shook her head.

"By God!" he said with a sort of dull wonder. "I don't think you're afraid of me, Dolores."

"Ah, *señor*," she murmured, "shall Dolores fear a man who dies for the sake of a woman?"

"Bah!" sneered the big man, "they've been filling your ears with chatter. All lies, Dolores, all lies. I did nothing for the sake of a woman. Well, if you won't tell me, go back to your father and give him my message. I've nothing but good will for El Tigre."

"*Señor*," she said, "I have been in the church. The *padre* has taught me prayers. I shall pray for you thrice every day." She remembered with a start and caught a hand to her eyes with a moan of horror. "But tomorrow night, *señor!*"

He waited eagerly.

"It is then that you die. Many men will come." She drew her dagger and offered it to him. He accepted the hilt and stood, staring at the long, keen blade.

"They will not kill you here. Let them take you and, when they have brought you out into the open, then spring on them with this knife. Can you use a knife, *señor?*"

"My girl," said Dix Van Dyck softly, "it's second nature to me. Use a knife?" His large head tilted back and he laughed softly.

The terror of the sound fascinated her, so that she still listened after the laughter died away. "*Señor, señor,*" she murmured, "you were not meant to die like a dog . . . in a kennel!" Then, checking herself, as one who said too much, she added: "I must leave you."

She held out her hand, and he caught it eagerly.

"Heart of gold!" he breathed. "Dolores, I'll be ready to welcome my executioners when they come tomorrow. This knife . . . it's teeth to me! Good bye, Dolores."

"No, no!" she cried. "Not good bye, *señor.* Only *adiós. Adiós amigo.*"

She fled up the stairs, panting, wild-eyed, like one who was being pursued.

El Tigre Covers
His Head   31

Straight back to the house of *Señor* Don Porfirio
Maria Oñate went Dolores. He was at the opening of
the main doorway to the patio, and, as she passed,
he merely lifted his glance to her and let it fall again
heavily. She knew he was very angry—angrier than she
had ever dreamed he could be.

She went straight back through the house and to the
room that had been assigned to El Tigre, apart from
the servants" quarters, for not even so great a man as
Señor Oñate could rank El Tigre among servants. She
found her father sitting on a mat, cross-legged, with his
arms folded. It was the first time they had been together
since the day he returned from the trail of Dix Van Dyck,
and now he rose and stood, looking out the window.

The girl set her teeth in silent fury and placed her hand
on the doorknob to retreat. She had actually swung the
door open, in fact, when something conquered her
pride. She closed it decisively, and walked up to the tall
Yaqui.

"It is I, Dolores," she said angrily.

He turned partially toward her at that, but his eyes still
avoided her. "El Tigre," he said solemnly, "is very weary.
He wishes to be alone and sleep."

"Bah!" cried the girl with sudden fury. "El Tigre has slept
for many days. His honor has slept with him."

His upper lip writhed back from his teeth, and his

hand shot across to the hilt of his knife. At that, a glint of terror came in the eyes of the girl, but she persisted with a perverse delight, like one who baits a bull, since here was one who would not charge blindly.

"The claws of El Tigre are bare," she went on, "but they are dull. The tiger is old. His claws are blunt. His teeth have fallen out. He is fat and slow. Very soon little boys will bait him in the streets and kick his fat ribs and laugh to see him grunt. El Tigre will dare not bite but lick their hands for crusts of bread. It is true!"

Half the length of the knife blade flashed and disappeared again in the sheath, a motion as swift as a winking of light.

"Does El Tigre still show his teeth?" went on the girl, though she had retreated half a pace, ready to flee like the wind for the door. "I do not fear him. There has been a hand on my shoulder that has three times the strength of El Tigre's paw. I felt that hand. Why should I fear El Tigre? The hand that was on my shoulder was the hand that dragged El Tigre out of the river. . . ."

"Dolores has spoken too much," said El Tigre, and turned upon her with eyes more deadly than his voice.

She said: "The hand drew El Tigre out of the river and threw him on the bank like a drowned cat to dry his fur. When El Tigre could stand again, he sneaked up on his white brother and bit the hand that had saved him. It is true!"

"It is true," repeated El Tigre and gave no sign of his torture.

"And now," said the girl, "Oñate is setting a trap for El Tigre. It may be that he will catch him and whip him and let him go . . . tamed."

"Ah," murmured El Tigre.

"Your master and mine," said the girl, "the master of El Tigre and his daughter."

The Indian drew himself a little more erect, if that were possible. "El Tigre has no daughter," he said calmly. "He dreamed he had a daughter named Dolores. Now El Tigre is awake."

"It is a lie," said Dolores. "El Tigre is not awake. He sleeps and waits for Oñate to catch him. A sleepy tiger, fat with too much eating. The boys of the town will bait him." She stepped a little closer, fearless, though she saw the death in the eyes of the Yaqui. "Why do you wait, El Tigre? Oñate has seen you stalk him with silent feet. He is a fool, but he knows. His eye is on you. Why do you wait? If you wish to find him, when he sleeps, I will open his door tonight. But there is little time."

"I would have killed him three times in three days," said the Yaqui calmly, "but every time, if I had struck, his blood would have fallen on Dolores."

She winced, as if under the whip, and her breath came sharply with a sort of stifling sob. "Now," she said, "it is too late. You may kill Oñate, but your white brother shall die."

For the first time he was roused past his self-restraint. "It is a lie," he said, "the father of lies."

"It is true," she answered. "I have heard Oñate talk with García. Tomorrow García will raise a crowd . . . a crowd to take the jail and carry off your white brother to the hills. There, they will pile up mesquite wood and burn him alive."

The last glow of the sunset struck through the window across the face of El Tigre and made it terrible. It gleamed on the sweat of his forehead.

"But why do I tell El Tigre?" she asked scornfully. "He loves his oppressors. They burned his village. They killed his son with fire. They butchered his brother with knives. They cut the throat of his father. But El Tigre has forgotten. He eats food from the hand of a Mexican. His teeth are so dull that, if he bit that hand, he would not break through the skin. He crouches before a master . . . he . . . El Tigre!

"Once he was wild and strong. The dark was like the day to El Tigre. His coming made no sound. It was like the plunge of the eagle through the air with wings closed. His going was as silent as the passing of a feather on the wind. When he struck, men died. His enemies feared him more than fire and bullets. His friends were tied closer to him than ropes can bind. But now El Tigre is fat and old. He would rather have a full belly than be called The Tiger. It is true. His white brother he leaves to rot in a dark place where the sun never strikes. But Oñate, who will hunt El Tigre before long, El Tigre crouches before Oñate and licks his hand. He has given Oñate the life of his white brother. He has given Oñate his daughter to keep."

"Ah!" said the Yaqui and made a step toward her, but checked himself and folded his arms tightly.

"Men see these things and laugh," said the girl. "Men smile at the name of El Tigre. They say that the soul of El Tigre has gone, and the soul of a coyote has come to live in his hide. He has nothing left but his growl. His teeth are fallen out, and his claws are blunt."

Her father's eyes, wherever they rested on her, were like the stroke of a knife, but otherwise he had endured her lashing tongue with marvelous strength. She changed her tone suddenly.

"I have been to your white brother. I have told him that I am the daughter of El Tigre, and I lied to him and told him that the heart of El Tigre bled for his sake. He is a man. He smiled on me and said that he forgave El Tigre. He made me come back to you. He made me swear to comfort my father and tell him that *Señor* Van Dyck holds him as his brother."

"Is it true?" said El Tigre hoarsely.

"By all the blood in my heart," she swore, "it is true. This and other things. What will you do, El Tigre?"

In place of answering, he turned his back on her again and sat down on the mat. As the girl looked at him, all the fire and fierceness went out of her face and left only the embers of her passion burning in her eyes. A little sound, no louder than the hum of a bee, came in her throat, and she stretched out her arms to the stiff, stern back of El Tigre. Then she stole back toward the door. As she opened it, she saw El Tigre raise an end of his blanket and wrap it about his head. The heart of Dolores stood still.

Sporting Chance

Straight overhead stood the sun. The shadow of the mesquite bush before the door of the shanty had shrunk to nothingness. A time of fierce heat—white heat. The shadow of the hut was hardly a relief, for it shut off the faint touch of the breeze. Perspiration trickled down the red nose of Bill Lawton, and the face of the girl was pale. There was silence in the hut, a deep, long silence as heavy as sleep, but more ominous than the silence of a man who watches a snake coiled within striking distance of his feet.

The meaning of the silence lay in the pile that mounted on the board on either side of it and in front of Jacqueline. In that stack were gold and silver coins, a few paper bills, the golden braid from the sombrero of Noony, the sombrero and bright bandanna of Bill Lawton, two pairs of spurs, two revolvers, a great hunting knife, a silver watch of great size, a diamond ring of respectable proportions, and a score of odds and ends.

The silence held. The eyes of the losers fixed as if fascinated on the pile of loot, and the eyes of the girl went from one to the other. They were stunned, grim. When they began to think, their thoughts would be dangerous. There was no such oblivion in the mind of the girl. Her brain was working hard and fast, and the thought of the loot was certainly not in it. Suddenly she pushed the pile of winnings to the center of the board.

"Gents," she said easily, "pick out your things."

Noony straightened with such a jerk that it forced a grunt through his set teeth. Bill Lawton stared at her with haggard eyes. He would rather have lost his right hand than the revolver that was among that loot. He pulled at his collar and loosened it, though it was already inches too large.

"Pick out your stuff," she said. "I been playing this game to kill time, not to pick up your coin. That's straight."

The hand of Bill Lawton flashed out for his gun, but he checked the hand halfway to the pile. For his heart was deeply troubled. "It can't be done," he said at last huskily. "Partner, I can see you're square, but I ain't never taken a gamblin' debt as a gift before, and I don't intend to do it now. That's final." To strengthen himself against temptation, he rose and turned his back on the pile of loot and stood at the door with his hands clenched behind his back.

"Well," said the girl, as if a new idea had suddenly come to her, "there's one thing left to play for. I'll stake everything here against a chance for me to break away and get to Double Bend before sunset."

Bill Lawton whirled, as if he were pulling a gun, and started to speak, Noony all the time begging him with his eyes to accept the chance, but the gunman shook his head.

"You being square," he said at last. "I can't make that play. Lady, you ain't got no ghost of a show to get to Double Bend before sunset. Dix Van Dyck is done. You can lay to that. They ain't no hoss in these parts can make that trip in that time."

"All I want is the chance," she said. "I don't ask for a sure thing. All I want is a sporting chance."

"A sporting chance?" repeated Bill Lawton.

"After all," she urged, "all the dope is against me to win this bet. I've won the last five straight. It's too much to expect. It's simply an easy way for you to win back your coin and things. . . . I'll have to stay here till sunset."

"Noony?" queried Lawton.

"Draw!" said the half-breed eagerly.

"Well," said Lawton, arguing with himself, "this is a sort of a compromise. You can't reach Double Bend before sunset. That's sure. All the big boss asks is to keep you away from there until that time. Am I right, Noony?"

"Sure," said the enthusiastic half-breed.

"Draw?" snapped Lawton, and dropped to his position.

"Two to one," said the girl, turning even paler than before. "I'll give you every chance. We draw for the first black ace. If either of you get it, you win. Draw, Noony!"

He drew, pulling the card out with a faltering hand. It was the seven of clubs. Lawton drew the five of hearts. They leaned forward with hushed breath to watch the girl. Her hand, as usual, was tightly clutched under the neck of her shirt. She drew the deuce of diamonds and groaned with disappointment. For the first time in the game, except at the very start, her nerve seemed to be breaking.

"Draw!" she urged.

She sat with her eyes half closed, seeing the cards as if through a mist, and her lips moved rapidly.

"What's she doin'?" whispered Noony to Lawton.

"Prayin' " answered Lawton. "I'll be damned!"

He drew an ace—the ace of hearts. Noony drew the king of spades. The girl rested her hand on the top of the deck, and it lay there for a long moment. It seemed to be trembling so much that she could not manage the cards.

"Draw for me," she said at last to Lawton. "I feel sort of sick."

She was a deadly white and Lawton, after a rather worried glance at her, turned up the card. It was the ace of spades. All three sat in a stunned silence. Then Lawton rose, removed his hat, and swept the dusty floor with it in his elaborate bow.

"Lady," he said, "I've played most all over this range,

but, when I meet a dead-game sport, I take off my hat. Take my saddlebag to help stow the loot. Your own ain't big enough."

But she rose in turn without a word and caught up her saddle. At the door of the hut she whistled, and the white stallion, with pricking ears, trotted up to her like a dog coming at the master's call. The two men leaned in the doorway and with gloomy eyes watched her saddle. But she gave them not a glance, working with feverish eagerness at the cinches. When they were taut, she leaped into the saddle, waved to them, and spurred in silence down the steep slope of the ravine. A tall boulder appeared before her. The white stallion rose like a hunting horse and sailed easily over it. It buried her from view on the other side.

"By God!" said Noony, pointing back at the winnings of the girl. "She forgot it."

Lawton stood with his hat off and stared down the ravine. "Forget it," he said slowly at length. "Noony, you was always mostly a fool, and you get worse the older you get. Me, speakin' personal, I guess I been a fool most of my life, too. I'm going to take a longer look at the next girl I meet."

He would not come back into the hut but stood bareheaded under the full blaze of the sun, staring into a vacuous distance lined with wavering streaks of heat.

Into that distance the girl rode at a desperate speed, swerving back and forth among the boulders. Yet, when the first rush of her eagerness had passed, she checked the stallion to a more even pace. She knew him as a student knows a well-conned book, every page by heart. The distance to Double Bend was vague in her mind, but she gauged it as well as she could and planned the use of the stallion's strength to fill that measured distance. There was no distant range around Double Bend by which she could test the length of her course. It was all by guess.

The rest at the shanty had freshened her horse. She felt the spring and drive of his stride, swinging onward tirelessly. It seemed as if no distance and no speed could exhaust that mount. Now and then, anxiously, she turned her head and glanced at the sun as it rolled westward. It had never seemed to move so rapidly. As if it lunged down the incline of the sky toward the sunset horizon, it sped faster and faster, and at every glance upward her heart beat faster, and the sickness came in her throat.

At sunset she knew something would happen to Dix Van Dyck. What it might be, she could not dream, but the very uncertainty increased her terror. Between those sudden and fearful glances at the course of the sun, she gave all her care to picking out the best possible course for the stallion. If it had been the new trail, the one that passed through Godfrey, she would have been able to ride it on a dark night, but every stone of this old trail was new to her.

She had reduced the pace of the stallion to a long, swinging gallop on the level stretches and to a sharp trot up the slighter inclines. But now and then they struck rough places that would have winded the horse if she had not let him take them at a walk. All the time she had the burden of caring for the stallion's strength. He was not like the average cattle pony that gauges a distance and strikes a pace that it can maintain all day. What that the great white horse wished for was freedom to take the bit between his teeth and race at full speed.

The sun rolled lower. Jack saw shadows growing deeper along the cañons and rising higher and higher up the slopes—shadows of death, she thought, and she knew now why death was so often likened to the oncoming of night. Still there was no sign of the approach to Double Bend, and the sun stood only an hour's distance above the western hills. Here she stopped the horse, dismounted. Forcing him to raise his head, she poured the last water from her canteen down his throat. His breathing frightened her. It came with a great gasp and wheeze, with a rattle toward the end, like the breath of a dying man.

When she leaped into the saddle again, the white stallion started ahead, not with his usual spring but breaking into a trot before he could reach a gallop. The lilt and spring were passing from his stride. His feet struck the earth as fast and as hard as ever, but there was none of that easy resiliency that tells of a resource of power. His ears were flattened now along his neck. His head stretched forth in a straight line from the shoulders. She knew all at once that the last strength of the gallant horse was going into his work. And, as if to break their hearts, the ground swept up into a long, steeply rising slope. She struck her hand across her eyes and groaned.

To the west the red sun, settling and bulging at the sides, was resting on the top of a peak and glaring at her like a great crimson eye of hate and mockery. She had ridden a course against it, and she had been beaten. She drove the spurs home, and the stallion, with sharpening panting, swept up the slope at a staggering gallop. His life was in every stride, but the life of Dix Van Dyck might be in them as well, so she rode cruelly, with a breaking heart. As the sun settled slowly, slowly behind that hill, she knew that Van Dyck was lost, and began to repeat aloud to herself, over and over again: "The cross! It is the cross!"

It would bring luck to her but never to Van Dyck.

The sun was down. The shadows swept with sudden dimness across the mountains; there was a deeper dark of hopelessness in the heart of Jacqueline. Then it was that she topped the slope. At the same time that a fresh cool breeze struck her face, she saw far below her the faint, uncertain lights of Double Bend.

Suspense   33

It was as if the spirit of a metropolitan city had descended upon Double Bend. Men, women, and children walked down the crooked street with quick steps as though each one had a business destination, a thing hitherto unprecedented, for usually the pedestrians loitered along, resting between steps, and even the horses trotted through the streets with shambling feet and hanging heads. Stranger still, the activity increased as evening approached. It was, indeed, as if Double Bend were that section of Broadway where the crowds of pleasure-seekers begin to swarm out at a certain late hour in the day, wakening as the sun sets.

So it was with Double Bend. Everyone in the town was on the streets. They gathered here and there in groups. There was a buzzing murmur like the swarming of many hives—the lowered voices of excited men. The cigarettes of the Mexicans, as the gloom of evening began, no longer hung pendant from their lips, requiring continual relighting, but now they glowed like live coals. As the light of day diminished the fire of the cigarettes made a halo on every dark, lean face.

The Mexicans were stirred up about something. The whites could not understand, and they consulted Marshal Phil Glasgow. He advised them to get inside their houses early and to keep guns handy. There might be hell to pay that night, but what was in the air he could not tell.

They followed the advice of Phil Glasgow, who was a prophet of some repute when it came to trouble. The result was that the complexion of the crowd waxed browner and browner after sunset. And then—as if at a preconcerted signal—the crowd drifted toward the center of the town. Numerous flasks had appeared from some quarter, and now they were distributed from hand to hand. One or two more industrious drinkers were already unsteady on their feet. The majority still carried a thirst, edged like a knife. The murmurs grew louder and louder. A rumor sprang up out of the earth that a white man had killed a Mexican on the outskirts of Double Bend. Some loud voices called for immediate vengeance. Others quieted them with the suggestion that there was something to be done right there in the heart of the town. Other rumors went the rounds—quickly—leaping from lip to lip, and leaving a sting of poison behind. Nothing human travels faster than rumor. It seems to be breathed in with the air.

The crowd began to grow more compacted. Finally it was almost impossible to cross any of the streets opening on the little square at one end of which the jail stood. It was at this time, just as the last glow of the sunset was fading, that a woman appeared on horseback, working her way toward the jail, and leading another horse of extraordinary size. She was stopped by the thickness of the crowd, and someone swung a lantern and flashed it in her face.

There was a cry: "She is all right. The daughter of El Tigre. The man who took the *gringo*. Let her pass."

As if by magic, the crowd melted away before her, and she started at a walk down the square. Almost at the same instant, at an opposite point on the square, someone recognized El Tigre. The Indian walked wrapped to the eyes in a large blanket. He strove to escape from the throng, but they stopped him, cheering. It was the first time perhaps in the history of the Southwest that a Yaqui had been cheered by Mexicans. But to them he was the captor of Dix Van Dyck first and a Yaqui second. They slipped flasks of whiskey and mescal into his hands. They bid him to supper.

He replied with grunts and continued to work his way among them with the agility of a snake, wriggling through tall grass. He also came to the open space around the jail and went directly toward it. The door was open, and deep in the hall paced the jailer, nervous and pale of face. He had been drinking to support his courage, and at sight of El Tigre he shrank back against the wall and raised his lantern for a surer view of the visitor.

The Indian held back the end of his blanket long enough to show his face, whereat the jailer lowered his lantern with a sigh of relief.

"I have come to see *Señor* Van Dyck," he said.

"From Oñate?" asked the jailer softly.

"Yes."

"Then it's not to be the crowd? You're going to do the work, and they're going to take the credit, eh?"

The Indian, who only vaguely understood this, shrugged his shoulders and grunted.

"Go ahead," said the jailer, handing over both key and lantern, "and remember that I haven't seen you come in. That's all. Down those steps . . . open the door at the end, and at the foot of the second flight you find the bars of Van Dyck. *Adiós.*"

He raised his flask to his lips with a shudder. The Indian had already veiled his face with his blanket and started down the first flight of steps to the basement. After he had opened the last door, he paused, as Dolores had done before him, and stared into the dark, scenting the light, disagreeable odor. His eyes brightened ominously as he descended that flight of steps. He raised his lantern at the foot of the stairs and, looking past the bars, saw the grim face of Van Dyck. He uncovered his face again.

"It is time," said El Tigre.

"Ah," said the captive, rearing his great height behind the bars, "they've sent the bloodhound again, eh?"

"The heart of El Tigre has been sick," said the Yaqui, "and he has thought of his white brother. *Señor* Oñate is a dog and the son of a dog. To him also El Tigre owes his life, but shall a dog receive a price? No, El Tigre has come to his white brother. Outside the jail the Mexicans are gathered. They are hungry for *Señor* Van Dyck. Therefore, I have come."

He unlocked the door of the cell and opened it wide. Dix Van Dyck stepped out and stretched his arms above his head.

"A square-shooter," he said. "El Tigre, your heart's white. D'you know the way to get out of this hell hole?"

The Indian raised his hand for silence. From the distance above them came a low mutter like the growl of a watchdog, but even a moment's perception showed that the sound came from many human throats.

"That is bad," said El Tigre simply.

"It is," nodded Dix Van Dyck. "I've heard it before. The Mexicans have been drinking, El Tigre?"

"It is true."

"They're going to rush the jail and get me?"

"It is true. They would lead you from the town and build a fire of mesquite in the hills and burn you . . . slowly."

Van Dyck shuddered violently, and then a fire burned up in his eyes. His captivity had increased his gauntness but had hardly weakened him. With his unshaven face and his hollow, lighted eyes, he might have stood for the picture of a gigantic madman, a Titan ready to wage war against Jove.

"They're waitin' for me, El Tigre," he said. "Let's go to meet 'em. I'm hungry, El Tigre. I haven't eaten for a month."

The face of the Indian lighted with a smile of infinite grimness. "El Tigre also," he said in his smooth Spanish, "has many debts to pay to the Mexicans. He thinks that the time has come. But we must have teeth before we can fight."

He threw down his blanket and exposed around his waist two belts, each with two revolvers suspended from the holsters. One of these he offered to Van Dyck, who buckled it about him instantly.

"And now?" said El Tigre softly.

"Wait," answered Van Dyck. "I'd rather be with a man I don't know than a gun I've never fingered." He whipped out the revolvers and balanced them in either hand. Then he spun the cylinders—pushed them open—glanced at the action. "They fit my hands like they were made to order," he announced as he shoved them back into the holsters. "Hark to 'em roaring, El Tigre! The dogs! They don't dream we're coming to feed 'em fat in another way than they think." He stopped with his foot on the stair. "But you can't go with me, El Tigre. Start out first and get safely from the jail. Then I'll follow you. This isn't your battle. You've done your share, giving me a fighting chance."

"My white brother forgets," said El Tigre. "He gave me my life even when his hands were empty. His honor could not be bought even by freedom. El Tigre, too, has a strong heart. He has a price to pay. He will fight at the side of his white brother. It is well."

"You hear me talk," said Van Dyck with profound emotion. "El Tigre, when we get past this mess, we'll team it to-gether. For a pal, you'll find me straight. Gimme your hand!"

The hand of the Indian closed hard over his.

"It is true," said El Tigre, "the spirit of El Tigre will follow his white brother, but his body shall lie on the street of Double Bend tonight, trampled by many feet with blood on his mouth."

"By God!" said Van Dyck. "It isn't possible!"

"It is true," said the Indian. "It shall be my last fight."

"You're thinking on a cold trail," said Van Dyck. "Buck up, El Tigre. We'll go through the Mexicans like a hot knife through butter. They can't stand close work, and I know how to play 'em. Die? Man, you'll live to a hundred."

"No," said the Indian, "there is no heart in El Tigre for living. Those he has loved have turned from him again. Those he would have kept as clean as the white snow have fallen in mud and grown black. He has lived alone, but he has lived long enough. He has found a man. He has found a white brother." He stiffened, and his head went back. Delirium lighted his eyes. "He has been a lone wolf. He has gone where no men have gone. He has been the tiger in the night. He has come without noise and killed, and without noise he has departed. Nothing has loved him, but there is nothing that has not feared him. El Tigre would rather be feared than loved. He is the tiger in the night. He is the lone wolf who hunts without giving voice on the trail. He will die with his teeth in the throat of his enemy. The Great Spirit shall lean from the clouds to welcome El Tigre when he dies. It is true. El Tigre has spoken."

He pointed above him with a stiff finger. "The dog pack howls. White brother, let us go to them."

El Tigre Pays All Debts　34

They passed quickly through the basement and up the stairs to the main floor of the jail. At the entrance to the corridor at the end of which the gate of the jail stood—wide to the night—El Tigre touched the shoulder of his companion.

"The jailer," he said, "sits in a chair down the hall. He is waiting for the dog pack. El Tigre will go to him and whisper in his ear. If El Tigre should miss his spring, his white brother must know that the daughter of El Tigre sits on a horse at the side of the square, to the left from the door. She holds another horse also, very tall. It is the horse of *Señor* Van Dyck."

"Good," nodded Van Dyck.

El Tigre stepped out into the hall and walked with a swift step down toward the jailer. At the end of the hall the jailer, waiting with beating heart for the coming of the mob, had so far fortified himself against the crisis that he was now past the stage of any fear. He raised his flask to his lips again and then leaned back in his chair. As El Tigre reached him, a patter of feet began, and the jailer sprang up. He stared back at the sight of El Tigre.

"For God's sake, they are coming!" he cried. "Protect me, El Tigre."

"It is true," said the Indian. "El Tigre is thirsty."

He took the flask from the hand of the unfortunate jailer, raised it toward his lips, and then completed the movement by swinging it sharply to the right. It struck the head of the jailer, crashed in a thousand pieces. After he had stared a stupid second at the tall form of the Indian, the Mexican sank in a formless heap on the floor. At the same instant the night beyond the open door was black with faces—black, for every man wore a mask.

"Now!" cried El Tigre, and Dix Van Dyck leaped into the hall.

First to enter the hall and leaders of the mob were the tall form of García and a stocky man beside him. They carried rifles. As for those behind the leaders, the majority brought no weapons whatever. The word had been passed by García that weapons were not wanted at this festival. All that was needed would be numbers to conceal identity, for a hundred men might do safely what six would never risk. Moreover, if many were armed, there would be great chances that one of them would send a bullet into the captive before he could be taken to the fire.

For these and other reasons García had issued his suggestion about arms, and the majority had followed his order. They had expected a helpless captive. Instead, they saw the most feared man on the range before them, armed to the teeth. Yet they were courageous men and quick with their weapons. In spite of the unnerving surprise, they jerked their weapons to their shoulder and fired. Both shots were wild. Van Dyck, standing tall and confident with the courage of the desperado who dares not miss, fired twice in return.

García sank to the floor without a word, but his squat, broad-shouldered companion tore at his face with both hands and staggered back through the open door, screaming horribly. He had been shot through the mouth. His fall back blocked the way of those behind and threw them into confusion. They had not dreamed of resistance.

Before they could recover, the Indian was at the door. He leaped low—among their very legs—and, dropping his revolver, he swung his heavy knife and buried it to the hilt again and again. Shrieks answered him, shrieks and the beginning of a panic. Those behind halted, dumbfounded at the check. Those in front swirled back with the picture of red death before them. Then the bull-like bellow of Dix Van Dyck ran on them like thunder, and the big man leaped through the door into their midst, a gun barking in each hand. Firing into that compacted swarm, the bullets could not miss. They ploughed their way through solid walls of flesh.

Shrieking rose to a ghastly crescendo. Those in front turned their backs on the horror in mad terror and fought to dive into the safety of the mob. They made a barrier of flesh through which it was impossible for those behind to fire effectively at Van Dyck or the Indian. They began to brandish knives and revolvers over their heads—the few that had them—and shots were fired wildly in the air.

Van Dyck loaded his guns again and emptied them a second time. Then he sprang like a Norseman, gone berserk with fighting madness, on the backs of all the fugitives. He used the barrels of his revolvers as heavy clubs, and in his strong hands every blow nearly brought down a man.

Not that they all fled blindly. There were brave men in that crowd, though all were at first unnerved by the unexpected attack. Here and there men began to turn—fire—or raise a knife. But they met either the bullet of Van Dyck or the deadly steel of the Indian. El Tigre was drunk with delight. He leaped here and there like a leaf jerked about by a crazy wind that blows from all directions. Wherever he leaped, he struck, and whenever he struck, he yelled in a way that curdled the blood and rose over the confused raging of the crowd.

The gigantic white man fought with his lips writhed back from set teeth, and through set teeth he laughed continually—a strange, ghastly sound. He broke the barrel of one gun, and then he threw them both aside and fought with his bare fists—weapons scarcely less terrible, for though they might not kill, they drove out with the force of pistons, and, where they struck, men groaned and fell.

It was one of these who had fallen who recovered his senses almost at once and, raising himself on his belly with his hands, saw the two destroyers, raging on the heels of the crowd that gave back in a rapidly widening semicircle. A thousand strange deeds had been performed, and yet the entire fight had covered only a small space of seconds. He saw them fleeing, struggling to get away from the nameless danger behind them. The little man noted that there were only two who drove so many. He noted that, and it gave him courage. His throat was burning with a recent draught of mescal. So he drew a long-bladed jackknife and, running low like a four-footed animal, came behind El Tigre in the midst of his work, leaped into the air, and smote the Indian in the middle of the back to the full length of his blade. The Indian turned and struck at his assailant, but the knife dropped from his hand. He coughed blood and fell forward on his face.

That was the turning point of the battle. The vast majority were fleeing. There remained only the armed men who had the courage to fight. These now turned their faces and rushed at Dix Van Dyck. A dozen shots whirred past him, but his thought was vengeance for El Tigre. It was not long in coming. The little man who had struck the blow came again and leaped once more into the air, like a cat. In the midst of his leap the piston-rod arm of Van Dyck plunged out and met him in the face. The blow smashed his nose and gashed his cheek. He went back as though recoiling from a spring and landed, head-first, on the ground.

A fury was on Van Dyck—a frenzy that trebled his enormous natural strength. For he caught up the fallen man by the heels, whirled him high over his head, and cast him into the faces of his foes. It checked them. It sent their shots wild, but the life of Van Dyck was limited to a matter of seconds when something like Providence struck for him. It was Dolores. At first she saw only a confused mass of struggling figures as the two men plunged out of the jail and met their assailants. Then the semicircle nearest the door cleared, and she watched the terrible fighting of her father and the big white man. A grim thing but glorious to the wild heart of Dolores. She had stood in her stirrups and yelled her delight. Now she saw the crowd surge back against the two men, saw her father struck down from behind, saw Van Dyck smite down the slayer, and then cast the senseless body in the faces of the crowd.

At that deed her blood drove from her heart to her brain. She swung the head of her horse about, looped the reins of the great charger of Dix Van Dyck over the pommel of her saddle. Driving the rowels of her spurs deep into the flanks of her own tall horse, she galloped against the fighters. She caught her own rein over the crook of her arm, snatched out her two revolvers, and fired blindly to left and right, yelling at the top of her shrill voice.

It was too much for the courage of the crowd. Already they saw the ground before them littered with the bodies of dead, wounded, and stunned men. There were some among them who had already felt the knife of El Tigre or the fist of Dix Van Dyck. At this sudden onslaught from the side, they raised a shout of dismay and split before the coming of Dolores like water before the prow of a ship.

Into the mass she drove. Her horse, rearing, struck out in a panic of terror, and men went down before those ponderous, armed hoofs. She felt the horse reel and stagger as his hoofs sank in something horribly soft—and then there stood before her only the bloody figure of Dix Van Dyck.

The tearing hands of a hundred men had rent his shirt from his back. He stood naked to the waist, splashed with crimson, his hands red as a butcher where he had taken a wounded man by the throat. He gave her a yell of welcome and, without touching the pommel, leaped into his saddle and caught his reins from Dolores.

"Now!" he cried. "Now, now!"

There were new guns in the holsters of his saddle. Dolores had seen to that. And with the yelling Indian girl at his side, he galloped straight through the crowd, firing to right and left among the last of the panic-stricken fugitives. Men melted away before them. The road stretched suddenly bare and blank. They thundered away into the thick heart of the night.

The Coming of Jack 35

35

The white stallion, at a reeling gallop, swung down the last long slope toward Double Bend. It was pitch dark now, and the horse was too exhausted to pick his footing by instinct. Twice he stepped on a loose stone and nearly fell. At last, with hanging head, at a shambling trot, he struck into the main street of Double Bend.

Jack had expected voices, noise, crowds. It was the time for the dance hall to be in full blast, but, when she passed it, she found closed doors and blank darkness. Something had happened, and she knew in her heart that it had something to do with Dix Van Dyck. But there was not a soul on the streets. The lights were out in every house. She could not hear the stirring of a step, not a voice, not a single burst of laughter. Yet, this was Double Bend! It was ghostly. She thought of some breath of pestilence that might have struck across the place. Certainly everything was as still as death. It was then that she caught the glimmer of light from the office of Marshal Phil Glasgow. She would rather have seen it in any other place. She spurred the stallion pitilessly to a staggering gallop. As she drew closer, she saw a huddle of horses in front of the office and men passing in, so she swung from the saddle and ran though the door.

Inside were a dozen white men, and at a table before them Marshal Phil Glasgow was reading. Every man stood with raised hand. They were taking the oath. A posse was being formed. It froze her heart. She knew the meaning well enough. A lawless mob had seized Dix Van Dyck and killed him. Now the marshal was forming a posse to follow the perpetrators of the crime. That was why Double Bend was plunged in darkness. The reading of the oath ended. The men answered as one in a deep-voiced chorus: "I do!"

It was then that Phil Glasgow looked up and saw the white face of the girl at the door. "What the hell?" asked Glasgow. "Jack, how'd you come here?"

"Dix," she said faintly, "Dix Van Dyck. They've killed him?"

"Have they?" growled the marshal. "Not that I know of."

"Thank God," she breathed and could do nothing but repeat it for a moment over and over. She said at last, light breaking on her: "This posse is to follow *him* . . . follow Van Dyck?"

"Maybe," said the sullen marshal.

"Send 'em home," said the girl. "There ain't no call for a posse. The governor has pardoned Dix Van Dyck. I got it here." She placed the pardon on the table before him.

It would have been hard to tell whether it was disappointment or relief that showed most plainly in the face of Phil Glasgow. "It's the old man's signature," he said, "and it reads like his lingo. Yep, it's straight stuff. Boys, you hunt your bunks. Thanks for turning out for me."

But they lingered, swearing. It was their way of expressing all emotions. They stared at Jacqueline who had slipped exhausted into a chair.

"What's happened?" she asked.

"I'll tell you that," said one of the men. "The prettiest little fight that was ever staged on the range. The Mexs started for the jail. They were in a gang . . . damn if I know how many there was in it. Old El Tigre went before 'em and turned Dix Van Dyck loose and give him guns. About the time the crowd hit the jail, Dix and El Tigre come out, Dix with his guns spittin' and El Tigre with a knife. Nacherally they was a heap of an argument between them two and the crowd. The Mexicans had numbers, but them two had the fighting heart. Finally El Tigre was knifed between the shoulders, and it looked black for Van Dyck, when little Dolores charged into the gang with two horses and got Van Dyck, aboard one of 'em. Then they beat it off. They left the ground considerable littered up. We picked up seven dead men, not counting El Tigre, and a dozen others hurt too bad to crawl away, besides the Lord knows how many that was able to run off. It looked like the floor of a slaughter house. Speaking personal, I'm glad Van Dyck got away. He showed like a man tonight."

"You talk like a fool," said the marshal. "They warn't nothing really to hold Dix Van Dyck for in the first place except for that shooting of the deputy from Guadalupe, and there was never any real charge against him for that to have happened. He never murdered anyone. He was tackled by a mob tonight, and all he done was in self-defense. But it's probably only days before he'll be on the trail of old Oñate."

"Is Oñate behind it?" asked someone.

"Are ye blind?" queried Glasgow fiercely. "Can't you see his hand behind all this? He come in here an hour ago with the fear of God in him. He demanded the protection of my men. Think of that! A sheriff asking for protection! I asked him what he feared, and he told me that during the fight Dix Van Dyck had made threats against him. I laughed at him and told him, if that was the case, he'd better order his coffin. But it wasn't any laughin' matter with old Oñate. He went off sick and yellow-faced, the dog! I hear he's called in a bunch and is payin' 'em to

guard his house. No, lads, it's only a question of time before we'll be on the trail of Van Dyck again for a reason.
He'll be coming for the hide of Oñate. I don't wish him
no bad luck, but, if he drops the sheriff, I've got to go after him, and there ain't no man that's got away from me
yet after I once started on his trail!"

"What'll you do?" asked one of the men.

"Sit here and wait," said the marshal. "Double Bend is
our trap. Oñate is our bait. Just takes time but in the end
we're sure to get Dix Van Dyck. Only it'll be a man-size job
to take him after he's cornered." He looked at the girl.
"Jack, you're his friend, ain't you?"

"I am," she answered.

"Then, if you can run across him, tell him to lay off
Oñate. It ain't healthy."

"Glasgow," she said scornfully, "d'you really think
there's a ghost of a show of getting Dix Van Dyck off a trail
he's once started?"

He leaned across the table and stared at her. "Jack" he
said, "I got an idea it'd be to your interest to get him off
this here trail of Oñate. They's been feudin' for some time
now, and no good has ever come of it. Oñate's lost some
of his kin in the fight so far. After tonight, and with this
pardon, maybe the feud could end peaceably for 'em
both."

Jack jumped from her chair and stood with flushed
face, glaring at him. "What d'you mean, Glasgow?"

"I dunno," said the marshal and grinned not unkindly
at her, "but just think it over. If he's worth saving, you got
to keep him away from the sheriff."

She turned slowly away. She was not thinking of the
marshal's words, but she was seeing again in her mind's
eye the careless, boyish recklessness of Van Dyck as she
had first watched him in the dance hall. How long ago it
seemed! The heart of a boy and the heavy hand of a

strong man. The two did not go safely together. She tried to define him. He was simply a grown-up mischief maker. Then the advice of the marshal struck home in her mind. She could have blessed him for it. She knew that Dix Van Dyck had followed her through the mountains on a long trail. Perhaps for her sake he would give up his vengeance on Oñate.

True, it was only a dim hope, for she remembered how he had sat at their table in the dance hall and actually waited for the pursuit to overtake him—waited in the hope and joyous expectation of a fight. Waited because he challenged the bad luck of the cross that she wore. She remembered how his agile hand had suddenly poised on the edge of the table, his eyes fixed and burning past her, so that she had known that the enemy was in the room. Then the down swoop of that hand, the flash of the revolver, the boom of the shot. How the deputy had staggered back with his hands across his face. It was terribly clear to her. And terribly clear were the misfortunes that the cross had brought upon him. First the outlawry. She had broken that, but now he was a known man, and at the first suspicion things would go hard with him again at the hands of the officers of the law.

The bad luck led him on toward Oñate. He was sure to strike at the Mexican. He was sure to succeed, and afterward there would be the inevitable outlawry again, and this time the pursuit must end in the death of Van Dyck. Once he had escaped. It would be impossible to do so twice. In the sense of helplessness that overwhelmed her, she brought her hand to the base of her throat to seize the little metal cross and throw it away from her, anywhere, into the night.

But at her touch the cross pressed cold against her flesh, and she remembered a thousand things. It had betrayed others, perhaps, but to her the cross had been a continual salvation. It was wealth and strength to her. It carried with it a host of associations. She felt that she would never have the strength to give it up, even for Van Dyck. But here her thoughts paused suddenly. It was necessary, first of all, to reach Van Dyck and tell him of the pardon and then of the necessity of keeping from the trail of Oñate.

She waited until after midnight to let the stallion rest. Then she started slowly on the trail for Guadalupe, keeping well to the right of the beaten track and among the hills. She believed Van Dyck would head toward Guadalupe to reach Oñate.

Oñate's Inspiration

36

In Double Bend *Señor* Don Porfirio Maria Oñate could neither sit nor stand in comfort. He could not walk without crossing a doorway, and, every time he crossed a doorway, there came over him a shuddering thought that the door might open and a giant spring out upon him. A giant such as his trembling friends had described to him: unkempt, unshaven, lean, hollow-eyed, swift, and terrible—with hands that crushed throats with a single grip and steel-faced fists that broke heads. It all seemed too frightful to contemplate.

Señor Oñate caressed his neck with his pudgy hands. He retired from the vicinity of the yawning doorway and sought refuge in the corner of his room. But here, with wall on two sides, it occurred to him that his own flight would be barred in case the foe should enter the room. He moved hastily to the center of the apartment and stood, casting fearful glances on all sides.

He was not an exceedingly timorous man, to be sure, but recent events had shattered his nerves. He was prepared for anything except failure. His plans had been so well laid that it had been more than improbable they would fail—it had seemed impossible. That was what broke his spirit. The impossible had occurred. Only a few hours ago the great enemy had lain helpless and hopeless in the jail. A mob had been gathering to crush him.

Now Van Dyck was free, loose in the hills, armed and ready for vengeance.

Thank God that for money guards could be hired. Oñate dropped back into his chair and sighed with sick-hearted relief when he remembered the stanch fighters whom he had employed. They patrolled his garden, up and down in every direction. They were posted at the four doors. But suddenly *Señor* Oñate leaped from the chair again. Fear had spurred him once more. It occurred to him that, though all these men had come highly recommended for fighting qualities, many of them were unknown to him personally. It might be that a few gold pieces dropped in their hands would undo all his prearranged precautions. After all, was it not simple? A man approached them softly in the dark and said to one of the sentinels: "Turn your back but an instant, my friend. Here is money to help you turn." What mercenary could resist that temptation?

Oñate stole from his room and crept along the hall to the main opening that passed in a vaulted hall from the path to the front of the house. Once in this passage, fears and whispers and the light-touching winds of the night beset him. He crouched in the throat of the black arch and peered forth into the night. There in the garden he peered cautiously, but he saw nothing. A pang of horror and cold rage beset him. Had the dogs already betrayed him and left their posts? Were they even then, perhaps, stealing up on him? At the very moment, when he was about to turn and fly back to the house, he perceived a shadow moving closer to the door. Then another, another, another. Four men walked their posts in the garden. He was safe, safe, safe! The sensation of relief was so great that a sob rose in his throat and tears trickled, one after another, down his face.

He went back into the house almost boldly, but, when

a door was snatched by the wind and loudly banged, he started and whirled in a fresh panic. At this point he discovered that he was very thirsty and called aloud: "Dolores! Ho, there, Dolores!"

It was not till his anger began to rise at her delay that he remembered that she had left him, that she was gone to the side of his great enemy. She had found the white man with the cruel, straight-lipped mouth, and she had followed him as she had threatened. It left a sense of bitter emptiness in Oñate. Moreover, it gave a new edge to his fear. For the girl knew him like a book. She knew all his tastes, all his weaknesses. She could read his mind. If she combined her brain with that of Dix Van Dyck, nothing between heaven and hell could keep him from falling before their combined attack.

"I hope he will beat her!" groaned Oñate. "Beat her till the blood flows down over her beautiful face. Beat her till welts rise on her back. Kick her in the mouth . . . so!"

He struck at the air in his wild fury. Then he remembered that such a man as Dix Van Dyck would never lay the weight of a finger on a woman. He remembered that for the sake of a woman Dix Van Dyck had allowed himself to be led, unresisting, into captivity. This strange truth still further disarmed Oñate. It was another miracle attributable to Van Dyck.

What we do not understand, we all fear. A child fears the night. Oñate feared Dix Van Dyck. If the man had been a plain scoundrel, he would have understood a little. He would not have felt so helpless. As it was, he was about to engage in a death struggle with an unknown power. He could not tell whether the man would hire others to fight his battle with him or make the attack alone. He did not know whether to look for many or for one. He did not know whether the stroke would come stealthily in the middle of the night with the silence of a crawling snake, or whether it would come in the middle of day with terrible boldness, when the bright sunlight wrapped him in a sense of false security.

The brain of Oñate reeled, and in his despair he reached automatically for his favorite flask of tequila and poured himself a stiff drink. The liquid fire warmed his throat and at least took some of the chill from his heart. It became possible for him to think. Thoughts sprang fully grown into the brain of Oñate. It was, indeed, the secret source of his power. He never had to fumble about in the dark, as many other men did. When a difficulty confronted him, he generally saw straight into the heart of the matter and knew instantly when and where to strike.

It happened now that he cast about in his mind to think what man would be sure to follow Dix Van Dyck in this war, and the first name that came to his lips was that of Joseph Van Dyck, the young brother in far south Guadalupe. First Oñate thought of him as a power to harm and remembered a tall youth of seventeen, rather darkly handsome, and with gentle eyes far different from the cold glance of Dix Van Dyck. The elder brother was an anomaly even to his family. He was a throw-back toward the primitive, an atavism. Joseph Van Dyck followed the natural course of family blood. He made up in his gentleness for the grim ferocity and tiger-hearted playfulness of his brother. Oñate regarded the elder brother as a menace, but the thought of Joseph Van Dyck's ever raising a hand to fight except in the most desperate case of self-defense was amusing. It was absurd.

Not a danger, then, and not a help to Dix Van Dyck? Then came the rapier thrust of inspiration. Not a help to Dix Van Dyck but a terrible and compromising weakness. To reach the terrible elder brother was not in the power of the sheriff in spite of his men, and he knew it. He could not have purchased the services of mercenaries to follow the trail of this redoubtable man-slayer. But the younger brother? There passed a trail of vague thoughts through the mind of Oñate—rumors he had heard in Guadalupe concerning a great love and tenderness that lay between the two brothers in spite of the differences between their natures. The rumors ran on to tell how the hard hand of Dix Van Dyck had warded the danger of the world from the shoulders of his younger brother. There were a score of anecdotes that flashed now across the mind of *Señor* Oñate, and now in the full flush of his inspiration he leaped to his feet and shouted aloud, again, again, and again.

Manuel and Pedro at the same instant showed their dark faces at the door. Their master redoubled his laughter and jovially hurled a stool at their heads.

"I am safe!" cried Oñate, and collapsed into his chair. "I am safe, Manuel, Pedro, good boys, worthy lads. Bring me yonder flask. God is on my side. But wait! First go to the telephone and get my new deputy at Guadalupe on the wire. Quick! Let everything wait for that!"

They disappeared, and, until his call came in, he sat in his chair, alternately shivering violently, like one seized with a palsy, and then laughing inordinately and rolling his fat body about in the chair. When his call came, the voice of José Remoso answered him on the end of the wire.

"José," called the sheriff sharply, "*Señor* Van Dyck is escaped from the jail. His pardon will be here at once from the governor. I am in danger."

In his astonishment the deputy swore. He had no other answer.

"I must be protected," went on the sheriff, "against this devil. José Remoso, my friend, there are still members of Van Dyck's family in Guadalupe."

"It is true," said the deputy.

"Do you see?"

"See what, *señor?*"

"You are a fool. Are there not brigands who kidnap men and children and hold them for ransom?"

"That also is true, *señor.*"

"And still you do not see?"

"Nothing, *señor.*"

"If Joseph Van Dyck disappears, will it not seem that some brigand, some outlaw has seized him?"

"That is true also."

"Blockhead, if the boy is in my power, I have nothing to fear from his brother . . . his devil of a fire-eating brother, Dix Van Dyck. Let the boy disappear. Then I send word to Dix Van Dyck that, if a hair of my head is injured, the boy will answer for it to my friends."

"*Señor*, the thought must have come to you from heaven."

"From heaven, indeed, Remoso. Let it be done at once."

"At once, *señor*. But how did the man break from the jail?"

"The treacherous dog, El Tigre . . . and then the two fought like demons and killed many men. *Adiós*, Remoso. Strike quickly in Guadalupe."

So saying, he hung up the receiver and went back to his chair. The terror was passing, leaving him only weak and weary from the long hysteria. Comfort was coming and with its coming a great thirst. He drank again and again until his brain hummed. Out of the humming grew a sound, and the sound after a time took on the semblance of a human voice. It was extremely odd. The drink, the sharp reaction, had thrown him into a sort of a delirium. He was conscious of a fever and a lightness of head for which the drink could only be partially responsible. A faintly singing voice chanted in his head. He canted his ear to it and listened with a frown. At last he made out that it was his own mind that kept repeating in his own voice, over and over: "Dolores! Dolores *mia*! Devil Dolores! Dolores, my beautiful!" The sheriff fell back helplessly in his chair. "She has come to haunt me," he groaned, "and I shall not sleep tonight."

s for Dolores, certainly she was never further from thoughts of *Señor* Don Porfirio Maria Oñate. She sat at this very time, staring with her great black eyes across the sullen red embers of the camp fire toward Dix Van Dyck. It was something past midnight, but they had only traveled as far as a convenient spring in the hollow of the hills, a little to the right of the main trail that led down toward Guadalupe. By the side of this spring they built their fire and screened it by rolling big rocks on all sides of the flame.

Then, after they had cooked and eaten, Dix Van Dyck threw off his clothes and she saw the faint white glimmer of his body in the distance while he bathed and shaved in the cold water that trickled down from the spring. She marveled with her childish mind at the dexterity of a man who could handle deadly steel and shave himself in the dark. She marveled still more when he came back beside the fire. With the unkempt growth of beard and the red marks of the battle gone, his face seemed singularly pale for one who had lived all his life in the open. The leanness of that face had now become almost cadaverous and suggestive of many things.

It seemed to Dolores, as he sat there with one of her dead father's blankets wrapped around his bare shoulders, that two men sat there confronting her in one form. When he sat with eyes lowered and staring at the flicker of the fire, she was conscious of the man's great weariness. He was tired, it seemed, body and soul. The thin face seemed thoughtful, sad. There was a suggestion that the straight set of the mouth inferred a repression and endurance of pain. It seemed the face of one who had borne through many bitter trials, whose trust in men and women had been burned away by hardship, who had fought the world and conquered it but found no value in his conquest. True, all these things did not come in sharp, clear words into the mind of Dolores, but the feeling was there. Yet, when the eyelids of the outlaw raised and she saw the unendurable keenness of the eyes, her own glance wavered and fell away. No matter what his body might be, his spirit was more terrible and unrelenting than ever. It was what set the fire in the eyes that made his glance something to be felt and shrunk from like the touch of a hot hand or like the drop of an acid. She understood, even more perfectly than when she had seen the big man in action against the crowd, why *Señor* Oñate had dreaded him like an incarnation of the devil. She also dreaded him fully as much, and yet the thrill of that terror was pleasant to the fierce Yaqui.

"*Señor*," she ventured timidly at length.

He turned his head silently toward her and waited.

"*¿Señorita?*" he queried.

"No. I am only Dolores," she answered.

"Dolores?" he repeated and almost smiled at her.

"You are thinking much and very quickly?" she suggested.

"No," said Dix Van Dyck, "I'm seeing the face of a man, Dolores, more clearly than I see yours."

"Oñate," she nodded.

"Oñate." His voice fell dry and hard on the name.

"That is why you take the road to Guadalupe?"

"Yes."

"But Oñate will remain in Double Bend."

"Why?"

"He stayed near the town," she answered, "to see the burning of my father's white brother from a distance. When he knows that *Señor* Van Dyck has escaped, he will be taken with a great fear. Yes, he will be afraid to leave Double Bend, and he will sit in his room surrounded by many men." She broke into rare laughter and hugged her knees in an ecstasy of childish, fierce delight. "He will pay many men money. He will set them about his garden and his house, and he will wait, shivering, for the coming of *Señor* Van Dyck. Pah, the dog!"

"The dog!" echoed Van Dyck. "You are sure, Dolores, that he will not try to go to Guadalupe?"

"It is true," she said. "Tonight he would rather take the road to hell than the trail to Guadalupe. No, he will sit in his house and drink tequila, and for all that he will be cold in his heart. I, Dolores, can see him shiver. Pah! I, a woman, have made him tremble till his knees knocked together."

"Aye," said the man curiously. "You are the daughter of El Tigre. I think, Dolores, that you have teeth and claws. I watched you coming through that crowd. By heaven, that was a man's work! I could see your eyes flash as clearly as I could see the fire of your guns. How did you have the heart for a job like that, Dolores?"

"It was not hard," she said simply. "It was for the white brother of my father. I was riding to you, *señor.*"

"Why did you come, Dolores? Why did you come to the jail and give me the knife? Was it all because I had helped El Tigre?"

"It is true," she said.

"Dolores, you lie to me."

"Ah," said the girl, delighted again, "the white brother

of my father sees to the heart of his daughter. It is true. I came because I had heard a strange story."

"So?"

"Yes. I had heard a story that *Señor* Van Dyck gave himself to his enemies for the sake of a woman. I knew it was a lie, but still I came to look. It was a great lie, was it not, *señor?*"

"Humph," grunted Dix Van Dyck, and he grinned broadly at the girl. "Is this to get a yarn out of me, Dolores?"

"It is true," she said frankly. "Dolores is hungry to learn. She is hungry for wisdom."

"Well," said Dix Van Dyck, "the story sounds queer, but it's straight."

She merely gaped at him, and then the smile dawned, the smile of bright wonder. "Tell!" she cried eagerly.

"About the girl?"

"Yes, yes!"

"Why," said the man, "she's about your height, Dolores, and beautiful as the devil."

"Ha!" said the Yaqui. "A beautiful woman makes great fools of men."

"Come to think of it," smiled Dix Van Dyck, "you're a bit good to look at yourself, Dolores."

"I?" she said with well-imitated surprise. "Alas, *señor*, I am a piece of 'dobe made into the shape of a woman and clothes in moldy rags. No man will look at me!" Her eyes glinted.

The white man, however, would carry the banter no further. "It wasn't her good looks, though, Dolores," he said, "that made me follow her."

"Ah?"

"She had a cross of silver that she wears around her neck. Now, I ain't superstitious, Dolores, but I got an idea that cross can do what people claim it can do. It brings good luck to Jack Boone and bad luck to everyone near her . . . everyone she likes, particularly. You see, Dolores, that cross has been tried out a lot of times, and it never fails. She always wins gambling, for instance, and she generally gets what she wants. In every way.

"But the people that go with her generally get their necks broke some time or other. There've been plenty of cases of that. She ain't been long in Double Bend, you see, but already two men have kicked off unexpected, sort of, just because they hung around Jack. Well, Dolores, I come to Double Bend while I was making a hurried trip north to get away from Oñate, who's sheriff of this county, you know. In the dance hall I saw Jack Boone, and I heard the story about the cross. Dolores, the minute I heard that yarn. . . ."

"You wanted to be with *Señorita* Jack?"

"How could you know?"

"A child," said the Indian girl, "will always do the one thing he is told he must not do."

"*Humph*," grinned Dix Van Dyck, "I'm a good deal of a child, eh, Dolores? Well, let that go. Anyway, I had to stick with Jack. I did it, and I got to like her a pile more'n I'd ever liked any other woman. When the pinch came, and I couldn't fight for my life except by throwing Jack to El Tigre and his hunting pack, I knuckled down for the sake of the girl." He was black with the reminiscence.

The Yaqui waited, wisely.

"Maybe," said the man, "it was a fool thing I done, because she left me in the hole and never come near me while I was in the jail. She got away with her skin safe and forgot plumb all about me, Dolores."

"I," said the Yaqui sternly, "would ride first on her trail and take her by the hair, so! And beat her till the blood ran and until she screamed and begged for pity. That is what Dolores would do."

"Would you?" queried the man curiously. "Sometimes I got a hunch that the heavy hand is what women need, Dolores, but I ain't ever had the heart to use it."

"You have never struck a woman?" she asked eagerly.

"Me?" he asked grimly. "Tell me what man ever said I did and I'll take him, skin him, and tan his hide for a saddle."

"Oñate is a great liar," she mused gently.

"Oñate again? Still spreading filthy talk about me, eh? Well, the longer the score the quicker the settling. But, when I take him, I wish I had the heart to kill him slow, the way he needs."

"You will not need," said the girl. "Give him to me. I will kill him, and you need not see . . . or hear."

"You hate him, Dolores?"

"Ah!" she said and fingered the knife at her girdle.

"Why?"

"Why? Truly, *señor*, Dolores cannot tell. Except that he is fat, and that he has been on the trail of the white brother of my father."

"You're a gentle thing, Dolores," grinned the big man, "a regular little pet lamb, you are. I'd rather meet a wild-cat bare-handed than have to mix with you, my girl."

"It is true," she assented sadly. "I am not like your woman, Jack. I am not gentle and soft."

"Gentle? Soft?" laughed Dix Van Dyck. "Dolores, that girl can ride any wild mustang on the range. She can fan a gun from the hip as good as I can . . . or better. She can throw a knife like El Tigre. There's no wearing out to her. She can ride that white hoss of hers all day and all night. I know, because I've tried to catch her. Tried for days."

"She was swifter than you? *Than you?*" asked the aston-ished girl.

"A whole pile," he answered emphatically. "But let's for-get her."

"It is good," said Dolores with much relish. "She was a coward. She did not stay with the white brother of my father when he fell in the trap for her sake. She is a devil, not a woman. *Señor* Van Dyck hates her. It is very good. The heart of Dolores is warm!"

But he pondered this question a moment seriously. "Hate her?" he answered at length. "I can't say that I do, Dolores. No, I got no reason to like her and a lot to dislike her, but somehow I can't get rid of the thought of her, and I can't say that it's hate that keeps me thinkin' of her. You know how some gents like whiskey? They can't get rid of the taste of it? Well, that's the way the thought of this Jack follows me, Dolores."

"So?" said the girl gloomily.

"That's straight. D'you know, after I'm through with Oñate, I s'pose I'll make a dead line for Jack and try to get on her trail."

The Yaqui drew her knife in a silent fury and drove it to the hilt in the dead stump on which she sat. "That is fool's talk!" she said furiously.

"Ain't it?" said the whimsical Van Dyck. "But it's straight talk, too."

Her glance narrowed, piercing the gloom of the cañon. "And this girl, she rides a white horse, *señor*?"

"Yes, why?"

"Nothing." But far away, through the gloom, she had seen the glint of a moving object. It must have been white to show so plainly at so great a distance.

Tears for El Tigre

38

To the sharpest eyes of a white man that glimmering form in the night would have been invisible, but the Indian saw and fell silent. She seemed to be brooding over the fire, with fallen head, oblivious of the world. Even the keen observation of Dix Van Dyck, trained to suspect everything and everybody, failed to note the glances that she sent now and again down the valley. But, by then, she had discovered very certainly that someone on a white horse was riding toward the red eye of the camp fire. As Dolores sat there with bowed, impassive face, a thousand emotions and impulses surged within her.

To speak as frankly as the Yaqui girl thought, she had decided that this *Señor* Van Dyck should be her man. It was a calm and great conviction that she could not be happy without him. The first necessity, therefore, was to stop the rider on that white horse. If the girl, Jack, should meet the man again, she, Dolores, would be cast at once into the outer night.

At first she thought of warning Dix Van Dyck that a horseman approached—that the pursuers were hard on their trail. It might mean that he would spring to his horse and gallop with her down the next slope and away toward Guadalupe. But a second of pondering assured Dolores that Dix van Dyck would never run away from a single horseman. On the other hand, it might be that he would attempt to stop the rider with a bullet. She herself would have ventured to bring down the night rider with a bullet, even at that distance, but here again she guessed this white man's ethics were different from hers. This man would not shoot at random on anyone. Moreover, if he once centered his glance on the approaching form, there was great danger that he would discover by the starlight what she had already seen—that the horse was white. That would be only hastening the catastrophe.

It was the slowness of the approach of the stranger that finally gave Dolores inspiration. If it were indeed the girl, Jack, her horse must be very weary, or she herself must be advancing cautiously, to reconnoiter. Possibly both things were true. In that case, the white woman would come within view of the camp fire unseen by Dix Van Dyck and would discover the white man sitting by the campfire with an Indian girl. Now, if it had been another Indian maiden approaching, the course of Dolores would have been to steal down the slope and shoot her rival as she approached. This would have been both brief and simple, and no man but a fool would waste regret over a dead body. The great fact remained that it was *not* an Indian girl. It was a white woman, and, when a woman is killed in the Southwest, there is a penalty to pay. A thing not to be understood by Dolores but known. Into her mind came another perception of the psychology of the white man. If the girl, Jack, stealing upon the camp fire, should have reason to suppose that Dix Van Dyck had taken Dolores as his partner, nothing in the world could bribe her to break in upon the two of them. Very faintly, like a thing described half by the eyes and half by the imagination, Dolores saw the white girl's pride in choice. On that she determined to bank.

She waited, timing her move cautiously. The rider had dismounted, for the figure of the horse was stationary some distance down the slope. It was fainter than the shadow of a ghost, but Dolores saw and understood. The rider of the horse was now stealing upon the camp fire. What if she should be wrong? What if it were another person on another white horse? What if it were one of the scouts of Oñate sent upon this bloody trail of the destroyer? What if it were some kinsman of one of those who fell in the square before the jail? In that case the life of Dix Van Dyck was about to end and her own life with his. A grim and terrible suspense—no one would guess it who has not been in danger in the trackless heart of the desert. There was very little time to make her final choice now, for the watcher must be stealing quickly upon them. Any second the eyes of the night-rider might spy upon them through the dark. A moan formed in the throat of Dolores and came tremulously on her lips. It was not at all assumed. Her very heart was stirred by the conflict of emotions within her. She interlaced her fingers and dropped her forehead upon them. From one side her glance probed the darkness toward the side from which the spy must approach. The little moan came again.

"Well?" said the low, strong voice of Dix Van Dyck.

"I am sick," said Dolores.

"The hell!" muttered Van Dyck and dropped instantly on his knees beside her.

To one out of earshot and not very clearly in view of his face that attitude of the man's might have said many unintended things.

"Where are you sick?" went on the big man. "What's the matter, Dolores?"

She raised her head slowly, with the dignity that befitted the daughter of El Tigre. The eyes she turned on Dix Van Dyck were both brightened and dimmed by tears; they flashed in the firelight. "I am sick here," she said and laid one of those dark, slender hands over her heart.

"Stomach?" queried the susceptible Van Dyck. "Been eating the wrong sort of chow?"

She closed her eyes, dropped her head back on her hands. It was not what she wanted to do, but she was forced to the move in order to conceal the smile that tugged suddenly at the corners of her mouth. After all, Dix Van Dyck was only some thirty years, more or less, of age. Dolores was as old as the ages.

He dropped a heavy but kindly hand on her shoulder. "I got a flask in my saddlebag," he said. "What say to a jolt of red-eye, Dolores? It ain't so bad for a stomach ache."

"It is not my stomach," said the girl, still unable to raise her head. "It is my heart, *señor.*"

"Oh," said Van Dyck, and settled back in his former position with great unconcern. "Oh, it's your heart, Dolores?"

He yawned widely, noisily. She had a great desire to spring to her feet and strike him across the face. Wisely she resisted the impulse. She was learning more of self-control in these few moments than she had ever dreamed in her life before.

"And what's the matter with your heart?" asked the big man lazily.

This would never do. The eyes of the watcher were waiting, guessing with all the shrewdness and all the blindness of a woman. How well Dolores knew! It must be a woman for only a woman would crouch out there in the dark to watch this scene.

"The white girl," said the Indian with a soft-throated sadness, "has a thousand brothers and a thousand fathers, but Dolores had only one . . . and he is dead."

"Oh," grunted Van Dyck, and then he leaned to stare into dark, steady eyes that rose to meet his glance unfalteringly. "By heaven, Dolores, is *that* what's riding you? I didn't dream . . . I didn't know . . . you see, I thought you were another kind . . . quite another kind."

"El Tigre," said the girl haughtily, "was a great chief. He killed more Mexicans than I have fingers and toes. He was a great chief. He was a great warrior. He was a tiger in the fight. And he loved me . . . me, Dolores. And he has left me alone!"

Her voice and her glance sank. Then her eyes rose and rested piteously on the face of Dix Van Dyck. What could he do? He was a man. The girl was beautiful, and above all she was a woman in trouble, and this was the Southwest. He started up.

"By heaven, Dolores!" he said, "it makes me feel a pile rotten to see you like this. I thought you were a sort of young tigress yourself . . . I thought you had teeth and maybe claws, too!"

"I?" said the girl softly, and she laid her soft, small hand in the mighty fingers of Dix Van Dyck. "See, *señor*, the strength of Dolores is very little, only her heart is great. But the death of El Tigre has made it small . . . so small and with such a hurt in the center of it, *señor*, that I know I shall die!"

He was staring blankly down at that slender hand, scowling in bewilderment. It was all very new to him. Suddenly he felt that she was only a child and needed comforting, as he had seen fathers comfort little children. He stooped from his rock and with a single sweep of those large arms carried her to his knees.

"Why, Dolores," he said gently, "you ain't no more'n a child, and you got no right to have troubles of your own. Tell 'em to me and I shall help."

"Alas, *señor*," she said bitterly, "how shall you help? My father is dead . . . dead . . . dead! Can you bring him back to me?"

"Me? Bring back El Tigre?" He pondered this obvious difficulty. "Dolores, I can't bring El Tigre back, but I'll tell you what. I'll take his place. I'll take care of you. Will you let me, poor kid?"

"Ah, *señor*," she said, "Dolores is only an Indian girl. Men would smile at the white brother of my father if he were seen with me."

"Smile?" said the big man fiercely. "By heaven, the man who smiles at me because of you, Dolores, will have to eat lead damned fast!"

His voice had risen with his sudden anger. Now it boomed and rang across the desert. The heart of Dolores swelled with intolerable joy. She knew those words had rung in the ears of the white girl with a differing connotation. To hide the wild happiness that was transfiguring her face, she slipped suddenly within the arms of Dix Van Dyck, buried her face on his shoulder, and wept heavily and long with great sobs. She had seen a white woman cry like that. She had never done so herself, but the inspiration came and with it even the tears to make her eyes wet. After all, the wisdom of Dolores was very old. All the while she wept, her eyes, over the vast shoulder of Dix Van Dyck, plumbed the darkness. The big hand of Van Dyck was patting her back with a measured cadence. He was attempting to reassure her with his deep, gentle voice.

Then out of the darkness, it seemed to Dolores, she heard an answering sound, a sob of choke-lipped agony. She wept only the louder, for she wanted to cover the retreat of the girl, Jack.

The Hunting

39

It seemed to Dix Van Dyck that he had scarcely laid down to sleep, warm with the consciousness of having comforted the Indian girl, when he was wide awake again. His eyes opened as suddenly as the eyes of a man who rouses from deep sleep with the consciousness that some danger is near. Only this was not danger. It was a fluttering sense of happiness tinged with vague regret such as comes from the interruption of a happy dream. He stared a moment into the black-blue depth of the sky, so low hanging and yet luring to the eye that it will draw the vision on from infinity to infinity until the soul seems somewhere up there, plunging through space, and the earth and the consciousness of this world are only a dwindling unreality far below. Up through those quiet stars Dix Van Dyck stared for a time, but the illusion pursued him so sharply that he almost thought he heard, or had heard a footstep on the slope of the hill.

Finally he sat up in his blanket and glanced at Dolores. She was sound asleep. She could not have touched him without getting up and moving several steps. Yet there lingered in Dix Van Dyck a definite and foolishly happy sensation. He could have almost sworn that a moment before a face had leaned above his. There was still a tingling sensation in his lips—he could almost breathe a faint scent of perfume. All the night was surcharged as with the feeling of watching eyes—happily watching eyes that surrounded him with care and tenderness.

Still sitting up, he canted back his head and listened for a repetition of that imaginary footstep on the cañon side. At last, shaking his head at this unaccustomed folly, he was about to turn on his side and lie down again in the fold of the blanket when his eyes dropped on a glitter of metal. It was merely a sparkle of two points of light and he thought, at first that it was the flare of the firelight on the eyes of a rattler coiled to strike. The shudder of that thought had scarcely passed over him, however, when he saw, by a taller flare of the fire, that it was a little piece of metal and, leaning closer, he observed with deep astonishment that it was a cross laid upon a small stone and holding down a small piece of paper. It was this that, fluttering in the wind, had made the singing, voice-like whisper that had intruded on his sleep. Someone had been here. Someone had withdrawn and left this singular memorial as what? A warning? A blessing?

Then light burst in upon him from every side, and his heart stood still. With an eager, faltering hand he took the cross and examined it closely. It was of purest silver, slightly carved, and it was suspended by a stout chain of silver. It was the great cross, the cross of good and ill luck—the cross of Jacqueline Boone—and there he held in his hand the strange attraction that had lured him after the girl and finally into hopeless slavery. He could not think. Why had she come, and why had she gone silently? Why had she left the cross? He cut short his dazed ponderings by lifting the scrap of paper. Holding it so that the light struck at an angle across the surface, he read:

I brought your pardon to Double Bend. You are safe. May you both be happy.

That was all. No signature. *Both be happy?* He stared from the paper in one hand to the cross in the other. It suddenly came to him that there was evil in this. He laid the paper carefully back upon the rock and dropped the cross over it. Still his mind was too dazed even to rejoice over his pardon. *Both be happy?*

He turned at last and stared into the unconscious face of the Indian girl. Then knowledge struck him like a physical blow. He ground his teeth and rose swiftly from his blankets, swiftly, never so fast in his life. Yet, he stepped silently, for the last thing he wanted in the world was to waken the Indian girl.

He understood. Jack stole in upon them to bring the happy news of the pardon, and she had seen him with Dolores in his arms. He ground his teeth again at that. If Dolores had wakened, he could not have ruled his tongue. Not that it was her fault, poor girl. He tried to convince himself of this while he slammed the saddle across the back of his great horse, but somehow the argument stuck in his throat. Much has been said about the faultless instinct of woman. A little might be noised abroad now and then concerning that of man.

He led his horse a little way down the hillside, after pausing to send a long, bitter glance at the cross. A drift of sand covered the sound of his departure as it must have covered the sound of the coming of Jacqueline. Now there was no trace of her anywhere. The night covered it perfectly. If he waited until day to trail, he would be helplessly left behind the white stallion. Yes, he might lose her forever by the horrible mischance of this night. For she was one of those who will move swiftly, without preparation, and cut themselves off from the life they had left behind them.

A sailor in a fog without a compass was not more helpless than was Dix Van Dyck as he sat his saddle in the heart of the cañon and searched the pitiless, thick heart of the night. Nothing was visible except the tall, cold outlines of the mountains. Suddenly he shouted like a hunter who sights his game. He drove in his spurs and made at a racing pace up the floor of the valley. Fool! Of course she would ride, feeling as she must, straight for the upper ranges of the mountains. That would be her impulse, and what was there to guide her except the first strong impulse? He rode hard, pitiless of the horse, for he was matching him in at least a short spurt against the white beauty that Jacqueline rode. A strange race, that, in the blind darkness, yet, as he rode, a gathering surety came to him that he was right. It was almost as if an encouraging voice were speaking continually at his ear.

The trail grew so steep that he had to bring his horse to a stumbling trot among the rocks and finally to a walk. So he came to the first crest and then, staring down into the valley beyond, he saw a glimmering form—a glimmering form that must have been white to be visible by the faint starlight. What a yell came to the teeth of Dix Van Dyck! It drove down the valley. It struck the faces of granite cliffs, and they sent long echoes leaping sharply from one side of the valley to the other. It was like the sudden, wild clamor of Indians on the trail and raising the scalp yell in full sight of the enemy. It was like the scream of a Highland Clan, Campbells with Stuarts or Camerons in view.

Then Dix Van Dyck went down the farther valley, and the thunder of the hoofs of the tall horse was like the charging of a company. Other sounds fled before him. But the white horse, the matchless white stallion, was galloping slowly, slowly, slowly. A common cattle pony could have overtaken the famous horse that night, and the steed of Dix Van Dyck gained greatly at every long stride.

He shouted again. The exultation overflowed his heart.

Then a clear, thin sound came back to him. It was like a whistling in the fierce wind that cut against his face.

"Dix!" cried the sound. "Keep back."

His wild laughter answered, booming down the rocky valley like the water of a spring freshet. It was her voice!

"Keep back!" sounded the shrill whistle.

His answer was another hunting yell. Then a gun cracked, sobering him, and there was an angered hum high above his head. She had fired wild the first time to warn him, but the second time . . . ?

He lowered his head with a growl of fury. He had become for the instant the same blind bull who charged up the valley after seeing the bloodstained sleeve of Jacqueline on the ground. In those days he had feared her. But now she did not have the cross. She had surrendered it to him. Yes, he saw the meaning of that pitiful tribute that still lay on the rock near the Indian girl. She had surrendered the cross and with it the power that had kept the range in awe. Now she was only a beautiful woman.

He plied whip and spur, and his horse grunted with effort. A stern chase is a long one, at sea or on horseback, but as Dix Van Dyck came closer he saw that the white stallion was hardly maintaining a gallop. It was the feeble effort of an exhausted horse. So it was that he whirled alongside. He saw the glitter of the girl's poised gun and laughed in furious triumph. He leaned from his saddle. His big arm caught at her reins. Then they came to a sliding halt that swerved his own mount around, and there they sat, face to face, though in the pitch black of the shadow of the valley he could make out only the outline of her head. What mattered that? He did not need light to help him remember. He leaned and set his hands on her shoulders.

"Jack" he said, "you're only a woman, and I'm only a man, and there ain't no damned cross between us."

"There's a greater thing than that," she answered faintly.

"Nothing that I can't explain . . . easy, Jack, you know why I'm here. How'd we stand?"

"Apart," she said.

"Once," growled Dix Van Dyck, "I was half afraid of you, Jack. But now you got no cross, and . . . here's where I take charge."

It was hardly a struggle.

"How'd we stand?" he repeated.

"Partners," said the girl.

The Man Who Beat McGurk

40

T he late moon, ragged through a low-lying mist along the western peaks, pushed up a glowing edge and looked at them. The slant light slid down the valley and outlined the black cliffs that had bellowed back the voice of Dix Van Dyck the moment before. Not a pleasant scene. No pleasant curves to the hills, but gaunt outlines, jutting, grotesque peaks, very black. Against that blackness the sky seemed marvelously blue, the sort of blue that paint cannot reproduce. The stars stared down with a queer, eye-like effect that stars never have except over the desert. The desert! The soul of ugliness, defying man. And these two with the smell of the sweating horses in their nostrils and the thought of love in their hearts.

No, it was not such stuff as poetry is made of. The ribs of the horses puffed and fell with their sharp breathing, and the souls of the two rose and fell in the same cadence. Not beautiful? Perhaps not, but life, stirring, commanding, overwhelming life. They should have talked. Instead, they were silent, growing into one another. They did not talk of the moon; they did not talk of the stars, or the gaunt cliffs, or the odor of the dry, deadly sand; they did not even think of them. The background against which they saw each other was nothingness. Their muscles were tired and aching from long labors. Their minds were fresh and young, bounding to meet a new emotion. Not beautiful. If you doubt, listen to their words.

He is saying: "Jack!"

She is saying: "Dix!"

Just those two words, many times repeated. What beauty is in that? Nothing. The chatter of two fools, meaningless. But how their hearts thunder and how their minds stand still!

At length: "How'd you come to give up the cross, Jack?"

"I dunno. I just had to. I thought you might use it."

"And bring bad luck on you?"

"You left it there?"

"Yes, with the Indian."

"Thank God!"

"Now I'm going to explain about the girl, Jack."

"I don't want to hear it. It doesn't matter, somehow. That's funny, isn't it! A moment ago it was the only thing in the world that *did* matter."

"Partners," said Dix Van Dyck, and repeated the word as if it were a poem.

"Where'd we go from here?"

"I got only one thing left."

"Well?"

"Oñate."

A silence and the first clash of their wills. One could feel it through the shadows of the moonlight and sense the hardening of their faces.

"Are you going after Oñate, Dix?" she queried softly at length.

"Yep."

Another silence, cruel and interminable.

"Dix, you can't do it. The governor was after you before. I had to hold him up with a gun under his nose before he'd sign your pardon. If you do this, nothin' this side of hell will keep him from outlawin' you again. You know what happens to outlaws in the end."

"I know."

"Well?"

"If you were me, could you stay clear of Oñate?"

"I dunno, Dix. All I know is that, if you go after Oñate, we're both done for."

"Both?"

"If they get you, they might as well get me. You know that, Dix."

"Never thought of it before."

"Neither did I."

"I *can't* let him go free, Jack."

"You've got to, Dix. For my sake."

"For your sake I'd do more'n I would for anything alive or dead. But. . . ."

"But not this?"

"Gimme time to think, Jack."

"I will. All the time you want. The more time the better. Oh, Dix, you dunno what it means, but I do. My father was an outlaw all my life. D'you know how he died?"

"Not exactly."

"I seen him sitting in a chair, looking as if he was laughing. The house was on fire. There he sat and seemed to laugh with the flames, bulging up through the floor so's I couldn't get to him. It was a dead man's laugh, Dix. That's the way he died. He was a good man, lots of ways, but they made him an outlaw, and he lived in hell and that's the way he died. It was McGurk, of course. D'you hear me, Dix?"

"Every word."

"Honey, you're not goin' to do it?"

"How can I leave Oñate? The whole range'd say I was takin' water!"

"Nobody that knows you, and what d'you care about the rest?"

"It ain't really what people think about me. It's what I think about myself. I owe Oñate a trip to hell, and I'm going to send him there!"

"Is that final, Dix?"

"I got an idea it is."

"Then, God help us!"

"Even that won't drive you away from me, Jack?"

"I thought it would, but it don't seem to."

"D'you know where I'll find Oñate?"

"Back in Double Bend. He knows you're free, and he knows that you're pardoned. So he's got his house full of men. He's about to ride down to his old house in Guadalupe, they say. He's waiting for you to come back to Double Bend and get him. Is that clear?"

"Then we start back on the double."

They turned their horses and jogged slowly up the rise of ground for the white stallion was wearied to the death.

"When we get into action, let me do the shooting, Dix."

"You!"

"Sure. They ain't so hard on a woman in these parts. Let me take my chances with Oñate, and I'll 'count for the Mexican."

"You?" he stammered. "D'you mean to say you'd even take a hand at the shooting yourself, Jack?"

"Oh, Dix," she said sadly, "I been raised with a gun in my hand. My whole life . . . it ain't been anything but one long fight. With a gun there ain't anybody better 'n me on the whole range."

"Even without the cross to help you?" he asked wonderingly.

"Even without the cross," she nodded. "There was once two men who could've beat me to the draw. One of them was McGurk. But his heart was broken and that's how I got his horse."

"I thought he was killed?" said the big man curiously.

"Nope. I met him after he was beat."

"Who beat him?"

"Another man."

"Well?"

"Dix, I'd rather talk about anything in the world better than about that one man."

"I got an idea," mused Dix Van Dyck, "that the feller that beat McGurk had something to do with the cross."

She would not answer. He gave up the riddle, and they rode side by side, slowly still, up the slope and down the next toward Double Bend.

The Waiting

41

To say that the town of Double Bend was in suspense would be to put it lightly. It was rather in a constant tension—the sort of tension that a steady pressure puts on a hair-trigger. Everyone knew that Dix Van Dyck was in the town to kill *Señor* Don Porfirio Maria Oñate. Everybody knew that Oñate knew it. And there was the singular spectacle of a sheriff besieged in his house. He had gathered trained fighters about him. Day and night they patrolled his house.

In the meantime the duties of the sheriff lapsed. There were complaints, and then Oñate called in a Mexican doctor, and the doctor gave out an interview and said that Oñate was suffering from a serious form of heart disease and that it might be some time before he could resume his official duties. Most of the *Americanos* agreed that Oñate was suffering from internal trouble, but most of them would have been disposed to call it "white liver" rather than heart trouble. Jokes were made and repeated on this subject. Even the *Mejicanos* enjoyed the dumb play of the sheriff's heart trouble.

The news was spread abroad. People began to come into Double Bend to wait for the catastrophe, for it was agreed that a man like Dix Van Dyck—especially since the exploit of the jail was now fully known—could not be kept away from his victim. Dix Van Dyck kept a room at the hotel, and Jacqueline Boone had a room in a private house. She had been strictly ordered by Dix not to take a hand in this business, but on that subject she had opinions of her own. She wore a gun, and she knew how to use it. A scheme for attack was gradually forming in her mind.

The first two days passed, and at the end of that time a strange event happened. A Mexican, known to be one of the sheriff's house guards, rode straight to the hotel and inquired for Dix Van Dyck. The bystanders looked for a gun play and a bold attempt at assassination, but, when Dix Van Dyck hove on the horizon, the Mexican thrust his hands eagerly above his head and in this position delivered his message in a low voice.

He said: "I, *señor*, have come from a man who is not your friend."

"You mean," said the big man, "that you're one of the hangers-on of Oñate?"

"I am working for *Señor* Oñate," answered the other and prepared for a quick jump for the door.

"Talk," said Dix Van Dyck, and fell into an attitude of patient waiting. "But maybe I can save you a long line of chatter. I suppose Oñate wants to buy me off?"

"It is true," said the Mexican, keeping his arms tirelessly above his head. "It is true that *Señor* Oñate thinks that *Señor* Van Dyck might be tempted by a price."

"It is true," responded Dix Van Dyck with a white anger, "that the swine could not buy me off for all the gold in Mexico. I'm here to get him, my friend, and I *mean* to get him. So just trot back to Oñate and tell him what I say. I'm in no hurry. Sooner or later he has to leave his hole, and then I'll be on the spot."

"Ah, *señor*," said the Mexican, "Don Porfirio would never dream of purchasing a peace with Dix Van Dyck with gold. But, *señor*, there are other things that pass as a price."

"It seems to me that somewhere in your heart you're laughing at me. Now I want to tell you straight that no one has laughed at me yet and got away with it. Understand?"

The pallor of death came over the messenger. "*Señor*," he pleaded eagerly, "there is no smile in my heart. I swear it. I could not laugh. My throat is too dry. I could not."

"Moisten your throat with a lie," said the implacable Dix Van Dyck, "and blaze away with your yarn. What's the price of *Señor* Oñate?"

"*Señor* Dix Van Dyck has a brother," said the messenger.

"Right," answered Van Dyck. "The finest lad that ever swung into a saddle within a hundred miles of Guadalupe. What of him? Does he owe a gambling debt to Oñate?"

"Alas! No, *señor*. It is more. The good *Señor* Joseph Van Dyck has fallen into a greater misfortune. You must know, *señor*, that the sheriff has many friends. Some of them have large hearts but small brains. They learned in a little while that *Señor* Oñate was in danger from Dix Van Dyck . . . a terrible man in killing . . . and they shuddered because they feared for their friend. Some of these simple men took thought among themselves how they could help the sheriff. Was it not so? Yes, they took thought, and then this is what they did. They went by night around the house of Joseph Van Dyck and made a calling such as a friend of his had been heard to make. When he came out of the house, they seized him with many hands, gagged and bound him, and they led him away into the hills where no man could ever follow them. Then they sat down and wrote a letter. . . ."

"God!" said Dix Van Dyck without breath in his voice, and sat down heavily in a chair.

"They wrote a letter," said the messenger, letting his triumph creep into his voice, though he kept it out of his eyes with a religious care, "saying to *Señor* Oñate that they had heard of his danger and that they had, therefore, taken a precaution to care for him. They had seized on young Joseph Van Dyck, and if the sheriff were in any way mistreated, killed, or in any way injured . . . understand, *señor*, in *any* way injured . . . they would do to *Señor* Joseph Van Dyck what was done to the sheriff . . . and perhaps a little bit more . . . *sí*, a little bit more. Is this clear, *Señor* Van Dyck?"

"I suppose," said the other slowly, "that the damned dog of a sheriff is now rubbing his fat hands?"

"It is true, *señor*," said the messenger, "that the sheriff is now enjoying a deep sleep. But he will doubtless awaken to hear the answer of the brave Dix Van Dyck."

"If I let Oñate alone, my brother will be sent back safe?"

"If reasonable surety is given," said the messenger cautiously. "If reasonable surety is given, *señor*. . . ."

"But in the meantime," said Van Dyck, "tell Oñate that he had better lie awake and keep thinking. I'm not done yet. How does he know that these men *he* could buy are safe from the price of somebody else, eh? Go back and tell him that I'll find their price and that I'll get Joseph free. After I've done it, I'll have another score to settle with Oñate. Tell him also that I'm in no hurry. That I have the patience of an Indian. Tell him that besides my own little troubles with him . . . which the death of Vincente balances, in a way . . . that I have the death of El Tigre to cross off the account. Tell him also that there are other ways of death than a quick one. Is that plain?"

"It is very clear," said the messenger anxiously, "but the *señor* should understand that these men who have carried your brother into the mountains are very rough men. You should consider that they are not safe men in any way and that they are, perhaps, liable to forget kind-

ness. That they are liable to point a gun toward Joseph
Van Dyck and perhaps grow so careless as to fire, for the
burden of keeping him safe is not small."

"Partner," said the big man calmly, "you make a good
talk. I allow that, and I'll tell the world that you talk better'n the sheriff himself could plead for his life. But your
bluff don't work with me. That's all. I like your lingo, but I
see ways through it. Now, my friend, I know that there
ain't a single one of you, from Oñate down, that wants to
get me on his trail unless he has to. Your kind friends up
there in the hills are among the rest of 'em. So go back
and tell Oñate that."

"Listen," said the other, dropping his caution in a burst
of blind anger, though still he kept his hands high, "if you
do this, you will have men against you. You are marked,
señor. You are a known man. You keep your back to the
wall. You dare not turn. Even suppose that you are able to
kill Oñate, how will that help you? Others will still be
alive, and we do not forget, *señor.* We do not forget!"

"Go back to Hole-in-the-Ground Oñate and tell him
that for the present there's a truce, but tell him to get out
all his wits and sharpen 'em up, for I'm going to get that
lad Joseph away from his men. Then I'm coming straight
for Oñate, and I'll nail him to the wall."

"Is that all?" said the messenger with ominous and furious calm.

"It's just about all, I guess," said Dix Van Dyck. "Except,
get out!"

He had raised his voice as he said this last, and with
every word the messenger had retreated a step across the
big room until at the parting injunction he leaped sidewise through the door and was gone.

Jacqueline   42

So the game continued day after day. Men ventured to ask Dix Van Dyck what he had up his sleeve, and his only reply was a broad and genial smile. So they drew upon their imaginations and figured up the possibilities that remained to him. It was commonly known that Joseph Van Dyck had been kidnapped, and it was at least commonly conjectured who had been the inspiration behind that act of violence. Some held that he dared make no move until his brother was out of danger. There were others who declared that he cared nothing for God, man, or devil, and that the safety of his brother would never make him postpone his vengeance.

This same clan pointed out that he delayed the killing of Oñate simply because it was humanly impossible for any man to break through the line of Oñate's guards. Others, on the other hand, vowed that, if his brother were only safe, Dix Van Dyck would make the attempt and either kill or be killed. Public opinion demanded action from him. The weight of this opinion, indeed, grew heavier and heavier as more and more men drifted in, coming with the avowed intention of being on the ground when the famous feud reached its *dénoûment*, even if they had to stay there all year. It was plain that Dix Van Dyck could not long delay action with such an audience waiting for him.

So the days crept on, a week—two weeks. Then a dusty

rider galloped to the door of Oñate and threw a sealed envelope to one of the loitering guards. It was addressed to Oñate, and, though the guard could not read, he carried the missive to the master of the house.

Señor Oñate had Manuel open the letter. He was far too wise to do that himself for he had heard unpleasant tales of poisons—dust concealed in an envelope that, when opened, filled the air, and a single breath was horrible death. But the missive was safely opened, and Manuel drew out a little slip of yellow paper, rough at the edges, and scrawled upon in a painful hand. Then *Señor* Oñate took it and read:

> Your woman, Dolores. . . .

The sheriff fell back in his chair. It was rather a collapse than a fall. His fat body seemed to have been turned to jelly that loosely filled the chair from arm to arm and overflowed. Manuel, skilled to the needs of the master, brought a drink. When it was disposed of, Oñate managed to continue past the fatal opening:

> Your woman, Dolores, came to the camp. We knew she could not have found us if you had not sent her. We trusted her, and she tricked us out of Joseph Van Dyck. We followed them fast, but the boy has some of the fighting blood of his brother. He wounded José and Baldorama. We had to turn back. The game is up. When you get Dolores in your hands again, skin her alive and then send her to me. I have some little things to whisper in her ear.

The paper fluttered from the sheriff's hand to the floor. He sat smiling. It was merely the relaxation of the muscles of his face, and the smile was like the smile of death.

It *was* death. He knew it. His mind worked through a daze slowly back toward life. The warm sunlight fell across his hand. He stretched out his fingers in it. It was good to feel. The bright colors on the wall—perhaps he was looking at them for the last time. His vague eyes turned to Manuel. Perhaps it would be those stubby fingers that washed the blood from his wounds. And yet, no wounds. No, Dix Van Dyck would use no weapon except his long-fingered hands. He remembered them as vividly as if he had painted them. They grew as terrible in his mind as the mandibles of a tarantula. He caressed his plump throat slowly. It was there that those hands would settle. It was said that a single pressure of Van Dyck's grip could crush a man's throat.

And he said, at last out of his stupor: "Manuel!"

The servant approached, trembling.

"Manuel, I am a dead man." The words were like a stimulant. He sprang up with a shriek. "Dead, in my own house? No, no, no! Call my guards . . . my men. I have been close-fisted with them. I shall open treasures to them. Dead! Help! But, no. There is no help. Dolores . . . the she-devil. She is with Van Dyck. She will teach him a way to reach me. Dolores! Demon! Manuel! Oh, God!"

His guards came running in and found him collapsed on the floor. In falling, he had struck his temple, and the crimson blood streaked slowly down across his flabby face. They looked to each other with round eyes grunting, and they worked over him until he came back to life—life that was a delirium.

"It is no matter," said Oñate. "Why did you not let me die? There was no pain in that. It was sleep. But tonight . . . tonight Van Dyck will come!"

And Dolores? It was evening before she rode into Double Bend with Joseph Van Dyck at her side. Throughout their long, hard journey she had not spoken to him once, aside from snapping brief orders and directions, and to all his proffers of gratitude she listened with a deaf ear, until they came close to the hotel where Dix Van Dyck lived.

"*Señor* Dix Van Dyck," said the Yaqui, halting her horse, "lives in that big house. Go find him there, *señor*. Your tongue has been pleasant to Dolores. The things you would have said to Dolores, remember them all and say them to *Señor* Dix Van Dyck. Now he will kill *Señor* Don Porfirio Maria Oñate. Tell him first to wait until Dolores comes. She will tell him a way. *Adiós, señor*." And she turned her horse down an alley.

Joseph Van Dyck rode straight on to the hotel. A man who knew him saw him cross the porch. The news spread from lip to lip—Joseph Van Dyck was free. Tonight, with his hands free from fear for his brother, Dix Van Dyck would kill Oñate. He could wait no longer. The time had come.

It was like the night of the rising of the mob against the jail, save that the conditions were reversed. On that night the *Mejicanos* had gathered in the streets, and the *Americanos* had kept to their houses. Now the *Americanos*, who had been drifting into Double Bend for days, gathered here and there in little knots, laughing, talking, waiting. When *Mejicanos* passed these little groups, they crossed to the other side of the street and went straight to their houses and waited there, ill at ease. All of this happened in the space of half an hour.

In the meantime Joseph Van Dyck was directed by the clerk of the hotel to the upper rear verandah of the rickety, old hotel and, coming out onto the little platform, he found a singular picture—Dix Van Dyck and Jacqueline Boone. It was a much more significant picture than Joseph Van Dyck could understand. What astonished him was to find his big brother alone with any woman—alone, and sitting in that silence that speaks more loudly than words.

And the woman? She no longer wore the divided skirt and the flaring bandanna around her throat. She had given up the short, divided riding-skirt. She had given up the boots with their big, jangling spurs. There was no longer the belt sagging across her hips and pulled far down by the heavy Forty-Five. Instead, she wore a small, soft hat of white cloth with a blue feather curling along one side, a white skirt, and a white shirtwaist, joining the skirt with a broad, black belt. Joseph Van Dyck saw white silk stockings and very small white shoes.

He saw these things and thought them very pleasant, for how could he know that this was Jack Boone? But, if he had known, he would have been most of all astonished by her occupation. For there was a sewing basket beside her, and she was sewing an edging of lace onto something soft and white and fluffy. Could this be Jack Boone? Where was the quick, cold, keen glance of the girl? Where was the calm aloofness? Where was the masculine poise that struck all comers with a sudden sense of respect and a little feeling of danger? It was all gone. In fact, it was no longer Jack, but Jacqueline. The eyes she turned on Joseph Van Dyck were wide and soft and infinitely gentle and with a light in them that old women and very young children understand. Sir Lancelot, says Mallory, laid down shield and spear and became a holy man in a monastery or, some say, an anchorite. With the losing of the cross, Jack Boone had given up the strength of horse and gun and knife and taken instead the disarming powers of a woman.

These things Joseph Van Dyck saw, in part, when he put foot on the verandah but hardly had that foot fallen, when Dix Van Dyck turned his leonine head and then shouted like a cowboy at a round up: "Heya, Joe!" He made one crashing bound and swept the boy into arms that would have strained the ribs of a bear. "You!" thundered Dix Van Dyck again.

"All that you've left of me," gasped Joseph Van Dyck, extricating himself from that terrible grip.

"Ha!" cried Dix Van Dyck. "They couldn't keep you, lad. The fighting Van Dycks! I'd forgotten that. And blood will out. Tell me, Joe, was it night work? How many d'you drop? Who? When? How'd they get you? Tell me everything. I. . . ."

"Gimme a chance, Dix," said the other, and he was aware, more than of the great voice of his brother, of the big, luminous, contented eyes of the girl. She had once more begun her sewing.

"Speaking personal," said Joe, "I'd never have had a chance alone ag'in' that gang. They were a pretty hard lot. They was too many for me, but that Yaqui friend of yours came in. . . ."

"What?"

"That girl, Dolores, she come to me. They thought she was strong with Oñate. So they let her come and go. It was she who worked me out of the place and gave me a running start. Dix, she's got the brains of a man."

"And a wolf," nodded Dix Van Dyck. "Was it a running fight?"

"Yep," said the boy, sighing at the memory. "They made it hot for a while, but we had the foot of 'em, and Dolores knew the country like a book. I winged two of the birds, and then they give up. So, here I am, but if it hadn't been for Dolores. . . ."

"Where is she?"

"She's coming here to see you, Dix, and for my sake. . . ."

"Oh?" said Dix Van Dyck.

"What's the matter?" cried the boy. "I'm not ashamed of liking her, Dix."

"You've had a long ride," said the big man. "Maybe you better hit some chow and then go to bed, Joe."

"See you in hell first," said the boy, and it was strange to hear talk like this to Dix Van Dyck.

"You young devil," growled Dix Van Dyck, "I'll. . . ."

"Before you fight," said the gentle voice of the girl, "I'd like to meet your brother, Dix."

They stood suddenly abashed, the big man and the slender, handsome, viciously graceful boy. The introduction came stammeringly, and then Joseph Van Dyck felt his fingers taken in a strong, cool, soft hand and felt a glance of strong, steady eyes pass into his own, not with criticism but with a calm understanding. His irritation left him. He sat down and felt, by little, slow degrees, the coolness of the evening and the oncoming of the dark. Then the anxious eyes of Jacqueline were on his brother. He thought he understood, and he leaned to her in a carefully chosen moment.

"Is it Oñate? Tonight?"

She answered with a whispering sigh. "God help us!"

And that was all.

The Song of the Heart   43

It was now that Dolores came again down the street, this time on foot. She caught the tenseness of waiting in the air—in the whispering of the little knots of men as she passed. The men turned and stared after her, and she heard them say: "Dolores . . . Oñate's woman."

"What does she know?"

"Everything!"

"El Tigre's daughter and worse than her father."

"There's a knife in her belt and another in her eye, lad."

She drank in the comments. The storm was about to strike Double Bend, and she was at the center of it. It was a proud place even for the daughter of El Tigre. She had dressed for the part of Dolores, daughter of El Tigre. She had dressed to conquer the heart of Dix Van Dyck. The emerald of Oñate glowed like an evil eye on her low, broad forehead; silks curled against her cheeks, or whispered about her body as she walked; and, above all, high on her breast she felt the chill touch of the cross—the mysterious cross that would bring her fortune—and ill luck to all others.

She knew that, when she stood in her glory of silks and jewels with her hand on the little metal cross and her eyes on the eyes of Dix Van Dyck, he would have to rise and follow her. It raised a mighty tide in her heart, that picture. He would have to rise and follow her. She would lead him to Oñate and please him by showing him how to destroy his foe in safety to himself. Then she would be his woman, and he would be her man. There would be no others on the ranges so swift and so rich and so terrible as they. A song formed in the heart of Dolores and came to her lips as a smile—a strange and stern and beautiful smile.

She came to the hotel and was told where to find Dix Van Dyck. She went up the stairs and straight toward the little upper rear verandah. But, with her hand on the knob of the screen door, she stopped and raised her head with a jerk. For what she heard was the same song that was rising within her and keeping time with the beating of her heart. It was a tune never written and a tune that had no words. It was light and faint and sweetly shrill. In her astonishment she thought at first that she had begun to sing it herself, but in a moment she was sure that the song came from the lips of another—not a song, really, but only a faint, humming croon. She flattened herself against the screen door and looked the length of the verandah.

There she saw the three. They were all seated. She saw the back of Joseph, the strong, cruel profile of Dix Van Dyck, and the full face of the girl. It was on this that her gaze centered—her cruel, hateful gaze. In her silent fury she made her mind cold and judged. The proud chin—it was not more perfectly carved than her own; the mouth—it was not more delicately curved; the nose—it was not so true and straight; the eyes—ah, there was the halting-place! For the eyes raised and turned full on Dix Van Dyck, and she saw him stiffen a little and his head almost jerk back, as though something shocked him fully in the face. She thought of her own eyes, dusky, smoky, with a promise of fire—passionate eyes, stern eyes, wildly loving eyes. But the eyes of the white girl would grow greater and greater, for she had set her eyes like a hand on the heart of Dix Van Dyck and made him blind in turn.

The noise of guns on that night when Dix Van Dyck broke free from the jail, the flash of knives, the yells of fear and pain, and the presence of death—that had been a tragedy. But I wonder if it were as great as the tragedy of the Yaqui girl as she stood with her face pressed against the screen of the door and stared her heart out and sent it against the eyes of Jacqueline.

The humming, the croon of the white girl went on, but there was no longer that same song in the heart of Dolores. It had died. She was full of silence to the lips—cold silence, like the night. How long she stood there did not matter. Seconds, perhaps, but they had the meaning of many years. For we must always remember that the age of Dolores was more than a matter of years, and her wisdom was something more than that of the mind only. She understood, I think, what all this story means. She had merely come to a crossroads—her own striking across the path of Dix Van Dyck. There they had met and lingered for an instant at the junction of the roads. They had talked, and she had listened but had not understood. Crossroads—ah, the bitterness of it! All she could carry away from this man was the little metal cross that hung about her throat, a victory for herself and a curse to all who were dear to her.

Crossroads! The road of Dix Van Dyck led somewhere up over the hills to happiness with the eyes of the white girl like a light to lead him. And her own road carried her out into the dark. It was that which made her think of death. She had never wasted much time on thought. Meditation crushed her. But now she wanted only a quick escape from life. Her road had passed the crossing, and now she wanted to travel it to the bitter end at a stride.

With all the silks rustling about her, she turned from the screen door with the humming of the girl still living at her ear. She went down the steps, out into the street, and turned straight toward the burial grounds. The body of El Tigre lay there, and now the soul of the Yaqui turned to her kind, even as the thought of the traitor turns to his country when he comes to die. She would die on the grave of El Tigre. It was not hard to do. A stroke of the knife—the heavy, needle-pointed knife at her girdle—would sweep her from the junction of the roads and carry her, in one breathless swoop, clear to the end of her journey. Her hand was strong for such a stroke. She began to hear again, deeply within her, the singing of the small voice—a different tune now and a different cadence. It kept time, not with the flutter of her heart but with the swift padding of her noiseless feet, a regular rhythm, a death song of a Yaqui, the daughter of a chief.

The knots of men were still standing on the streets, here and there. They were increasing in number. The tenseness of waiting grew more keen, but it all meant nothing to Dolores, daughter of El Tigre. Her thoughts were far away with her father. Her course through the streets led her past the house of *Señor* Don Porfirio Maria Oñate, and here, where the gate opened in the old hedge, she paused a moment and stared curiously at the low, broad front of the building. Squat and ugly it seemed now, but she remembered how she had first entered it, not so many days ago, with a sense of power and command.

She walked on again more slowly. She was thinking of the interior of that house, the spacious rooms, the coolness, the sense of order, the pattering feet of the swift servants, their eyes of fear and hatred following her. Suddenly Dolores tilted her head and laughed softly. The sound of her own laugh startled her to a halt, and she remembered with a sharp discomfort that she was walking toward her own death. There she paused, frowning into the night. At last she retraced her steps to the gate in the hedge and stood, listening. A shadowy form crossed the line of her vision, a guard. Another form passed.

A voice in Spanish asked: "Who is there?"

She opened the gate and stepped inside. After all, would it not be an exciting way to meet death?—alone, surrounded by the hatred of Oñate and his many men?

"It is I, Dolores, daughter of El Tigre," she said, "and I have come to see *Señor* Oñate."

Oñate Smiles

Who shall say that there is not mental telepathy? There had been no sound in the coming of Dolores, daughter of El Tigre, and there had been no sound in her departure from the screen door. But, while she stood there, waiting and listening and passing down the crossroads of her life away from the fate of Dix Van Dyck, there was a heavy silence on the verandah, broken only by the light humming of the girl, Jacqueline. Scarcely had she gone when Dix Van Dyck rose to his full height and stretched himself, muscle by muscle, like a great cat that dozes by the hearth all day. When the night comes and all of the people of the house sleep, he rouses himself, stretches his muscles, and turns his yellow eyes on the darkness, ready for adventure. So it was with Dix Van Dyck, and the others rose in turn. The girl sat down again almost at once, and her hands glimmered on the arms of her chair that they were gripping hard. As for Joseph, he shook his revolver butt as though to make sure that it was loose in the sheath, then he ranged himself silently beside his great-shouldered brother.

The white teeth of Dix Van Dyck gleamed through the gathering dusk of the evening, but he said, after his smile: "This ain't a party for a crowd. It ain't by force of numbers that I'm going to reach Oñate, Joe. If I wanted a crowd, I could raise one in ten minutes with the boys that are waiting in the saloons and on the street corners. But they could never rush Oñate's house. He's got men with rifles behind his walls. The only way he can be reached is by a soft foot. D'you see?"

"D'you want me to sit here . . . like a woman?" asked the boy fiercely. "Ain't I a Van Dyck? Ain't I your brother?"

"Thank God you are," said the big man, "and that's why you're going to sit here . . . beside a woman, Joe. If things go wrong, she'll need you more'n you could help me tonight. 'S that clear, Joe?"

"I s'pose it is."

"Maybe you better get a lamp for Jack if she wants to sew some more."

"No," she answered, "I think I'll just sit here and wait, Dix."

And that was all she said, no remonstrance, no appeal. She sat there with her hands folded in her lap. Surely this was not the Jack Boone of old, whose gun spoke more often than her lips! Or perhaps she, too, had come to a crossroads, like Dolores, and was waiting to see in which way the hand on the milestone pointed.

The screen door banged after Dix Van Dyck, and his soft but heavy footfall went down the stairs. He could make his stride, at need, as silent as the padding foot of a panther. He left the hotel by the back entrance, for he dared not let himself be seen on the streets. It would have meant that he would be followed, and the escort would have proved his ruin. So he cut across the back way and slipped from the shadow of one building to the shadow of the next and loitered in the black shade of a tree—a shade cast by the dull starlight—till a pedestrian passed by. At last he lay almost prone underneath the hedge in front of Oñate's house.

A light step passed him. He dared not turn in his narrow street covert along the base of the bushy hedge. The step went on, and paused. In the pause he breathed the scent of irrigated soil—the stinging pungency of newly wetted sand. In the garden there was the regular whish and rattle and whisper—very light—of a circular water spray, playing upon the grass of the lawn, a cool sound, infinitely peaceful, infinitely restful. The light step returned toward him, as it would have returned if he had been discovered, and he slipped his hand down to the butt of his gun.

But the step paused again, and he heard a voice ask sharply in Spanish: "Who is there?"

Then the soft answer of Dolores, careless and low: "It is I, Dolores, daughter of El Tigre, and I have come to see *Señor* Oñate."

There followed a mumble of astonished cursing. The message was repeated by muffled voices in the distance. Dix van Dyck, grinning to himself in the dark, crawled slowly, like a winding snake, to a hole in the hedge near the gate and passed through. He was on the inside, committed finally to the test.

Now the door of the house fell wide, and a blast of light shot down the path straight upon Dolores. She stood, a flare of color, tall and slender—like some graceful, tropical flower, and he knew what sort of a smile was on her lips. For the thousandth time Dix Van Dyck strove to read her mind. But what white man has ever succeeded in reading the mind of an Indian?

Two guards followed her to the door at which stood Manuel, grinning at the approach of Dolores like an evil spirit at the gate of a small hell. She paused beside him on the threshold, and he whispered in her ear. She snapped her fingers and passed within, shrugging her graceful shoulders. The door closed with a jarring sound—like teeth, when a morsel has been swallowed. The two guards remained on the doorstep, chattering quickly with voices of wonder.

It was this moment Dix Van Dyck chose to dart, on hands and knees, across the lawn.

"Who's there?" rang out a sharp voice.

He flattened himself on the lawn, his head turned from the guards. For, strange as it may seem, even in the night it is easier to find a hidden man if his face is turned toward you. It is as if men can feel the challenge of eyes through the darkness. A silence fell.

"It was nothing . . . the swaying of that palm tree," said one of the guards at last, and they walked out to resume their beat.

Van Dyck went on in another rush toward the house. There, he reached a corner of the wall and flattened himself again in the soft soil of the garden mold that ran around the edge of the building. What he would do next, he had no idea. The first and only thing that had filled his mind was to pass the outer line of guards. It remained to get entrance to the house. Through the door? That was guarded. Through a window? They also must be locked and guarded. How, then? It occurred to him that the whole house lay open on the patio—but was he a bird to descend on it? The roof was unguarded, surely.

He looked up. A stout old climbing vine with many twisted stems wound up the side of the house just before him and curved under the narrow edge of the eaves. The architect had placed something like eaves there as an ornament, even in that land of little rain. He must try that. Noiselessness was the first requisite of success. So he rose and flattened himself against the wall, reaching the full length of his arm above his head and gripping the twisted stems of the vine. Few men can handle their own weight with one arm, far less with such a faulty grip. It was a mighty labor, but he drew himself slowly up and up. A final jerk and his chin came on a level with his gripping right hand. He flung his left hand high above—and barely reached the edge of the eaves.

He made his finger-hold secure, whipped up his right hand, and hung there a moment, suspended at full length. He began to swing his body from side to side like the pendulum of a clock. Once, twice, thrice, the swing increased, and with a final heave he whirled himself far to the right. His heel caught on the edge of the eaves. In an instant he lay flat and panting on the gradually sloping roof.

He lay for a moment, listening. There was a whispering of the guard below—just below him. When he peered cautiously over the edge, he made out a faint glimmer through the starlight. A revolver? No, another sound, a gurgling sound, reached him. They were drinking from a flask. He could have reached down and jerked the hats from their heads, and a perversely foolish impulse came to do it. He had to set his teeth to resist the inclination.

When they passed on, he worked his way along the edge of the eaves to the side of the house and then up, slowly, softly over the ridge of the roof and down toward the patio. There was one thought, one picture in his mind now, and that was the fat throat of *Señor* Don Porfirio Maria Oñate. He stopped his progress at a corner point from which he could overlook three quarters of the ground space below. It was very pleasant. Green things, here and there, and the blur of bright blossoms faintly illumined by paper lanterns that stirred and swung in every touch of the wind and brushed faint shadows across the bloom of the garden. A scentless garden of the semi-tropics. Brilliancy, but no perfume. It made Dix Van Dyck think of a lovely woman without heart or soul.

Now a door opened. Voices sounded. Dolores walked out into the very center of the patio like a tragic actress to the center of the stage. An armed guard stood on either side of her, holding a hand. They had torn away her *re-*

bozo, and the hilt of her knife no longer glinted at her waist. She was disarmed, helpless. In the arched shadow of the opposite doorway stood *Señor* Oñate. He was nodding and grinning and rubbing his fat palms together— just as he had on the day when he had asked Dix Van Dyck for his vote.

He stepped out and walked slowly in a circle about her, and she all the time standing proudly with her eyes straight before her, as if she were quite unaware of his presence. Dix Van Dyck drew a revolver slowly and cautiously and held it ready, the butt snuggled against the palm of his hand like the pressure of a friend's fingers. But there was no apparent treachery in this slow, circular movement of *Señor* Oñate's. He was simply viewing his victim from all angles. Revenge, after all, to a connoisseur like Oñate is not sweet in the final blow so much as in the delightful anticipation. Still, in the same nodding silence, he went over to the little corner table and sat down in the big armchair. He poured himself a drink of tequila, swallowed it drop by drop, his eyes all the while lingering on the form of Dolores, and then rolled back his head. He might have been preparing for a little *siesta*.

This movement raised his face fully to the light for the first time, and Dix Van Dyck perceived a singular change in the countenance of the great sheriff. It was still round, but it sagged here and there. It was like a balloon from which half the wind is gone. His mouth, usually pursed up at the corners with superfluous flesh, now drooped in those places, and below his eyes the flesh was pouched and purple, as if he had been struck there by a heavy hand. He had the worn, battered look of a man who has been thumped by a crowd in a riot. His body lived, but his spirit was half dead.

He revived, however, in the presence of Dolores. His very body seemed to puff and bloat out like that of some ancient hero, swelling his chest to relate his exploits at the board of the king's banquet. New light came in his eye. There was a steady and most unpleasant grin on his lips. At length, he leaned leisurely forward on the table and drew out a revolver that he held daintily poised.

"Is she searched?" he asked.

"We called in the women," said one of the guards with a grin, "and she's searched to the skin."

"You may go," said Oñate.

"Go?" repeated the guard in astonishment.

"Go!" screamed Oñate with a sudden fury. He beat on the table with the muzzle of his gun.

The guard fled but with a backward eye over his shoulder, like a boy forced to leave pleasant company at bedtime.

"Ah," said Oñate, "it is good to be with you . . . alone again, Dolores *mia.*"

She turned to him for the first time, walked to the table, poured herself a very small glass of tequila, raised it to her lips, drank it in small swallows, looking Oñate up and down between them. Not a scared look, certainly. It was rather one of not unpleasant meditation.

He nodded, delighted. "I see it in your snake eyes," he said with a sympathetic grin, "you are seeing where you can wriggle through the grass. But there is no opening, Dolores, my darling. Every door is guarded, every window. The house is full of men, and they are all warned. They are ready for you. And I am." He tapped his gun. "So the white dog turned you out. He beat you, and he threw you out into the street, and you come whining to the door of old Oñate?"

Dolores sat down, and, resting her elbow on the edge of the table, she tapped her slender fingers against her chin. All the while her wide, dull eyes surveyed Oñate, like one who looks upon a familiar and wearisome landscape. "Yes," she said, "he turned me out." She paused, seeming to hunt for the words that would irritate Oñate the most. "He . . . used me . . . and threw me out. He found a white woman more beautiful than an Indian girl. So I came back to my sty. It is true." And she nodded casually. "Yet, I had tried to buy his love and paid a great price. I had freed Joseph Van Dyck. That leaves the hand of Dix Van Dyck free to take you by your fat throat, *Señor* Don Porfirio Maria Oñate. It is true!"

Oñate blinked, and his face wrinkled like that of a sick man under the knife of a doctor. The exquisite pain, the paralyzing fear left him with a heaving chest. He blinked again, as if to shut out the doom, and shrugged his fat shoulders. "We will forget that," he said. "First there is the death of Dolores. We will think of that."

"Why," said the girl, "think of something so far away? It is very tiresome."

"Yes," he said with a sort of vicious wonder, "you came, thinking to escape?"

"I came," she corrected him, "to see the fingers of Dix Van Dyck sink in your swine's throat, Oñate. Aha!" She gave a little brief laugh of fierce exultation. "As your eyes grow dim, I will snap my fingers under your nose."

He shrank away from her in real fear. "You are mad!" he said at last. "You have always been mad. Fool! Do you think I will delay with you? No, no, Dolores, tonight is the time! Tonight is your last on earth!"

"It is you who are the fool," said the girl. "Do you think I would risk myself here without protection?"

"Protection?" he asked curiously. "My men surround you . . . *mine!*"

"Have you guarded the air above you, *señor*?" And she pointed up.

He drew in his breath with a little gasp of horror, and his round eyes flashed up. In an instant, however, he regained some self-possession. "You are very clever, Dolores *mia*."

"Listen," said the girl, "have you heard of the cross of the girl, Jack?"

"The she-devil who took the pardon from the governor? What of the cross? Yes, I have heard of it."

"It is here," said the Indian calmly, and she raised the glittering trinket on its chain at the base of her throat. "Are you stronger than this luck, *Señor* Oñate?"

He leaned forward and stared at it with fascinated eyes. "It is true," he whispered at last. "It is the cross! I have heard it described!"

"And now, Oñate?"

"Dolores, we will try the power of that cross. Now!"

"Bah!" she said scornfully, "you have already wasted much time. You will waste still more, Oñate. You have dreamed of me while I was gone. Is it true?"

"I have wakened in the night to curse you!" he said angrily.

She nodded, satisfied. "There are many things in me to curse. But, *señor*, could you live without your tequila?"

"I have no need."

"No, you could not. Can you live without Dolores, *Señor* Oñate?"

"You have the eyes of a snake," he muttered, "but I will not look at them."

"But you will, Oñate, my fat bird. You will look in the eyes of the snake and wait to be swallowed. Besides, you have not much time to live. *Señor* Dix Van Dyck, remember him?"

The sheriff edged his chair back into the corner and

gripped his revolver with a shaking hand. His eyes wandered past the girl to every side and then came back to her.

"So you see, Oñate, your time of life is short. You will try to make it merry, will you not? With tequila, yes, and with Dolores."

"You shall die," he said hoarsely, "by inches! By little inches, Dolores. There is fire . . . there is the knife. I can use them both."

She laughed softly. "But not yet, *señor!* No, you will wait a while. It is pleasant to sit here in the garden in the cool with Dolores, is it not?"

"If I have no power myself, I will call a guard. He will do for you what. . . ."

"If you called him, Oñate, could you bribe him with money as much as I could bribe him with this little cross?"

He started to his feet, rolling suddenly from his chair. "It is true," he cried, half scream and half groan. "They will betray me! It shall be my own hand."

"It shakes, Oñate, does it not?"

He raised the gun and covered her breast with the wavering muzzle.

Dix Van Dyck, on the roof above, raised his own revolver likewise and drew a careful bead on the point where the fat neck of Oñate joined his body. Yet he delayed his shot for an instant. If he fired, the devil of a girl would be seized by the law.

"Steadier, Oñate, my hero," she urged.

"Oh, devil," he breathed. "Oh, devil Dolores!"

"Remember Van Dyck!"

"Now!" he said, and squinted his eyes for the shot but did not fire.

She rose. "Sit down, *señor.*"

She approached him, and he pressed the muzzle of

the gun against her breast. There was no question of missing now, and even from that distance Dix Van Dyck could see the eyes of the girl lighted as if all the fires of a small hell burned green and yellow in them.

"This would be too easy a death for me, would it not, *señor?*"

"Too easy, yes!"

"Then sit down and wait. Think of a better way."

She laid both her hands on his shoulders and literally pushed him back. He fell with a jar into the chair. And she? She turned her back, deliberately, and poured a glass of tequila that she held to his lips.

It was nature. It was habit. He swallowed a mouthful. Remembering what she was with a start, he raised the gun with a jerk and then turned sad eyes upon her.

"Dolores, you have tortured me."

"It is ended, *señor.*"

She took the revolver from his hand and laid it on the table behind her. The man seemed to have grown perfectly nerveless.

"Van Dyck!" he whispered and, overcome by the horror, gradually closed his eyes.

At that instant the face of Dolores grew positively demonic, but, when he opened his eyes again, her face was again gentle. "Suppose I save you from him?"

"Dolores!" He clutched her by either arm. "I will robe you in silks . . . gold on your wrists and diamonds on your fingers . . . jewels in your hair. You shall walk on the petals of roses and sleep in satins and down. Dolores, Dolores, Dolores! Save me! He is the devil . . . not a man. He walks on me in my sleep. I die every night. No walls and no guards can save me!"

"I will," said the girl.

"Ah, God!" breathed the sheriff. "You mock me again!"

"With this cross," said the girl, "I will save you, my Oñate."

"The cross?" he whispered, in breathless hope, like a child hearing the tale of a curse—a tale of horror and unreal marvels.

"But the carriage and beautiful horses, Oñate?"

"You shall have them all . . . all! And horsemen . . . I swear it!"

"If I wish to go north and east to great cities?"

"I will send you. I will take you myself. But the fiend . . . the devil? Van Dyck . . . you will keep his hand from my throat?"

Dix Van Dyck did not wait for the answer. He was already working his way across the roof with the gun back in its holster. The return was easier. The guards had ceased walking their beats, as if they realized that there was little to guard against from the outside as long as Dolores was within, and Van Dyck reached the street in safety.

At the hotel he found Joseph and Jacqueline, waiting even as he had left them, and they rose and stood stiffly, faint figures through the dark.

"You could not reach him?" asked Joseph at length.

"I reached him," said Dix Van Dyck, "and I went away again and left him. I do not need to send him to hell. He is already there."

About the Author

Max Brand is the best-known pen name of Frederick Faust, creator of Dr. Kildare, Destry, and many other fictional characters popular with readers and viewers worldwide. Faust wrote for a variety of audiences in many genres. His enormous output, totaling approximately thirty million words or the equivalent of 530 ordinary books, covered nearly every field: crime, fantasy, historical romance, espionage, Westerns, science fiction, adventure, animal stories, love, war, and fashionable society, big business, and big medicine. Eighty motion pictures have been based on his work along with many radio and television programs. For good measure he also published four volumes of poetry. Perhaps no other author has reached more people in more different ways.

Born in Seattle in 1892, orphaned early, Faust grew up in the rural San Joaquin Valley of California. At Berkeley he became a student rebel and one-man literary movement, contributing prodigiously to all campus publications. Denied a degree because of unconventional conduct, he embarked on a series of adventures culminating in New York City where, after a period of near starvation, he received simultaneous recognition as a serious poet and successful popular-prose writer. Later, he traveled widely, making his home in New York, then in Florence, and finally in Los Angeles.

Once the United States entered the Second World War,

Faust abandoned his lucrative writing career and his work as a screenwriter to serve as a war correspondent with the infantry in Italy, despite his fifty-one years and a bad heart. He was killed during a night attack on a hilltop village held by the German army. New books based on magazine serials or unpublished manuscripts or restored versions continue to appear so that, alive or dead, he has averaged a new book every four months for seventy-five years. In the United States alone nine publishers now issue his work. Beyond this, some work by him is newly reprinted every week of every year in one or another format somewhere in the world. Yet, only recently have the full dimensions of this extraordinarily versatile and prolific writer come to be recognized and his stature as a protean literary figure in the twentieth century acknowledged. His popularity continues to grow throughout the world.

☐ **YES!**

Sign me up for the Leisure Western Book Club and send
my FREE BOOKS! If I choose to stay in the club, I will pay
only $14.00* each month, a savings of $9.96!

NAME: _____

ADDRESS: _____

TELEPHONE: _____

EMAIL: _____

☐ I want to pay by credit card.

☐ **VISA**   ☐ **MasterCard.**   ☐ **DISCOVER**

ACCOUNT #: _____

EXPIRATION DATE: _____

SIGNATURE: _____

Mail this page along with $2.00 shipping and handling to
Leisure Western Book Club
PO Box 6640
Wayne, PA 19087
Or fax (must include credit card information) to:
610-995-9274

You can also sign up online at **www.dorchesterpub.com**

*Plus $2.00 for shipping. Offer open to residents of the U.S. and Canada only. Canadian
residents please call 1-800-481-9191 for pricing information.
If under 18, a parent or guardian must sign. Terms, prices and conditions subject to
change. Subscription subject to acceptance. Dorchester Publishing reserves the right to
reject any order or cancel any subscription.